Legal

Vengeance

A Novel By

E. Wright Davis

DEDICATION

I must dedicate this book to my mother, Evelyn H. Davis,

the eternal optimist and a true angel sent from God,

and to my late father, Dr. Elmo W. Davis, who is with God.

He taught me to never give up.

ACKNOWLEDGMENTS

I am grateful to many people, all of whom were equally important in this book's creation. First, I would like to acknowledge and thank all of my law partners throughout my fifteen years of law practice, our associates, secretaries, employees, paralegals, and law clerks. There are too many to name them individually. Thank you. I love you all.

The heart of this book belongs to the wonderful people we called our clients. They paid our bills and they provided the real life experiences that made this book possible.

I must thank the wonderful members of the State Bar of Georgia.

I would like to say a special thanks to Susan P. Fossett, without whose excellent secretarial skills this book would have never been produced. Thanks, Susan.

Much thanks to my friend, Michael Harris, the great photographer who makes me look my best with his photography.

A very special thanks and deep appreciation must go to Mrs. Gladys C. Crabb, my high school English teacher, who reviewed and edited this work. After all these years she still doesn't miss a comma, misspelled word, or a dangling participle, and to her son Tabby, my dearest childhood friend for his great knowledge and assistance in making this novel possible.

To my wife, Cynthia, I love you. You were most patient and understanding during the challenges to get this book published.

And thank you "Kelli" and "Terri Beth" wherever you are today.

And last but not least, my deepest gratitude to the ladies of United Writers Press, Vally Sharpe and Jan Lowe for making this book possible.

One

I didn't know why anyone would want to practice law in Conecuh, but there I was, driving down Versailles Boulevard past row after row of cheap motels, pawn shops, tattoo parlors, honky-tonks, and used car lots that are the typical scenery of a military town. Conecuh's main industries were textile mills where the "barons" kept the wages low and the unions out, and the United States Army with an abundance of hookers, gambling joints, and adult bookstores. Like it or not, in a town like Conecuh, the criminal defense lawyers had plenty of business, and there were plenty of "brown lung" cases for the workers compensation lawyers to make their fortunes.

Conecuh was located on the Chattahoochee River, on the Alabama border, and was controlled by five old blue-blood families who controlled everything from who got elected to political office to who got admitted to the local country club, a money losing hundred year old golf and social club. Barrett, Ferguson and Thomas was a five-member law firm, and, fresh out of law school, it seemed like a good place to start.

The firm had been founded by a man named Jack Owens, who had recently died, leaving Hilton Foley Barrett the senior partner in the firm. Or so I assumed.

"Barron," as he was nicknamed, had been my mother's classmate in high school and a friend of my father's. He had grown up in my hometown sixty miles away, his family bordering on the aristocratic. A former United States attorney, he was known for his honesty, sarcastic wit, and intelligence. Methodical and calculating in his manner, he was not known as a rainmaker, but he was an Emory University graduate with impeccable credentials and an excellent reputation. I had worked with his older brother, Marvin, and sister-in-law, Jesse, in a gubernatorial political campaign while in high school. Our candidate, the last of a dying breed of fire breathing, stump-speaking politicians, lost in a landslide.

I didn't know the other partners in the firm, but I knew one of them, Kelli D. Ferguson, was a forty-two year old female. Martindale Hubble, the legal directory, was sketchy about her education, but she did most of the domestic relations and bankruptcy work, the chief source of income for the firm. The third partner, Roland B. Thomas, was a thirty-seven-year-old Emory University graduate who specialized in criminal defense and personal injury.

The law offices of Barrett, Ferguson and Thomas were located on Fourth Avenue across the street from the county courthouse. They were housed in a one-story, flat-roofed building of yellow brick, the front door of which opened onto the sidewalk.

It was time for my interview so I pulled into a parking place, got out of the car, and straightened my tie in the window glass. After a few short steps around to the front of the building, I opened the door and stepped inside. The reception area of Barrett, Ferguson, and Thomas reminded me of a shoe store, not unlike the shoe department at the Belks where I'd worked as a teenager. The walls were lined with worn vinyl chairs, all of them occupied by blue-collar types. None wore a coat or tie and I wondered what kinds of legal problems these poor souls suffered.

"Hey." A middle-aged lady with short bleached blond hair greeted me with a pleasant smile and a sweet southern accent. I glanced at the nameplate on her desk. Juanita Anderson.

"Hello, Juanita," I said. "I'm Jake McDonald. I have an eleven o'clock appointment with Mr. Barrett."

"Oh, yes. Mr. Barrett is expecting you. I'll tell him you're here. Please have a seat."

I found a seat next to a large black man who was catching some winks in the corner. I figured he had worked the graveyard shift at one of the mills. Minutes later I was ushered into the office of Hilton Foley Barrett by a cute young thing named Kim.

"Jake, how are you?" asked Mr. Barrett, extending a warm right hand. "Can I get you something to drink? Coffee or coke?"

"No, thank you, sir. I'm fine."

"Tell me, how are your folks? Gosh, I haven't seen your mom and dad in ten years, I guess. Hope they're doing well."

We exchanged a few more pleasantries and then Barrett got down to the reason I was there. "You have a very impressive resume, Jake. How'd you do in law school?"

"I was in the upper third of my class, Mr. Barrett, but to tell you the truth, I was glad to get out."

"We all were," he said, grinning. "You know what they used to say. In the first year of law school they scare you to death, the second year they work you to death and the third year they bore you to death. So, how was the bar exam?"

"It was pretty tough. A real endurance test." I was trying to conceal the fact that I had probably flunked it.

"Oh, I'm sure you did well. Say, Kelli Ferguson and Brook Thomas will be joining us in a few minutes. Jake, this is a family practice firm. We handle a lot of divorces, adoptions, bankruptcies, criminal cases, personal injury - plaintiff only, probate, and all kinds of litigation."

After twenty minutes of polite conversation had expired, Kelli D. Ferguson bounded through the door. All I could think was that the legal directories had not done justice to this striking blonde with piercing pale blue-green eyes. I could tell by the way she moved that she had boundless energy, and was confident to the point of being cocky. Slightly built with a northern accent, I knew she could strike terror in her opponents in the courtroom.

"Hi, Jake. I'm Kelli Ferguson. It was so good of you drive over this morning. I guess Barron has told you a little about the firm—"

"Mrs. Ferguson, You have a call on line two," interrupted Juanita.

"Who is it?" Kelli replied, looking at me and rolling her eyes.

"It's Judge Braxton's office."

"Okay, but hold my calls after this. We're in a conference." She pressed the speaker phone button on the phone. "Kelli Ferguson."

The voice on the phone was perky but matter of fact. "Hello, Mrs. Ferguson, this is Sandy in Judge Braxton's office. The judge wants to move the case of Johnson vs. Johnson from this afternoon until Tuesday at two o'clock."

"That's fine, Sandy. I always have other things to do on Friday afternoons. We'll see him Tuesday." Pressing the button again, she turned back to me. "Sorry about that Jake. I think you can see from my reception room that we stay real busy around here.

"So, tell me something about yourself. I hear you're engaged. Is she a local girl?"

"No, she's from Florida. I met her during my senior year in law school. We plan on getting married in August of next year when she finishes college."

"I see you were a salesman in a department store once."

"Yes, I worked my way through college with that job. That, and a newspaper route."

"Anybody that sold shoes and delivered newspapers knows how to work, and that's good. One thing you'll find out about this firm is that we represent the little guy and we're not afraid of anybody—big corporations, insurance companies, banks, or hot shots. The bigger they are, the harder they fall." She stopped and looked at Barron. "I wanted Brook to meet Jake. Where is he?" she said, obviously irritated. "He's always late." She hit the intercom button. "Sarah, where's Brook?"

"He's on the phone, Ms. Ferguson. He's about through."

"Slip him a message that we had an appointment with Jake McDonald at eleven o'clock. He drove over an hour to get here and we're waiting on him." It was clear who ran this law firm.

"Any questions for us?" Kelli asked.

"Yes, who are all those people in the lobby?"

"My dear, those wonderful people are called clients. They pay the bills and just may be paying your salary." She winked at me and smiled.

"Why so many? Do you see that many every day?"

Barron laughed. "Sometimes more. This is an average day. Come around here about five o'clock when all of Kelli's five o'clock appointments show up." Barron and Kelli glanced at each other grinning. Inside joke.

When the frivolity was over, Kelli glanced toward the door. "Where the hell is Brook?"

Before she could finish, the door opened and in walked a short, stocky man. Roland Brookings Thomas was slightly balding and his most notable feature was his ears, which stuck straight out from his head at ninety degree angles. I imagined that, as a youngster, he had been picked on unmercifully. I would have felt remorse for him except for one thing—his eyes. They contained the look of a fearless man, a man born with the killer instinct, one who would not back away from a fight. I would find out later that my first impression was correct.

"Sorry I'm late," he said. "I had to get a bail bondsman to get a DUI client out of jail before the weekend."

Kelli ignored his apology. "Brook, this is Jake McDonald."

"Hi, I'm Brook Thomas. I read your resume. There's only one thing wrong with it. You went to that off-brand law school in Macon." He extended his hand.

"Brook!" Kelli said, once again rolling her eyes.

"Well," I said, "you know what they say. A Mercer graduate is one that's too poor to go to Emory and too proud to go to the University of Georgia."

They all burst into laughter. I knew at that moment I would receive an offer.

"We always have a firm luncheon on Fridays," said Barron. "It gives us a chance to get our lawyers together at one time. Strictly business, of course. Strictly tax deductible." He winked at Brook and then turned to Kelli. "See if you can round up Phillip and Parnell and let's get going. Our table has been reserved for twelve o'clock."

*****

"Jake, meet Phillip Jackson."

I looked up to see a young attorney in his late twenties. He had blond hair, and was losing it fast. An affable person, it was obvious that he had been in sales sometime during his career.

"Where did you go to law school?" he asked.

"Mercer," I replied.

"Say, I like Macon. I had a case over there not long ago. It was worker's compensation case with the Barkley firm. I didn't think too much of those defense snobs though. They acted as if it were a personal insult to bring a claim against one of their insurance companies."

"Yeah," I said. "They're strictly the blue-blood, silk stocking types. A few of my classmates clerked for them."

The door opened again. Kelli nodded toward the guy who stepped through. "And this is Parnell Walters."

This guy was the real oddball of the firm. The largest member of the firm in terms of physical stature—six foot four and at least two hundred and fifty pounds, he paused between every sentence as if he were trying to figure out what to say next. I definitely didn't want to meet him in a dark alley at night. I would learn later that his nickname around the firm was appropriate. Lurch.

We all walked outside. Kelli and I climbed into Barron's Park Avenue while Phillip and Parnell chose to ride in Phillip's Oldsmobile. After a fifteen minute drive, Barron turned on his blinker and turned between two huge rusty gates guarding the entrance way, which was fairly visible from the street. The Conecuh Country Club was a stately place on a hill overlooking one of the finer and older neighborhoods in town. The club consisted of a well-kept golf course, the typical tennis courts in front of the main clubhouse, and an Olympic swimming pool in the rear.

A parking valet met us at the front door and whisked the Park Avenue away. Soon we were standing in the palace of the blue-bloods of Conecuh. Ornately carved mahogany paneling and mirrors decorated the walls. The hallway that led into the dining room was covered with oil portraits of every former president of the Conecuh Country Club. There must have been eighty of them.

"Right this way, Mr. Barrett." A white-jacketed black man in his sixties ushered us to our table.

"Thank you, Stone," Barron said, acknowledging an obviously long-time employee.

Stella, a light-skinned black waitress, quickly appeared. "May I get you folks something to drink?"

Kelli spoke up. "An extra dry martini for me." She turned to explain. "We usually have a little libation on Fridays. It makes the day go faster."

Barron also ordered a dry martini, as did Phillip Jackson. Brook ordered a Manhattan, but Parnell Walters ordered iced tea. He mumbled something about having to be in court that afternoon. "I think I'll have iced tea too," I said. "I have a long drive home."

We ordered and once everything had settled down, Kelli turned to me. "So, where else have you interviewed?"

"I talked with a firm in Brunswick and one in Camellia. The firm in Brunswick made me an offer but those people are insurance defense attorneys and holy rollers. Just the opposite of you guys."

They all laughed and I continued. "The firm in Camellia was a sole practitioner-plaintiff-oriented and a good law practice. He made me a generous offer, but my fiancée has reservations about such a small town. I'm used to small towns, but she's not."

The steak and baked potato luncheon was delicious. The rest of the meal passed by uneventfully and it was time for me to go home.

As it happened, the drive passed quickly, during which I daydreamed about what it would be like to work for Kelli Ferguson. I had clerked for a female attorney in Macon as a law student but I had never met a woman with the drive, determination, and confidence this one exuded.

*****

Three days went by and no news. The long hot days of a Georgia August seemed to drag on. My thoughts kept drifting back to Conecuh. Had I blown the interview? Had I pissed somebody off?

I spent most of Tuesday cleaning out my old law school files and the papers I had accumulated over the three years of school. It's amazing how much junk you accumulate in law school. On Wednesday, I slept in. I'd stayed out past two in the morning with some friends. The phone rang about ten a.m. and my mother answered. "Let me see if he's here. Can I say whose calling? Yes, just a minute, Mrs. Ferguson."

I shot up in bed, instantly awake. It took me no time at all to get to my mother's side. The voice on the other end of the phone was professional but warm.

"Hello, Jake. Kelli Ferguson here. We all enjoyed the interview Friday. Look, I know you're busy, so I won't beat around the bush."

"Yeah," I fibbed.

"We had a firm meeting after you left and everybody liked you. We let the associates have a say-so too, because any lawyer we hire must work with them very closely. We want you to join our firm. We know what the other two firms offered you, and we're willing to start you out at five thousand more a year. When you pass the bar exam, we'll raise it another five thousand dollars. We'll provide full medical and life insurance, a pension and profit-sharing plan, bar dues, and civic club dues, if you decide to join one of those groups. Personally, I don't have time for civic clubs. Barron does that. Oh, yes, we'll move you over here. Phillip Jackson can help you find a place to live. He represents a number of good realtors. What do you think?"

"It sounds great, but I need to ask you for one favor. I have to run this by my fiancée and show her the town."

"Smart man, Jake. I don't want you to have a domestic relations problem before you're married. You can't afford my fees on the salary we're going to pay you." We both laughed. "How about this Friday? Can you make it over here?"

"I'll be there. Same time?"

"Yes, and bring your special lady with you. We're all anxious to meet her."

*****

Kelli hung up the phone with confidence and looked at the man behind the desk. "Barron, I think we've got him. Let's pray his fiancée doesn't get turned off when they drive down Versailles Boulevard."

The old man laughed. "What, and see where all of our clients hang out? I just hope he passed the bar exam. We've got plenty of work for him to do."

"Yeah, he can start by straightening out the Owens estate and all of Brook's messes."

*****

Kathy had been out looking at wedding dresses all morning. When she drove into the driveway, the telephone was ringing off the hook. "Hello."

"Where have you been, sweetheart?"

"What do you mean? Where do you think I've been? I've been out looking at wedding dresses."

"Listen, you know the firm that I told you about in Conecuh where I interviewed last week?"

"The one with the hot shot blond bomber?"

"Yeah. They made me an offer. One I can't refuse. Five thousand dollars a year more than the other two and more benefits. And listen to this. They'll even move me over there."

"You mean *us*, Mister Attorney. They'll move *us*."

"Yeah, that's right. They want us to meet with them this Friday for lunch. You can look the town over."

*****

I hadn't been in Conecuh long before I began to get a feel for my new colleagues. I was assigned the middle office across the hall from Brook's secretary— Sarah, a tall, skinny blonde. Brook and Sarah were made for each other. It was obvious that neither had seen the top of their desks in years.

It was rumored that Brook hadn't turned down any cases in over a year—that he would take a case for a twenty-five dollar retainer. This drove Kelli crazy. I was surprised that one of those blood-sucking insurance firms hadn't attracted her. She was a woman who loved money and would milk every dime she could out of a case.

Kelli's secretary, Neva Gullihorn, was just the opposite of Sarah—the most organized human being alive. She had a place for everything. She delighted in details and was a perfectionist—just what her hard driving boss needed.

I was unpacking a box when the intercom rang and Kelli's voice called out, "Jake, I'd like to see you." I immediately hurried down the hall and into her office.

"Sit down. We need to discuss getting you a secretary. We have a good working relationship with Carolyn Clements' employment service. I'll have her send us some applicants. She screens them the best she can. Once in a while we get an airhead, but not often. I'll talk to them about money, but let Neva, Kim, and Sarah check their secretarial skills. The worst mistake you can make in practicing law is hiring the wrong secretary. What is your schedule this morning?"

"I have a docket call in Superior Court in Judge Braxton's court at ten o'clock, then I'm sitting in with Brook on a motion to suppress in State Court."

"Good, I'll have Clemmie start sending us applicants at two o'clock."

*****

Judge Lamar H. Braxton's courtroom was abuzz with the usual jostling of lawyers on both sides of cases trying to out-posture their opponents.

Lots of whining and whimpering goes on at a docket call. Plaintiffs' attorneys want their cases tried immediately because they don't get paid until they win. Defendants' attorneys use every excuse they can create to get their cases passed so they'll have more time to run up the bill for their insurance company clients, or worse still, to avoid the inevitability of losing a hopeless case.

A loud buzzer sounded somewhere behind the judge's bench. "All rise," the deputy sheriff announced in a booming voice.

Judge Braxton was an imposing figure in his black robe. Very tall, he had huge hands that looked like meat hooks, and he wore a perpetual war face. He had once had a reputation as a tough prosecutor, a reputation he'd been building for ten years. He'd sent more men to the electric chair than any other district attorney in Georgia—sixteen in all. He hadn't lost his prosecutorial demeanor when he was elevated to the bench, as the result of a political appointment arranged by a political friend of his.

When he favored your side of the case, it was an easy day in court. If he didn't like the case, the lawyers were in for a miserable experience. I had been warned by the lawyers in the firm not to get cross-wise with Judge Lamar H. Braxton. If you ever made it on his list, you would never get off.

"Please be seated, ladies and gentlemen," Judge Braxton commanded. He wasted no time getting right into the docket call. He was impatient and didn't believe in messing around. "First case is Johnson vs. State Farm Fire and Casualty Insurance Company."

"Ready for the plaintiff," announced Fred Stopleton.

"Judge, we still have some discovery pending," said John Lee, a defense attorney with one of the largest firms in town. "We would like this case passed until next term."

"Your honor, this is the same excuse he gave at the last docket call."

"Mr. Lee, how long has this case been pending?"

"Thirteen months, Judge."

"You've had plenty of time, Mr. Lee. Set it down for next Monday morning at nine a.m. You've got a week to get your discovery done, Mr. Lee. The next case is Johnson vs. Johnson."

No announcement was made for either side.

"Is Mr. Evans in the courtroom? How about Mr. Jones? Steve Jones? "He turned to his clerk. "What kind of case is this?"

"It's a will contest, your Honor."

"Case dismissed. Ladies and gentlemen, you know my rule. If you're not here when your case is called, I'll dismiss it."

Thirteen more cases were called with the same dispatch before he finally got to ours. It was one of Barron's cases—a finance company rip-off that Barron wanted me to announce ready. There was one thing you could say about Barron. When he announced ready in a case, he was ready.

"Golding vs. General Finance Company."

"Ready for the plaintiff, your honor." Those were my first spoken words in a courtroom.

"Discovery's pending, your honor," announced a sandy-haired attorney on the other side.

"What about that, Mr. . . . uh..."

"McDonald, Judge, Jake McDonald."

"And what firm are you with?"

"Barrett, Ferguson and Thomas, your honor."

"Mr. Berry says discovery's pending. What do you say about that?"

"Well, this is one of Mr. Barrett's cases. I assumed discovery had been completed."

A snicker was heard from the back of the courtroom.

"Assume? Mr. McDonald, we don't 'assume' anything in my courtroom. You *do* understand that, don't you?"

"Yes, sir."

"Knowing Barron Barrett the way I do, I'm going to set it down for trial. Mr. Berry, if discovery is pending, and I mean, serious discovery, and not some flimsy excuse for discovery, then we will pass it. You can get together with Mr. Barrett and work it out."

I was glad to get out of Judge Braxton's courtroom. If he was that tough in a routine docket call, God help the lawyers who were trying a case before him.

*****

The snack bar was located on the ground floor of the courthouse. I figured I'd get a cup of coffee before I met Brook in State Court for the motion to suppress hearing. I had forty-five minutes.

Inside the snack bar were some women I recognized as employees in the office of the Clerk of the Superior Court. They were part of the usual group who formed the courthouse crowd. I noticed the sandy-haired attorney in the line right in front of me who had represented the other side of my case at the docket call.

"Hi, I'm Jake McDonald. I'm the new guy with the Barrett firm."

"Good to meet you," he said. "I'm Porter Berry, with King, Golden and Bonner. Was that your first experience with Judge Braxton?"

"Yes," I said. "I didn't know what to expect."

He laughed. "Don't take it personally. Judge Braxton picks on all attorneys equally. It doesn't matter if you represent the plaintiff or the defendant. Maybe Mr. Barrett and Mr. King can get together and settle this case. I'll have him call Mr. Barrett. See you later. I've got a deposition in five minutes."

King, Golden and Bonner was one of the largest law firms in town, and Bradford L. King was their star litigator. Their clients included all the major insurance companies— twenty-six, by last count according to their listing in the Martindale Hubble legal directory. All the large corporations in town somehow found their way to their front door. Their largest and most lucrative client was First Fidelity Bank and Trust, a large banking empire that had its tentacles into every major project in Conecuh.

L. Porter Berry was the great-grandson of one of the five textile baron families in Conecuh. The Berry family had appeared in Conecuh shortly after the War Between the States with loads of money. Genealogical studies indicated that the Berrys came from the garment district in New York, though no member of the Berry family ever admitted this publicly. The less polite blue-collar workers who worked in their cotton mills said they were suspected carpetbaggers. L. Porter Berry, a Harvard graduate, was, no doubt, hired because of his last name more than his legal skills.

I picked up my coffee and moved towards the table in the corner. I noticed a woman's purse on the counter. "Hey, somebody left her pocketbook," I said.

The cashier said it belonged to the lady in the back corner booth.

"I'll be glad to take it to her if you want." I picked it up and strode to the back.

"Ma'am, did you leave your pocket book on the counter?"

"Oh, my goodness, thank you," she said. "I guess I've got too many things on my mind right now."

"Hi, I'm Jake McDonald."

"Good to meet you. I'm Terri Beth Flynt."

"You must be new around here. I haven't seen you in here before."

"I am. I just moved here from Goldsboro, North Carolina. I'm looking for a job."

"What do you do?" I asked.

"I'm a legal secretary with extensive experience in banking. I worked as a bank examiner in Washington in one of my other careers."

"That's a coincidence. I'm *looking* for a legal secretary. What brings a lady from Goldsboro, North Carolina, to Conecuh?"

"My husband was killed in a plane crash, and I have an aunt who lives here. She's my only living relative."

"Oh, I'm so sorry about your husband."

"I just settled with the airline. I had to get away from a lot of memories, so I moved here."

"Say, have you interviewed with a law firm yet?"

"No."

"Do you have a resume with you?"

"Yeah, here's one. Take it."

"I have a motion hearing in a few minutes. Could you meet me at, say, two o'clock this afternoon? My office is located right across the street. Here's my card." I slipped her resume in my briefcase, hoping to read it during lunch.

Judge Jenkins was known as the policeman's judge. A former State Court solicitor, he had never granted a motion to suppress evidence. Brook tried hard, but he knew what the decision would be. After thirty minutes of argument, Judge Jenkins said, "Motion denied. We will set this case for trial at the next term of court."

*****

When I finally got a look at Terri Beth Flynt's resume, I thought I had died and gone to heaven. She was a Certified Professional Secretary, a designation given to only a very few by Professional Secretaries International. She had worked for six years at a five-man law firm in Goldsboro. Her boss was a plaintiff's attorney who was the past president of the North

26

Carolina Academy of Trial Lawyers. She was proficient with computers, word processors, knew shorthand, and could type a hundred words per minute. Her resume revealed that she had worked for the Office of the Comptroller of the Currency as a banking examiner, an odd combination for a plaintiff attorney's secretary. *Well, she's good with numbers*, I thought. She seemed perfect. If only Kelli would pay her enough.

Terri Beth arrived promptly at two o'clock. There were two other applicants in the reception room, applicants sent over by Clemmie. One was an older lady, about forty-five, the other very young.

"Mrs. Flynt, you have an impressive resume."

"Thank you, Mr. McDonald. Please call me Terri Beth."

"Please call me Jake. My real name is W. Lancaster McDonald, but I was nicknamed Jake in high school and it stuck."

Her eyes met mine. It was as if we were reading each other's minds. "I'd like for you to meet some of the other secretaries and take a little typing test. I'm afraid you *do* have to type here." We both laughed.

"I think I can handle it." she replied. "I worked for five slave drivers in North Carolina."

*****

Neva and Terri Beth hit it off immediately. Even Kim liked her. She was always standoffish when we hired new personnel.

Sarah gave her the typing test on the word processor. The keyboard clicked like a machine gun. Precisely one hundred words a minute with just one error. I knew Kelli was a stickler about shorthand so Neva gave her a shorthand test. Perfect.

"Would you mind waiting around for a little while? I have a couple of people to talk to and then I want you to meet Kelli. She's the boss."

"Sure."

I interviewed the other two candidates quickly. The older applicant had no legal experience. Her secretarial skills were marginal. The younger applicant was right out of high school with no work experience. I told them we would get back to them. I knew who my choice was.

When Kelli reviewed Terri Beth's application she was impressed. "Terri Beth, Jake says you're the one."

"Thank you, Mrs. Ferguson."

"Did he show you around the firm?"

"Yes, ma'am."

"We're a general practice law firm with a strong emphasis on personal injury, domestic relations, bankruptcy and criminal law. What are your salary requirements?"

"Well, I was earning two thousand dollars a month in North Carolina."

Kelli winced. "I'm afraid you might be out of our range."

"What could you pay me?"

"Our top salary is fifteen hundred a month plus benefits-medical, life insurance, profit sharing, two weeks of paid vacation, sick leave, and a bonus."

"I'll tell you what I'm willing to do. I just settled my husband's death claim with the airline. I'll work for fifteen hundred, and if I prove I'm worth every penny and more, will you give me a raise or bonus?"

Kelli smiled. "You've got it."

My heart beat with excitement. I had just hired my secretary.

I contacted all the references Terri Beth had listed on her resume. They all gave glowing reports. Sam Clegg, the former president of the North Carolina Academy of Trial Lawyers, said that I was the "luckiest sonofabitch alive." He would hire her back in a minute, and he was sick when her husband was killed. Her husband had been a regional sales manager for a computer firm and was killed when a DC-9 crashed outside of Dallas. Pilot error was the cause. Sam told me never to repeat the fact that the case was quickly settled out of court for three million dollars. Terri Beth netted two million and some change. Sam said, "Jake, you've got a gold mine in Terri Beth. Treat her right. She's a real hurt puppy right now. She was deeply in love with her husband."

"Thank you, Mr. Clegg. We'll keep you posted."

"Hell! Do better than that—send her back."

Her boss at the Office of the Comptroller of the Currency, Karl Flick, was pleasant enough. He was very positive about her job performance. But I had the feeling that there was something he wasn't telling me.

*****

29

September flew by quickly. I was up to my neck in the estate of Jack Owens. At the time of his death, he had a mean ex-wife and a mean current wife, and two children—one by each wife. He owned over ninety-two parcels of real estate, seven corporations, and millions of dollars in stocks and bonds, and Kelli had been appointed the executrix of his estate.

After months of frivolous litigation between the wives, the court appointed First Fidelity Bank and Trust as Trustee in an attempt to settle the disputes. I regularly met with the bank's attorneys, King, Golden and Bonner, and their paralegals. The bank's attorneys were billing the estate at $250 per hour and $100 per hour for their paralegals. The legal expenses were horrendous. King, Golden and Bonner no doubt trained their associates to dream about the Owens estate at night and then to bill the estate for their dreams.

It was October 26th, and I was in another endless meeting with the attorneys of King, Golden and Bonner to discuss the guardianship fees for Owens' fourteen-year-old daughter when I was interrupted by a phone call. It was Brook.

"Jake, get out of that meeting as quickly as you can. The bar exam results are out. Get over here now."

"Did I pass?" I asked.

"We don't know. We don't know your bar exam number. Get over here quick. I have their telephone number."

"Gentlemen, something very important has come up and I have to leave. No emergency, but I have to leave." I ran back to my office and almost knocked Terri Beth over running down the hall.

"Jake, what's the matter?" she asked.

"Tell you later, Terri Beth. Where's Brook?"

"In his office."

I bounded in to find Brook standing behind his desk holding a piece of paper out to me. "Here's the number."

My heart was pounding. This was it. My mouth was dry and my stomach was in knots.

"State Board of Bar Examiners," said the lady on the other end of the line.

I could hardly get it out. "Are the results of the most recent bar exam out?"

"Yes, sir. If you'll give me your name and your exam number—"

"Jake, I mean W. Lancaster. That's L-A-N-C-A-S-T-E-R, McDonald. M-C-D-O-N-A-L-D. Exam number 170."

"Just a minute, please..." A week went by while we were on hold. Then a voice came back on the line. "Yes, sir, Mr. McDonald, you passed. You will get your official notification in the mail within a week."

You could have heard the rebel yell clear across Georgia. I'm sure the clients in the waiting room thought someone had been murdered. Kelli and Barron ran in to see what was going on.

"What the hell is going on?" Barron asked, frowning.

"My fellow partners, please meet the newest member of the State Bar of Georgia, W. Lancaster McDonald, Attorney at Law." Brook grinned.

My head was spinning. Everybody congratulated me. I got kisses from all the secretaries, including the prude Kim. "I passed that damn test," was all I could say.

"Phillip, you and Parnell go down to Cherio's and get us some good champagne. This calls for a celebration," said Kelli.

It was 6:30 p.m. and all the congratulations that could have been said had been said. We were down to the last bottle of Dom Perignon. Everyone else had left and Sarah was taking trash out to the dumpster. Terri Beth was typing something on the word processor. "What are you doing?" I asked.

She turned and smiled. "I just wanted to give you something special on this special day."

I poured her a glass of champagne and refilled mine. She smiled, took a sip, and said, "Here."

"What's this?" I asked.

"It's a poem, dummy."

I laughed and then cried when I finished reading it. "It's beautiful." It was a poem about life and death and the uncertainties in between. I could tell she had put a lot of feeling into it.

"I wrote this for my husband on our wedding day. He's no longer around to share it with, so it now belongs to you."

"Oh, Terri Beth, you can't."

"Yes, it belongs to a very special person who has given me new hope—you. Congratulations, Mr. Attorney at Law. See you in the morning. And drive safely."

******

I began to detest the way King, Golden and Bonner and First Fidelity Bank and Trust were ripping off the Owens estate. A man works all his life to accumulate enough wealth so his family can live comfortably. Now these lawyers and bankers were squandering it away in fees for frivolous legal work. I only wished somebody would sue the bloodsuckers.

I arrived at King, Golden and Bonner a few minutes early and was ushered into the conference room, a place I had spent many hours before. The other attorneys had not yet arrived. Somebody had left a file on the table. I couldn't help but notice the note attached to it.

The C Boys are coming in from Chicago Friday and they want this problem taken care of immediately.

Anthony C. Jacobs

The note grabbed my attention because it was attached to a file labeled First Fidelity Bank and Trust vs. Perkins

Construction Co. I was stunned. I represented Randy Perkins and Perkins Construction Company and wasn't aware of a lawsuit by First Fidelity against him. I made a mental note to ask about it.

Bradford King's secretary, Cassy, came in and started preparing the coffee for what was going to be another long, boring and expensive meeting with the First Fidelity lawyers. The Owens estate once again would be the loser. She picked up the mysterious file and left the room.

The morning was again consumed with wrangling over non-essential estate matters that could have been resolved in five minutes. First Fidelity's attorneys chose to drag it out for the tidy sum of $950 and there was nothing I could do about it.

Two

Randy Perkins was the avant garde builder in town. He was not afraid to take risks. Perkins Construction Company had built the most unique projects in town and was the first to introduce the condominium concept—the Vistas Project—to Conecuh. Perkins Construction Company, like all other construction companies, sustained heavy financial losses in the early seventies and almost went into bankruptcy. It had been Jack Owens' finesse and threats to creditors that saved it from the predators and banks. Owens had the reputation for taking on banks and loved to do it in front of juries. He had never lost a case against a bank—they usually settled out of court.

I inherited Randy Perkins as a client from Kelli, who had brought the business into the firm. She had handled the adoption of Perkins' child and eventually represented his construction company. I had handled a few minor legal matters for Perkins but did not know the intimate details of his company.

"Randy, this is Jake McDonald. Are you free for lunch?"

"Yeah. What's up? Where do you want to meet?"

"How about Sandy's at 12:30?"

"Okay, I'll see you there."

Twelve-thirty arrived and there was Randy Perkins standing in front of Sandy's Restaurant wearing his typical work attire, a blue denim shirt with the name Perkins Construction Company embroidered on the left pocket. He was also wearing a pair of khaki trousers with heavy construction shoes.

"Hi, Jake. What's up?"

"Let's see if we can get a private room in the back."

Sandy's family had owned the restaurant for forty years. All of the local crowd ate there. The food was good, the prices were reasonable and the waitresses were friendly. The waitress ushered us into the back room that was usually reserved for civic groups that met there every week.

"Say, Randy, this is in the strictest of confidence, you know. Attorney-client privilege, you understand?"

"Yeah. Is something the matter?"

"Randy, you need to tell me the truth about what's going on with your business."

"What are you talking about?" he said.

"I was in a meeting at King, Golden and Bonner this morning on another matter. Nobody else was in the room. I noticed a file on the table that was labeled First Fidelity Bank and Trust vs. Perkins Construction Company. Are these guys suing you?"

"Uh...uh, no. Why?"

"Well, what really got my attention was a note attached to the file that said 'The C Boys are coming in from Chicago on Friday, and they want this problem taken care of immediately.' It was signed Anthony C. Jacobs, the president of First Fidelity."

Randy Perkins turned white as a ghost.

"Randy, as your lawyer I need to know everything—the good, the bad, and the ugly."

He took a deep breath and looked around before speaking. "Nobody knows this but First Fidelity and me. And now you. Perkins Construction Company is in deep financial trouble. We're leveraged to the hilt and we had to do something. Robert Banks, the commercial loan VP at First Fidelity said he could get me a million dollar line of credit, but it would cost me. It did—twenty-five percent interest and a first lien on everything, including all the stock in my company. They even charged me ten points."

"Whew!" I whistled. "My God, Randy, that's rape!"

"We had no choice, Jake. We couldn't meet payroll and we were halfway through the Vistas project. Our whole company was on the line. Apparently the money didn't come through traditional banking sources. Robert kept saying that his money source was not happy with the way the Vistas project was going and they threatened to cut off the line of credit."

"Who are the C Boys from Chicago, Randy?"

He turned white again. "I'm scared, Jake."

"Who are the C Boys?" I insisted..

"Jake, I'm afraid I'm dealing with the mob."

There was silence. We finished our meal quickly, paid the check, and left.

The rest of my afternoon was consumed by hearings in bankruptcy court—the usual first meeting of creditors, with each hearing taking about five minutes. We had twelve hearings, all no-asset cases. But I couldn't keep my mind off my luncheon meeting with Randy Perkins.

At six o'clock Thursday morning, the phone rang just as I was getting out of the shower.

It was Terri Beth. "Hey, Boss, have you seen the morning paper?"

"No. What is it?"

"Get a paper, quick. Front page. Randy Perkins' Vista Villas burned to the ground last night."

"You're kidding me."

"No. Over four million dollars in damage. Ten fire trucks. A total loss."

A shiver went down my spine. "Did they say what caused it?"

"They said arson investigators are on the scene now. It looks suspicious. You don't believe Randy Perkins burned it, do you?"

What caused her to ask a question like that? I hadn't told her about my meeting with Randy. "I don't know what to believe. The man has poured his heart and soul into that project. Listen, get to the office as quickly as you can and gather up everything we're doing now and everything we've ever done in the past for Perkins. Don't let anybody near those files."

"What do you suspect, Boss?"

"Nothing good," I said.

38

I got to the office at 7:30 and Terri Beth was already there and making coffee. "I got all the files together," she whispered. "They're locked in your credenza."

"Thanks."

"Oh, and Randy called a few minutes ago. He's distraught. Here's his number."

I hurried into my office and looked at the number. This was strange—a long distance number with an Atlanta exchange. I dialed the number and Randy answered. "Randy, this is Jake." I could hear him sobbing in the background.

"They've done it, Jake. The bastards have ruined me. I'm finished. It's over."

"Where *are* you?"

"In a motel outside of Alpharetta. Jake, believe me, I didn't burn my own damn buildings down. They were my only hope of pulling out of this mess."

"Well, the insurance company will take care of the losses."

There was silence on the other end of the telephone. My heart sunk.

"You *did* have insurance, didn't you?"

More silence. "It was all payable to First Fidelity Bank and Trust."

I was stunned. "Give me a number where I can reach you later and don't go anywhere. I'm sure the investigators will want to ask you some questions."

"I swear, Jake, I didn't burn it down."

*****

It was ten a.m. I had read the story of Vista Villas' fire four times when Juanita buzzed in, "Mr. McDonald, Donald Pollard is on line one."

Donald Lewis Pollard and I had graduated from the same law school. He had been an assistant district attorney in Conecuh for ten years, and for the last five, he had been the DA. He was a Democrat, but he'd probably received as many Republican votes as Democrat. The toughest prosecutor in the circuit since Judge Lamar Braxton, there were eleven men and one woman on death row as a result of his prosecutorial skills. Three men had already gone to the electric chair and he had personally attended each one of the executions. He was as mean as a rattlesnake but honest. I didn't want to take his call.

"Hello, Jake. Don Pollard."

"Hello, Don. What can I do for you?"

"I think you know. I'm sure you read the morning paper. Somebody got a little careless with fire last night at your client's place."

"If you're accusing my client I believe you are jumping to conclusions."

"I don't think so, Jake. I've prosecuted quite a few arson cases in my time. We want to talk to Randy Perkins as soon as possible. Do you know where he is?"

"I could probably find him," I said.

"See if you can round him up as soon as possible."

"I would like to be present."

"Okay, that's your right. I want Johnny Harbuck present, too."

Johnny Harbuck was the best investigator the DA had. A Green Beret in Vietnam, he had graduated from law school and became an FBI agent. He was one of the best agents the Bureau had until a bank robber had shortened his career in a shoot out. Drawing a nice disability pension from the federal government, he'd retired to his native Georgia and gone to work for the DA's office fifteen years before. Every case was a challenge to him. Cool and collected with stone cold blue eyes, he could smell a rat ten miles away. He had sent plenty of our clients to the penitentiary. If Randy Perkins committed arson, Johnny Harbuck would know it.

I called Perkins with the bad news and we agreed to meet at the DA's office on Friday at eight a.m.

At eleven o'clock Kelli ushered two people into my office, a Ronald Eugene Cochran and his wife, Betty. They were obviously blue collar. His reddish brown hair was slicked back with heavy hair tonic that reeked of the stuff I used to smell in the barbershop as a kid. He wore a mustache and had a tattoo on his right hand. Two of Betty's front teeth were missing and her jet-black hair was coiffured in a 50's-style bouffant. Kelli had extracted a thousand-dollar retainer from them for us to handle a fraud case against a finance company.

She was always doing this to me. I was the newest attorney in the firm, so she would take a retainer and shuttle the undesirable cases down the hall to me.

Gene and Betty Cochran were door-to-door vacuum cleaner salespeople who operated a franchise of a well-known vacuum cleaner company. The vacuum cleaners were overpriced but financing was available if one was willing to pay the price.

They were difficult. Betty was a know-it-all, and kept interrupting. Eventually I had to insist that they speak one at a time. After much inane chatter, I finally learned that their usual way to sell a vacuum cleaner was to get a small down payment and finance the rest. They would sell the installment agreement at a discount to various finance companies, primarily Southern Finance of Georgia, Inc. SFG would then advance funds on the contract and hold back 25 percent against any future default in payment by the customer.

Things went well for the first two years, and then the charge-backs became more frequent. Soon the retention funds ran out and Southern began to keep all of the proceeds of the sales. The Cochrans were working for Southern for free.

Gene and Betty brought in a pile of unorganized paperwork. This was the kind of case a lawyer doesn't want. It was obvious from a cursory look that they had been cheated, but for how much, nobody knew. I told them I would need to investigate their case more thoroughly. I finally got them out of my office. I was relieved when they were gone.

My thoughts turned back to Randy Perkins and I buzzed Teri Beth. "Is Dixie in the building?"

"She's in the library, boss."

Dixie, as we nicknamed her, was our law clerk. A senior in law school at Mercer, she had a nose like a bird-dog and the ability to ferret out facts in a hurry. The Cochran case was just her type of case. I walked into the library.

"Dixie, how about getting on PHOL—Prentice Hall On Line—and see what you can find out about Southern Finance of Georgia, Inc. I need to know everything about them—their officers, directors, Dun and Bradstreet, where they get their money."

"Sure. When do you need it?" she asked.

"Well, they just paid a thousand dollars in retainer, so as soon as possible."

"Okay." She scurried off to the computer in the library.

*****

Randy Perkins and I showed up at Donald Pollard's office at five minutes to eight. Randy wasn't wearing his normal contractor attire. He was dressed in a dark navy blue suit with a power tie and his hair was neatly combed. His eyes were bloodshot- He had either not slept in quite a while or had been drinking a lot; probably both.

Donald Pollard greeted us at the door. I shook hands with Johnny Harbuck and another assistant DA who was present. After the usual pleasantries were exchanged, Don got to the point. "Mr. Perkins, I want to record this conversation. Let the record show that you have your lawyer present, Mr. W. Lancaster McDonald. Is that right?"

"Yes, sir."

"At any time you wish to confer with your attorney, please feel free to do so. Do you understand? We are not accusing you of anything at this point. We are still in the investigatory stage of the fire that destroyed your property Wednesday night."

Randy revealed that he had been in Alpharetta on the night of the fire and that he could provide alibi witnesses. He also revealed his financial difficulties, which Pollard already knew. He stated that all the insurance proceeds were payable to First Fidelity Bank and Trust and that he would get nothing. Johnny Harbuck perked up and leaned forward when he heard this. Pollard looked at his assistant DA and then back at Harbuck. Their exchange of looks indicated that they knew something we didn't.

The interview lasted until 11:30 a.m. Don said he would get back with us and we left.

As we were leaving the courthouse, Randy turned to me and said, "I swear Jake, what I said is true. I didn't burn down my own building."

"Okay," I said, "but don't go anywhere, and keep me informed of where you are. The DA isn't through with you."

I walked in the front door and Kelli was prancing around her office. "Let's go. It's time to go to the club. How did it go with Pollard?"

"As well as could be expected," I said. "You know how Pollard is. He indicts everybody."

"Yeah," said Kelli. "He's one mean sonofabitch."

The lunch at the country club was a sweet reprieve from the morning's activities. No phones, no clients, no interruptions.

"How did you do with the Cochrans?" Kelli asked.

"I'll never forgive you, Kelli," I said, laughing. "You take in a thousand dollars and you put those turkeys on me."

She said, "I suppose you want me to give the thousand dollars back. I seem to recall you're due for a raise this month."

"That won't be necessary. I'll handle the case."

"That's what I thought."

Dixie had placed a thick manila envelope on my desk. It was a lengthy report from Prentice Hall. I flipped through it rapidly, but stopped on page 26. I was stunned at what I saw in front of me. Southern Finance of Georgia, Inc. was a wholly owned subsidiary of First Fidelity Bank and Trust.

These guys weren't satisfied to just screw people over as bankers. Now they were operating as loan sharks. They were totally corrupt. I would hold this information until Monday, when Kelli had a clearer head. Suddenly the Cochran's case became more interesting to me.

I headed out for Fort Walton Beach, Florida, to be with my fiancée Kathy for the weekend. It was hard for me to realize that in two weeks I would be married.

We spent some time on the beach. There's nothing like the sound of waves to calm frenzied nerves. We talked about our final wedding plans and about the house in Conecuh that we were remodeling. We had bought a house in an old, established neighborhood near the country club, which was rapidly being occupied by yuppies. I had hired a re-modeler to do the job—Rudy Tolbert. I liked his innovative style and the way he combined colors.

I dreaded the long drive home from Fort Walton Beach. I dreaded having to deal with the Randy Perkins case and telling Kelli about Southern Finance and its connection with First Fidelity. I especially dreaded my pre-trial motions with Judge Braxton at ten Monday morning.

Terri Beth was usually the first person to arrive at the office, but I arrived before she did on Monday morning. Rudy Tolbert was waiting at the office doorstep. Tolbert was a stocky guy with black curly hair.

"Mr. McDonald," Rudy said, extending his right hand.

"Call me Jake."

"Yes, sir."

"You do good work remodeling houses. Come on in. Can I get you some coffee?"

"No sir. Had all I could drink about five o'clock this morning."

I got right to the point. "I'm getting married in two weeks and I'm giving my bride a wedding present—a house." I outlined the floor plans and showed him some pictures. His eyes glowed with excitement. He started rolling off the tip of his tongue all the things he could do with the house. "Look, get me a plan and an estimate and get back with me as quickly as you can," I said.

Terri Beth peered around the corner. "How was your weekend, boss?"

"Wonderful. I wish I lived on the beach."

"Win a big damage suit and you just might."

*****

The motion hearings went quite well. Judge Braxton was civil for a change and ruled in our favor in two of the three motions. He must have had a good weekend, too.

I returned to the firm just as a divorce client was leaving Kelli's office. "Hey, Kelli, I'd like to see you when you get a break."

"How about now?" she said.

"Okay," I said, and stepped in and closed the door. "You know the Cochran case you gave me Friday? It's more serious than we thought. Dixie did an investigation and it turns out that Southern Finance of Georgia, Inc., is a wholly owned subsidiary of First Fidelity Bank and Trust."

Her expression didn't change.

I continued. "When did they get into loan sharking?"

Kelli looked away. "Jake, I'm not surprised. Anthony Jacobs and First Fidelity have their fingers into everything. But be careful. Before you go and sue them, we need to have a law firm meeting about it."

"Are you scared of them?" I asked.

"Hell, no. I never got a dime's worth of help from those bandits. You see what they're doing to the Owens estate."

"Will this create a conflict of interest?"

"I don't see one. We didn't hire them. The court appointed them."

"Hell, if we sue them maybe they'll be more honest with Jack's estate."

Rudy had a really creative plan for the remodeling of the old house. He said he could get the gut rehab work done in two weeks and it would be another month for completion. The price was right, but I had to check with Kathy. I would overnight the plans to her.

When I returned from the mailroom, Rudy was still waiting in my office. "We're through for now, aren't we?" I asked.

"I appreciate your hiring me to remodel your house, Mr. McDonald, but I need to ask you a question. Can I hire you as my lawyer?"

"What for?"

He said, "Well, first, I need to know if you're afraid to sue a big bank."

"Hell, no," I said. "So long as *I* don't owe them money," I laughed at my own joke, but Rudy didn't smile.

He pulled out a set of papers wrapped in a blue binder. I had seen hundreds of these before. "The bank is trying to take away my house," he said.

"What bank?" I asked.

"First Fidelity Bank and Trust."

"Those bastards," I blurted out. "Do you owe them money?"

"Yes and no," Rudy replied.

"What kind of answer is that?"

"Well, I owe them money from my business, but somehow they tied my house up on the loan."

"How did they do that?"

"I don't know. I just signed the papers they stuck in front of me in the lawyer's office. You see, I don't read too good."

"What lawyer?"

"King, Golden and Bonner."

What a surprise.

Rudy Tolbert was the product of what used to be called the "social promotion" system of Georgia's school system. Illiterate, he had dropped out of school in the tenth grade and could hardly read a comic book.

"Look, Rudy, I want to help you, but this is going to be a tough case. I'm gonna need all your closing papers. Can you get them to me in a hurry? I mean, like, today. When is the foreclosure?"

"Tomorrow morning at eleven."

" We're going to have to move it."

Rudy returned with the closing papers within an hour.

It seemed that First Fidelity had taken a second mortgage against his house for twenty thousand dollars. Rudy had remodeled the house himself and probably had eighty thousand in equity in it. He brought me a note, a security deed and a copy of a hazard insurance policy naming the bank as the insured.

Something was missing. I called Rudy. "Rudy, are these all the papers you have?"

"Yeah."

"Are you sure you didn't sign anything like a closing statement?"

"I'm sure."

"Do you know what a closing statement looks like?"

"Yeah, I've signed lots of them."

"Are you positive you signed no closing statement?"

"I'm sure."

*****

I burned the midnight oil. After a quick hamburger at the Burger King, I found what I was looking for—a statute known as the Secondary Security Deed law that provides that if a second security deed is placed on a person's house, he must be given a signed statement detailing all of the itemized closing costs at the time of closing. If this doesn't happen the mortgage is canceled by law. The interest is forfeited, the lender loses its principal, and the borrower is entitled to attorney's fees.

I quickly found a form book that had what I wanted. I drafted a basic complaint alleging the violation of the Secondary Security Deed law, the facts as they applied to Rudy Tolbert's case, and petitioned the court for an ex-parte temporary restraining order prohibiting foreclosure.

It was 10:30 p.m. I called Terri Beth at home and outlined the situation. "We've got to get a temporary restraining order in the Tolbert case as soon as possible." She promised to be in by seven. I apologized again and hung up.

I called Rudy Tolbert at home. I told him what I had done and told him to be in my office by 8:30 in the morning.

Promptly at ten o'clock the next morning Rudy Tolbert and I marched into the chambers of the chief judge, J. Robert Lanier. I briefly outlined the facts and put Rudy under oath. Judge Lanier signed the restraining order and I ran downstairs to the courthouse steps where the reading of foreclosures was being held. There stood L. Porter Berry of King, Golden and Bonner poised and ready to read the foreclosure ad and take Rudy's house away from him.

I stepped forward proudly and served him the papers. "Porter, I have a temporary restraining order from Judge J. Robert Lanier stopping the foreclosure of the property of Rudy Tolbert."

"What the hell is this?" he said.

"Read it and you'll see."

"I'll see you in court."

"The hearing is in two weeks."

God, it felt good for once to stop the self-righteous Pharisees in their tracks. Rudy was amazed at what we had just done. I could tell he would be my friend for life.

*****

Friday afternoon was the annual circuit barbecue at Snyder Lake. The stated purpose of the meeting was to elect the new officers of the Circuit Bar Association, but the real reason was to drink, posture egos, and settle cases. It was the time all lawyers and judges got together, got drunk, ate barbecue and shot craps under the protection of the sheriffs of the seven counties in the judicial circuit. This was the one event of the year that no lawyer missed. One could learn all the gossip, settle more cases, and soothe more feathers with beer and barbecue than all the pleadings and hearings in any courtroom. This was one event where Judge Lamar Braxton liked to let his hair down and show the members of the bar that he was indeed a human being.

I arrived about five o'clock and parked my Buick Skylark under the shade of an old live oak tree. Jim Horne, one of our kind of lawyers, was getting out of his car. "How's it going, Jake?" he said.

"Pretty good, Jim. Did you finish your case today?"

"Yeah, we got a verdict for thirty thousand. State Farm only offered five."

"Congratulations."

"Say, I'm sorry to read about Randy Perkins' project going up in flames."

"Yeah, I think it's going to kill the poor guy."

"Any word on what caused it?"

"The DA's office is sniffing around. Looks like arson.

"Hello, Colonel." It was Judge Kidd. The small claims judge, he addressed all lawyers as "Colonel," especially the ones he liked.

"Hello, Judge."

After talking to him for a moment, I wandered over to where Don Pollard and another criminal defense attorney were engaged in a lively conversation. The other attorney was obviously glad I had interrupted them. It was evident that Don was getting the best of him. He excused himself to get another beer.

"Hey, Don."

"Jake."

"You scared the hell out of my client Monday."

"I hope so," he said. "Maybe he'll tell the truth."

"He *was* telling the truth."

"They *all* say that. Even when they are sitting in the electric chair."

"You aren't going to send my client to the chair, are you?" I said laughing.

"Not him. But maybe you." He laughed, too.

"Listen, about this fire thing. Something was bugging me even before it happened. If I give you a lead, will you keep it in the strictest confidence and never let it be known where it came from?"

"What? Does your client want to confess?"

"Hell no, you fool. Listen, can I meet with you and Johnny Harbuck?"

"Sure. We'll be working in the office tomorrow morning, assuming we don't all have hangovers."

"You government boys work on Saturdays?"

"We try to give the taxpayers their money's worth."

The get-together dragged on until late into the night. I left early around nine p.m.

Saturday morning, I arrived bright and early at the courthouse. The deputy sheriff on duty recognized me and unlocked the elevator. I went to the fourth floor and knocked on the door. Johnny Harbuck let me in. He was dressed in blue jeans and a blue denim work shirt, just like Don.

"Coffee?"

"Yeah, I need to wake up. How late did you guys stay?"

"Till about ten. I get tired of seeing Bill Brady lose his ass at craps. He needs to learn how to play or quit." He shook his head. "What's on your mind? I know you're not up here to drink coffee with us."

"Gentlemen, I don't know how to say this, so I'm going to shoot straight."

"Okay, shoot."

"Two days before the Perkins fire I was in the offices of King, Golden and Bonner. It was another one of those damn meetings on the Jack Owens' estate. Strictly a billable fiesta, if you know what I mean."

Don and Johnny both laughed.

"Anyway, I got there early and the secretary put me in the conference room where the meeting was to take place. I noticed a file on the table with a label on it that said, 'First Fidelity Savings and Loan vs. Perkins Construction Company.' Attached to the file was a handwritten note from Anthony Jacobs that said, 'The C Boys from Chicago are coming down on Friday. They want this matter taken care of immediately.'

"As you know, my firm has represented Randy Perkins for a long time. I've looked through all the firm's files for everything we've ever done for him. I am aware of no case against him by First Fidelity. He swears that no action is pending."

"What's your point?" asked Don.

"I know you are already aware of his financial condition. He is strung out. Unknown to me he was paying those bloodsuckers twenty-five percent interest and they had a lien on everything he owned. He indicated that the bankers told him on more than one occasion that the lenders were very unhappy with his repayment performance and threatened to cut off his line of credit.

"Don, we're not talking about the bank. Somebody else was fronting the money. The *insurance* proceeds were payable to the bank. He won't get a dime.

"The point is that I think there is a mob connection. Should I go to the Feds? Clements is a good friend of mine." Barksdale Clements was the United States attorney and a good prosecutor.

Don raised his head to look at me. "Don't do anything yet. We're too early into the investigation. If the Feds move in, we might lose valuable time and control over the case.

"I can't give you all the information yet but we know a crime was committed. I *can* tell you this—we *know* it was arson. If your client was involved, we'll do the decent thing and let you bring him in to surrender as quietly as possible.

"This information is indeed valuable." He glanced toward Johnny. "I'll put Johnny on it. He's the best. Right, Johnny?"

Johnny shook his head.

I left and went back to my office to dictate some letters. Terri Beth would have a lot to do on Monday morning.

*****

Don Pollard watched out the window as Jake walked back to his car. He looked at his detective. "Well, what do you think?"

Johnny raised his eyebrows. "I think Jake is telling the truth. He may be onto something."

"I know. He wouldn't make up crap like that, not for any client."

Johnny was silent for a moment. "We know how the fire was started. We just don't know who did it yet. I haven't seen one of these incendiary devices since Vietnam. They'll burn a hole through six inches of steel in a New York minute. But where would Jake's client get a 'cindy'?"

"From an Army post, I guess. That's easy enough. But why would he burn his own place down if he couldn't collect the insurance? He certainly wouldn't do it to help the bank. He hated them."

"You know what I believe?"

"What?"

"I believe Jake's client has been set up. The 'C Boys' just might be the Costellano crime family from Chicago. Let's put our intelligence unit on it right away. But I don't think we need to call in the Feds until we have more proof."

*****

I made one last trip to Fort Walton Beach before the wedding to get my mind off all the events of the past week. Kathy was excited to see me. I told her that Rudy was doing a wonderful job with the house and that hopefully we would be able to move into it within the month.

We had a cookout with some of her bridesmaids who were in town, and I got in some surf fishing. It sure beat handling divorce and custody cases.

My final week at the firm as a single man was hectic. Along with all the last minute details of the wedding, I had to contend with the Cochrans. They bugged me every day about their case. My mind was totally focused on getting married, and *not* the law practice. I left the whole thing in Dixie's hands.

The whole law firm came to Florida to attend the wedding. It was a gala affair. Kathy could not have looked more beautiful. We were ushered into a reception hall where some friends of my new mother-in-law had prepared a beautiful wedding reception. I was anxious to get on with the honeymoon.

Dixie came up to congratulate us. "No shop talk, Jake, but I just wanted you to know that your Cochran clients are driving me nuts."

"You mean *our* clients, Dixie. Give 'em back to Kelli as a wedding present to me." We laughed.

"They may be crazy, but I think you should know that in all that mess of paperwork they left us with there's evidence that they've been ripped off on twenty-two separate occasions. Their payments have been misapplied and the finance company has misappropriated the funds."

"Dixie, I've been thinking maybe we ought to look into filing a RICO action against First Fidelity in the form of a class action. We could bring in Perkins, Talbot, Cochran, and anybody else the bank has screwed. Don't mention it to Kelli yet but look into it, will ya?"

"Jake," exclaimed my new better half, "you've been married thirty minutes and you're still at the office. No more lawyer talk. Promise me!"

"I promise. Thanks, Dixie."

We took a cruise ship to the western Caribbean. I now know why they call it a honeymoon. The best food in the world. No phones. No faxes. No television. No calls from the Cochrans. I didn't want to go home. I determined that my secret ambition was to win a multi-million dollar verdict and retire permanently on a cruise ship.

Three

Neva Gullihorn suggested that I attend the Chamber of Commerce monthly breakfast. Our law firm was a member of the Chamber but none of our lawyers ever went. I agreed to go if she would go with me. I met her at 6:45 a.m. at the office. She looked elegant in her white dress and her long dark hair. "You look gorgeous, Neva."

She grinned. "I see you're wearing your suing suit this morning, Jake." That was what she called my navy blue Brooks Brothers.

The room was full of business people; all net workers looking for a new buck. A few I recognized. Everybody stood around drinking coffee and orange juice and doing the usual glad-handing until a bell rang and breakfast was served.

Every month the Chamber breakfast had a different sponsor. The sponsor paid the costs and got to give a ten-minute commercial. Ironically, First Fidelity Bank and Trust's Matt Young, First Fidelity's Executive VP, was head of the Chamber and presided over the breakfast. I laughed to myself. Here I was having breakfast with the bunch of bastards I was about to sue. The Last Breakfast.

Neva selected a table for us. There were two women at the table from Georgia Power, a television executive wearing a Rotary pin, a man who owned a carpet mill store, and Ronald Sherman, a vice-president from First Fidelity. The television man introduced himself as Ford Ashton. He was the anchorman at Channel 6 and knew Kelli. "Is this your wife?" he asked me.

"She's *one* of them," I said. "I keep a harem at the law firm."

They all laughed.

"No, this is Neva Gullihorn. She's one of the best legal secretaries God ever created."

"And one of the prettiest," Ashton added.

Neva blushed.

The Georgia Power women were polite but quiet. Ronald Sherman tried to impress everyone with his knowledge of business and finance. I wondered what part he played in the rip-off of my clients.

Neva and I returned to the office at 8:30 a.m. The office was buzzing already.

"Coffee, boss?" Terri Beth asked.

"No, thank you. I'm coffee-ed out after the chamber breakfast."

"How did it go?" she inquired.

"It was sponsored by First Fidelity, and the Chamber president is a First Fidelity man. They control the Chamber of Commerce in addition to the loan sharking business."

I looked into the library. "Where's Dixie?"

"Making copies of the brief."

Dixie was a methodical workaholic. When you gave her something to work on she wouldn't quit until it was sliced and diced from every angle. She had prepared a twenty-page brief outlining the state and federal RICO statutes.

RICO stands for Racketeer Influenced Corrupt Organizations Act that began as a federal criminal statute to seize the assets of the mob. Various states, including Georgia, had adopted a civil version of it to break up corrupt business organizations. It was a nightmare for businesses but it was a plaintiff lawyer's dream. It scared the hell out of the chamber of commerce types. They lobbied the state legislature every year to abolish it, without success. The speaker of the Georgia House of Representatives was a trial lawyer, and as the most powerful political figure in Georgia, he had blocked its abolition every year.

Dixie had included in her brief a synopsis of the Georgia foreclosure statues, the Secondary Security Deed Law, and the usury statues. There was little legal precedent interpreting the Secondary Security Deed Law. It looked as if Rudy Tolbert's case would be the first on the books when it was appealed.

"Dixie, you do good work," I said.

She smiled. On the Law Review at Mercer University, she was a serious student and didn't find time for dating. I hoped she hadn't had time to talk about the project she'd been working on.

"Dixie, you haven't mentioned what we're doing with Kelli, Barron, or Brook, have you?"

"No," she said.

"Don't, until we get further along. I want you to get on our real estate database and pull up all of the foreclosures of security deeds by First Fidelity in the last five years. I'm especially interested in anything that's not a first mortgage.

Also, pull up all foreclosures against businesses by First Fidelity in the last year. And then check the litigation history of Southern Finance of Georgia, Inc. I want to know whom they have sued, who has sued them, and the outcomes. It's a big task, Miss Dixie, but it's important. You got the picture?"

She smiled. "Yeah. Our motto is 'Sue the bastards.'"

The injunction hearing on Rudy Tolbert's case was scheduled for ten a.m. in the chambers of Judge J. Robert Lanier. Rudy was dressed in blue slacks and a white shirt with no tie. The defendant, First Fidelity, was represented by Bradford L. King, the senior partner of King, Golden and Bonner, and L. Porter Berry, the attorney to whom I served the restraining order. He was there, no doubt, to carry King's briefcase.

We had the burden of proof. I outlined the facts in my opening statement, arguing that Rudy gave a second mortgage on his house, that he was illiterate, and that he was not given a closing statement as required by the Georgia Secondary Security Deed Law.

King argued that Rudy knew what he was signing, that he had done business with First Fidelity many times before, and that the fact that he didn't receive a closing statement was harmless error and should not cause a forfeiture. And that if it did, then the law was unconstitutional, and it deprived the bank of property without due process of law and in violation of the U.S. Constitution and the Constitution of the State of Georgia.

I put Rudy on the stand. He testified that he had dropped out of school in the tenth grade. I asked him to read the security deed and note. He stumbled through it. It was obvious that he was illiterate. I asked him if he had received a closing statement at the closing. He testified that he had not. We introduced into evidence all the documents he had received at closing.

On cross examination King tore into Rudy, contending that he knew what he was doing, and that he had given First Fidelity a second mortgage on his house many times before and he had never objected. A heated argument erupted between Brad and me. Judge Lanier stopped us.

"Gentlemen, I understand the facts of this case. What I need is more illumination and less heat. I want both of you parties to submit briefs on the law within ten days and I'll make a ruling."

We left the hearing. Brad King turned to me and said, "You don't really think the bank is going to roll over and kiss twenty thousand dollars goodbye, do you?"

"I don't care what the bank does. I'm just representing my client. But for the record, he's not going to roll over and kiss his home goodbye either."

I returned to the office at eleven o'clock. There was a stack of phone messages. Two were from the Cochrans. They knew almost to the minute when I had returned from my honeymoon. Three divorce clients, a new client, and a call from Don Pollard, also awaited my return to the office. My heart sank. Were they about to indict Randy Perkins?

I called Pollard first. The receptionist in the district attorney's office said he was in a conference. She took my name and number and said he would call me back.

I got on the telephone with the Cochrans to field the usual one hundred questions about what was going on with their case. I assured them we were going to research the law and the facts carefully before we did anything. I asked them to be patient.

Juanita buzzed me on the intercom. Don Pollard was on the line. "Jake. It's Don. I need to talk with you today. How about 1:30?"

"In your office?" I asked.

"Yes."

"See you then."

Lunch was not pleasant. I lost my appetite, imagining that I could see Randy Perkins in handcuffs, charged with arson, splashed all over the front page of the newspaper. At 1:30 p.m. sharp I walked into Don's office. Johnny Harbuck was there.

"Our investigation reveals that your client may be telling the truth. We want to give him a polygraph."

"Hell, Don, you know they aren't admissible as evidence."

"We believe in them even if the appellate courts don't. If he passes, we'll drop our investigation against him."

"And what if he doesn't?" I asked.

"Well, we'll have a different case then."

"I don't think I can recommend it to him, Don."

"It's his life."

"I'll ask him."

When I returned to the office, I instructed Terri Beth to get Randy Perkins on the phone. "What do we have for this afternoon?"

"You have to prepare three people for hearings tomorrow."

"See if you can get Phillip or Brook to prepare them. We need to get Randy Perkins in as soon as possible."

At four o'clock Perkins arrived at the office. He looked as if he had aged ten years in the past ten days. "Sit down, Randy," I said. "We've got a lot to talk about. I had a meeting with the district attorney this afternoon. He says their investigation shows you might be telling the truth."

"Damn it, Jake. I *am* telling the truth."

"It's not that simple, Randy. They want you to take a polygraph."

"I'll do it."

"Wait a minute, Randy. Not so fast. The appellant courts have held that polygraph tests aren't admissible in criminal trials and besides, they're not always accurate. It depends on who administers them. You can have two different operators and get two different results.

"I believe you, but we're dealing with the law and burden of proof here. If you flunk the damn thing, you can count on being indicted and you'll spend the rest of what you've got left fighting it. On the other hand, if you refuse they can't put the fact that you refused to take the polygraph in evidence. Quite frankly, I don't think they have a case against you. If they did, I guarantee you that Don Pollard would have already indicted you. I know him quite well."

"Jake, I want to take it and get it over with. I tell you, I'm innocent."

"Randy, as your lawyer, I am advising you not to."

A loud and explosive argument followed. I yelled at Randy and he yelled at me. We were oblivious to the fact that there were other people in the office. The door opened abruptly and Kelli stuck her head in the door. "What's going on in here?"

I quickly outlined what had transpired and Kelli sided with me. "Randy, you need to listen to Jake. You're gambling with your life."

Randy was as stubborn as a mule. Finally, seeing it was useless, I said, "Okay. It's your life. You take the damn polygraph, but I want you to sign a statement that I advised you against this. And if you get indicted you'll need to get a new lawyer—one whose advice you'll follow."

I dictated a two-paragraph statement to Terri Beth. She took it in shorthand. I learned that if you practice any criminal law at all you learn to use these statements. It keeps the ACLU off your back if your client goes to jail.

Randy signed the statement stating that I had advised him not to take the polygraph and we both calmed down. "What's happening with the fire?" I asked.

"We took a total loss. The only thing we have left is the four-acre lot. You won't believe this, Jake, but Robert Banks, the commercial vice president at First Fidelity, said the bank was willing to buy the land for $250,000."

"Wow," I said. "That's only about a tenth of its value."

"I know, but they've got me over a barrel."

"Hell, Randy, what else do they want? They've got all the insurance money and now they want the land too? Listen, Randy, this might not apply to your case, but we've got another case in which First Fidelity took a second mortgage on a client's home and started foreclosure. Do you remember if they ever took a mortgage on your house?"

"Damn right they did. Every time I got a construction loan from them."

"Listen, Randy. This is very important. It may affect your case. Would you bring in every scrap of paper that you ever signed at any closing with First Fidelity in which they took a mortgage against your house?"

"What's up?"

"It may be nothing, but we're working on a theory that could be of great benefit to you."

*****

The polygraph with the district attorney's office was scheduled for Friday at nine a.m. We were ushered into a room used for grand juries. "Jake, I'd like to introduce you to Bob

Devson, chief polygraph examiner for the Georgia Bureau of Investigation. You know Johnny Harbuck, of course."

"Yeah this is my client, Randy Perkins. I think he's met everybody but Bob." The two men shook hands.

"Bob is going to explain the procedure. If at any time you wish to bail out of this, we're willing to stop the examination. But if you do, we can't promise any deals. Okay?"

"Okay."

The GBI agent explained the procedure, and Randy signed the consent form to take the test. I read it carefully to confirm there was no hanky panky and then Devson went through the usual background questions to test Randy's truth tolerance. After an hour into the polygraph, he began to center in on the night of the fire. Sweat rolled down my back as he asked Randy point blank if he had set the fire. Randy calmly answered no. I could see the needle move on the polygraph machine, but I didn't know what the movement meant. From the outside, Randy seemed cool as a cucumber. Another half-hour went by and the test ended.

"When will you let us know something?" I asked the GBI agent.

"We'll notify Don's office by next Wednesday and he'll take it from there. Thank you, gentlemen," he said, and left.

"How did I do, Jake?" Randy asked as we were leaving the courthouse.

"I have no idea because I don't trust these tests. We'll know Wednesday."

It was a quarter to twelve and I was looking forward to the firm luncheon at the country club. Phillip and Parnell had already left. I rode over with Barron, Kelli and Brook. "How did it go?" Brook asked.

"I felt pretty uncomfortable. Randy said the right things, but you have no control over polygraphs. You know that."

"Did you get him to sign a CYA statement?"

"You bet I did. Kelli and I told him if he flunked and was indicted, he should get other legal counsel."

"Good. At least the ACLU won't be on our backs."

*****

Saturday was an exciting day for Kathy and me. We were finally ending our apartment life and moving into our very first home. Rudy had done an excellent job remodeling. The movers worked quickly and carefully, placing each piece of furniture where Kathy instructed. I was in the back yard near the spot I had selected for a garden. Kathy and I had done a trade-off. She got her dining room set and I got my Troy Bilt tiller.

I cranked up the tiller and started to work on the thirty by fifteen-foot garden plot I had selected. The black soil turned quickly under my feet. I could see the lush vegetables growing already. Nothing has the smell of fresh turned soil.

Rudy's truck pulled into the driveway behind the moving van. He and another man I didn't recognize got out of the truck.

"Hey, Jake, I want you to meet Dick Shelton. Dick is another re-modeler in town. Dick, this is my lawyer, Jake McDonald."

"Rudy, you did a great job with the house. Kathy and I are really pleased."

"If there are any things that need fixing just make a list and I'll be over," Rudy said. "But that's not why we're here. I told Dick what you did for me. He wants to talk with you about something."

"Mr. McDonald —"

"Please, call me Jake."

"Rudy told me about the second mortgage deal on his house and how you stopped his foreclosure. First Fidelity took a second mortgage on my house too. They didn't foreclose, but I still owe them. My brother Phil's in the remodeling business too. Same deal."

Hmmm, I thought. *How many of these deals are there?* "I don't know where this is going, Dick, but briefs are due in the court next week. We think we're right on the law. If we win, the bank will surely appeal. I'll be glad to look at your paperwork if you'll bring it all in. I'll need every paper you were given at the closing. Tell your brother to do the same."

*****

I picked up the mail Saturday morning. In it was a letter from Judge Lanier's office. J. Robert Lanier was a judge who didn't waste time. I read the last page of the order first—the one where the decision is always located—and saw the words,

"A permanent injunction is granted. Signed, J. Robert Lanier, Superior Court Judge."

I was ecstatic. We had whipped First Fidelity! I knew it wouldn't take them long to strike back, though. In Tuesday's mail we got the notice of appeal.

I felt anxious all day Tuesday, but not about Rudy's case, for I knew the final decision was months away. At least he wouldn't lose his house during the wait. My mind kept racing back to Randy Perkins and the fire. Wednesday, at 8:30 a.m., the phone rang. It was Don Pollard "Jake, come on over and bring the bail bondsman with you."

Oh hell, I thought. I couldn't tell if Don was serious or not. He had a cynical, sick sense of humor at times. I was in his office in five minutes.

"Jake, sit down. How about some coffee?"

"I'd rather have bourbon."

He laughed. "Not this early, pal. Jake, it's apparent that your client Randy Perkins is a cold-blooded pathological liar."

My heart sank and I could feel the nausea setting in. My face must've been green, 'cause the next thing I knew, Don exploded with laughter. "Buddy, I'm joking. The bastard beat the polygraph. The GBI says he's telling the truth."

Just as quickly as I'd been sick to my stomach, the weight of the world was lifted from my shoulders. "Does that mean you're not going to indict him?"

"It looks that way...but we're not through with him."

"What do you mean?" I asked.

"Jake, *somebody* burned down the Vista Villas condos and we need Perkins' help.

"Whoever did this is very sophisticated when it comes to the use of incendiaries. Johnny Harbuck says the device was one like they used to use in Vietnam—one that could burn through six inches of steel in five minutes. The state fire marshal's office has confirmed all of this.

"We could probably list a hundred Vietnam veterans around here that know how to use the device. The problem with the case is motive. Now, it's obvious that your client did not gain economically. And I don't think he would burn his own project down because he was in debt. As he told us, he won't collect a dime of insurance.

"We've known each other for a while, man. I think we can shoot straight with one another. I'm going to tell you something, but if you ever repeat it I'll deny it under oath." He paused and looked around nervously. "I believe the bank did it or they know who did. We just can't prove it yet. We tried to pass off your little discovery the other week at King, Golden and Bonner as nothing.

"But Johnny agrees with me. He's an old FBI man and has a nose like a bird dog. We need your client's cooperation to catch these firebugs."

I debated whether to tell Don about the newest development and then decided to go ahead with it. "There's something else. Fidelity offered Randy $250,000 for his land. That's only about a tenth of what it's worth."

"Very interesting," said Don. "Keep me informed, but be careful about it."

*****

The Cochrans kept calling me every single day about their case. and they were driving me crazy. Terri Beth and I had worked out a signal. If I wanted to talk with them, I would give her the thumbs up. If I didn't, thumbs down. She was a real pro in handling them. "I'm sorry, but he's in court...I'm sorry, but he's in a deposition...He's with a client." All good legal secretaries know how to tell these kinds of little lies. Hopefully, God will forgive them. Then they started calling me at home at night. Kathy finally insisted we install an answering machine. with Caller I.D.

Thursday was one of the lightest days we had experienced in a long time. Barron was goofing off fishing in Florida. Brook was on an investigation—his "code" for taking the afternoon off to play golf. Parnell was at a legal seminar in Atlanta and Phillip was in North Carolina taking depositions. Kelli and I held down the shop. At about 5:30 she got out the ice bucket and poured herself a scotch and water. I knew something was up by the way she settled back in her chair.

"Jake, I think it's time we talk about what you've been working on. I know you have Dixie running around on something big, and I need to know."

I began to outline the case against First Fidelity, starting with the Cochrans, the Rudy Tolbert case and then those of his brother and friend. I went into detail about Randy Perkins and the evidence of how he had been screwed by the bank.

"Dixie pulled off the computer a list of potential clients in a RICO class action against First Fidelity. I hope this won't leave these walls, but between you and me, I believe First Fidelity had something to do with Randy Perkins' fire, and so does Don Pollard."

"You're kidding me."

"Nope. I've got a funny feeling they're doing business with the mob." I told her about seeing the file in King, Golden and Bonner, and watched as her face turned red and then white. "Are you scared, Kelli?"

"Hell, no! Somebody has to stop these criminals."

I swallowed hard. "It'll be one hell of a fight. Maybe we ought to associate some other attorneys. What bothers me is how this will affect the Jack Owens estate. You know King, Golden and Bonner are ripping them off."

"Let's let the chips fall where they may. At least we'll get their attention."

"How do you think the other partners will feel about such a suit?"

"Barron will be against it. He doesn't believe in doing anything that would rock the establishment in this town. Hell, he might get pissed off and leave."

"That bad, huh?"

Kelli leaned back in her chair. I could tell she was trying to decide whether or not to tell me something. "Jake, I've carried this law firm for years. I brought Barron in after Jack died. I thought I needed a strong, well-respected attorney to lead our firm. You see who the clients come to see. I don't even have a law degree; I took the Bar after studying law on my own."

"I didn't know you didn't go to law school."

"Does it bother you?"

"Not at all. You're one hell of a lawyer. Much smarter than those silk stocking thugs at King, Golden and Bonner."

She laughed. "Thanks, Jake. I needed that." She hesitated, obviously thinking. "Brook will bitch and worry, but he'll ultimately do what I tell him to do.

"Don't worry about the partners. You're the one we need to worry about. If we file this suit, you'd better be prepared for the worst kind of pressure you've ever been under in your life. Prepare Kathy for it too. If we take a shot at the king, we better be able to knock him out. Do your research, and make damn sure it's right. First Fidelity owns this town. They control everything financial, political, civic, and social. If you lose, be prepared to fold up your tent and leave. And I'll probably not be far behind."

"That bad, huh?"

"Yes, sir. I'll start preparing you a chart of who's who in this town, and how they are owned by First Fidelity."

Monday morning was unusually gloomy at the office. Barron was gentlemanly polite, but cold when I met him in the hall. Brook seemed as if he was trying to avoid me. Kelli was frazzled, and not her usual enthusiastic self. It was apparent that the partners had had a powwow over the weekend.

The only redeeming ray of sunshine was Terri Beth. Always pleasant and smiling, one would never guess that she had lost her husband in a terrible plane crash. I was lucky she was my secretary.

I escaped to my office and got involved in dictating interrogatories and motions that I had been putting off. Just before lunch, Kelli stopped by my office. "Let's have lunch—just you and me."

We went to one of our favorite restaurants six blocks down the street in the historic district and got a back table in an out-of-the-way corner of the room.

"Well," she said, "I laid it on the line with them Saturday afternoon. Just as I expected, Barron exploded. He would have nothing to do with a suit against First Fidelity. Brook about had a heart attack. He came around, however. We took a vote; it was two to one in favor of going ahead with it. I think Barron is going to leave the firm. Brook wants us all to work on it, but he wants to move with extreme caution. I agree with him. Let's don't fly off the handle." She ordered a second martini.

I nodded and tried to reassure her. "Kelli, we've got plenty of time. There's a four-year statute of limitations. I figure we've got at least three years to do this."

Four

After lunch, I stopped by Dixie's office. Her desk was covered with a stack of computer printouts and more were coming off the printer. "What's all this?" I asked.

"It's your project, Jake. These are all the second mortgages that have been foreclosed on by First Fidelity. Now I'm printing all the litigation involving Southern Finance of Georgia."

"My God, there must be hundreds of them! Can you sort all that out? We need to get good addresses on all of the people involved in the foreclosures. Maybe Carl Schiff, our detective friend down the street, can help us find these people. Start with the telephone directory and the city directory. Those you can't find, let Carl skip-trace them." We had started the process to attack and take down the king.

Barron was very cold and in the next few weeks, he got downright mean. He began to find all kinds of nuisance cases to assign me in order to waste my time—sending me running off to police court for drunk driving cases, and attending docket calls in small claims court where the total claims were less than $2500. He had me taking his depositions on hopeless dog bite cases. I sensed a deliberate attempt on his part to sabotage my efforts. He pictured me as the demon that was about to wreck his legal career.

Then luck struck. I had been handling a horrible rear end collision against a trucking company. After discovery, the insurance company threw in the towel and paid the policy limits of $300,000, and the firm received a $100,000 legal fee. I was a hero at the firm—at least for a week. Even Barron was pleased and backed off for a while.

*****

The law firm of King, Golden and Bonner consisted of seventeen lawyers, nineteen secretaries, seven paralegals, five law clerks, a receptionist and three investigators—a total of fifty-two employees. It had grown by recruiting the brightest and the most industrious attorneys, because the firm had the money and the prestige to do so. Then, after years of limelight, it acquiesced to the sins of all monarchies, inbreeding. Legacy upon legacy, cousin upon cousin, blue blood upon blue blood, it began to rot internally, no longer driven by principle or character or anything else of honor—only money.

On Monday morning, Anthony Jacobs, the president and CEO of First Fidelity Savings and Loan, demanded a meeting with his attorneys at King, Golden, and Bonner. Bradford L. King, the senior partner, Ken Golden, the managing partner, L. Porter Berry, a junior partner who handled their minority business, and Shug Golden, their rainmaker, were all present when Anthony Jacobs arrived. They all congregated in the firm's main conference room. All their other appointments had been canceled for the day and their secretaries had been fully warned against interruptions.

Jacobs, as usual, took charge. "Gentlemen, I think we need to clear the air about a few things. For the last thirty-two years your law firm has been the exclusive legal counsel for First Fidelity Bank and Trust. My accounting department has advised me that we have paid your firm over sixty-five million dollars in attorneys' fees over these years. I hope that translates into some form of loyalty. I have received word that we have lost a $20,000 case to a small-time illiterate painter represented by some neophyte lawyer just out of law school. What the hell is going on?"

Brad King spoke up. "Tony, we haven't lost the case yet. It's on appeal."

"Appeal! Hell, we pay you guys enough to win these cases without an appeal. Now I get a bill for $11,360 for a case we lost that's going on appeal. What's the appeal going to cost? What's going on here? What's the bottom line?"

King flinched but plowed on. "Bottom line is we could lose the $20,000 First Fidelity lent to Rudy Tolbert, plus interest, plus attorneys' fees. But more importantly, we could lose a legal precedent, which could cost First Fidelity and the banking industry millions."

"We need to stop this crap now!" Jacobs thundered. What about the insurance? Do we have full coverage on our loan?"

"Yes," replied Brad King.

"Then let's take our loss out of the loop. This is a job for our friends in Chicago. You know what I mean. How about our little excess insurance coverage? Is it in place?"

"Yes, it is," replied King.

*****

It was Friday evening and I was sitting on my front porch in a rocking chair next to the most beautiful woman in the world. Out of nowhere, deafening sirens sounded, seeming to come from everywhere. Three fire trucks raced past the front of our house. Everyone ran outside to see what was happening.

The trucks stopped somewhere in the 1700 block of 17th Avenue, only seven blocks from where our house stood. Kathy and I raced down the street, only to be horror-stricken. It was Rudy Tolbert's house – the one I'd kept out of foreclosure - and it was embroiled in flames.

Firemen were running everywhere. I saw Rudy's wife, Angela, and two of their daughters, Connie and Samantha, but Rudy and their eighteen-month-old daughter, Angel, were nowhere to be seen. Suddenly, I saw Rudy run screaming between two fire trucks carrying the toddler. Badly burned, the child was rushed to the pediatric intensive care unit with second degree burns over a third of her body. We watched as the firemen tried everything to save the house, but in the end it was totally destroyed.

They had nothing left. Kathy and I had my $10,000 bonus from the truck wreck settlement. We wanted a lot of things as newlyweds, but our little bonus check meant nothing compared to the Tolberts' losses and we decided together to give them all of it. Kelli gave $10,000, Barron $1,000, Brook $2,000, Phillip

$1,000, and Parnell $1,000. Another $10,000 came anonymously from our firm. I didn't ask where it came from—but I knew. Terri Beth.

Rudy and Angela were, of course, distraught—they had nowhere to go. Kathy and I had four bedrooms, so we let them move into our house until they could find another place to live. While Rudy and Angela camped out in the pediatric intensive burn unit at Catholic Hospital, Kathy spent the day buying replacement clothes for the children. Angel teetered close to death all day long—IVs connected to all four of her limbs.

I talked with the city fire marshal who was on the scene with his investigators. He said it looked like an electrical fire that had started near the fuse box. They would send the results of their investigation to the state fire marshal's office. He said in a house that old there were probably a thousand electrical problems. I had my doubts.

Little Angel Tolbert was in and out of a coma all weekend. Rudy and Angela stayed by her bedside throughout the whole ordeal. Kathy and I took care of the other children. Kathy and I agreed that all parents should be given the Medal of Honor.

I decided to take the bull by the horns, and call the county's premier arson attorney to get a list of his experts. He recommended Dr. Craig Utz, the best arson investigator around. Dr. Utz was expensive, requiring a $10,000 retainer, so I cashed a CD to make the payment and arranged with the fire marshal for him to examine Rudy's burned-out home on Monday.

Dr. Utz wasted no time with his investigation. He spent four hours at the scene of what remained of Rudy and Angela's home, poking and prodding and taking samples of evidence.

The call came on Wednesday morning. "Go and stand by your fax machine. I want to fax you something that is very confidential. After you get it, I'll call you back and we can review it."

The fax was a lengthy one, some 24 pages, consisting primarily of scientific charts and numbers. On the last five pages was a narrative summary of his findings and conclusions. When Dr. Utz called, he walked me through his investigation step by step, detailing all the procedures necessary in the case of a suspicious fire. When he finished, I felt as if I had earned a Ph.D. in arson investigation.

"This fire was caused by an electrical malfunction. And yes, the fire marshal's preliminary conclusion was correct. The origin of the fire *was* near the fuse box. But we didn't stop there.

"In their defense, most of the state fire marshal offices don't have the latest scientific equipment. Our company does because it's the way we make our living. Our conclusions are cross-examined by the best trial lawyers in the country. We have to be right."

Dr. Utz continued. "We went a step further and examined the actual wiring we found at the fire scene with a spectro-chronometer. A spectro-chronometer is sort of like the carbon dating devices you've read about.

"Here is where it gets interesting. All of the wires were copper, as is the wiring in all the houses that age. Our tests reveal that the in-going wire that fed the current into the house was vintage 1944, which coincides with when the house was built, but the outgoing main lead was most unusual. Two portions of the wire were vintage 1944, but a third piece of wire was spliced in between. *It* was manufactured in 2002. This splice created an electrical arc, which undoubtedly caused the fire.

"Mr. McDonald, electricians don't splice incoming hot wire cable. Not only is it dangerous, but it violates all the fire codes in the country. All contractors know this. And certainly Rudy Tolbert knew it. He was a re-modeler. He surely wouldn't jerry-rig his own house. We checked all the construction permits ever issued on his house and there were no electrical permits ever issued for this type of work. This was deliberately done by someone who knew what he was doing. And it was done very recently, too. We have an arson case on our hands."

I was stunned. The $10,000 I had spent to retain Dr. Utz was worth every penny. We had a lunatic out there who would not stop at killing even children to accomplish his purpose. "Should I turn your findings over to the district attorney?" I asked.

"Not just yet. I'm working with the state fire marshal's office now. It would look better if this information came from them and not some hired gun like me. You know what I mean. We're better on the stand."

"I got you. We'll get the same results in time."

Dixie was making good headway locating people who had been foreclosed on by First Fidelity. She and Carl Schiff, our private investigator, had already located twenty-three people who would qualify as plaintiffs in a RICO class action suit.

Barron sensed that we were getting closer to filing the suit, and he began his diversionary tactics again, throwing a docket call in small claims court and a case in police court at me. He gave me a case that he thought was a "dog,"— a slip and fall case against a major department store. Most of these cases have no liability and wind up with a defendant's verdict, but for some strange reason the defense attorneys wanted to settle and they paid us $30,000. Barron was amazed and ticked off. I received the glory for his "dog" case.

On Friday, I took a break from the law practice to attend a continuing legal education seminar in Atlanta. The state bar requires eighteen hours of continuing legal education each year and I hadn't done anything about it. Most of the seminars are on subjects worthless in the practice of law, but this one was timely—it was on prosecuting and defending civil RICO cases. I recognized another attendee across the room—Porter Berry of King, Golden and Bonner. He came up to me during the coffee break and engaged in the usual polite chitchat. Then something he said caught my attention.

"How's Angel?" he asked. "Has your expert witness found out anything about the fire?"

I did my best to present a poker face, but I felt a chill run down my spine. No one but me knew there *was* an expert witness. Not even Terri Beth had known that I'd hired Dr. Utz.

Although the conversation kept running through my mind, I still learned a lot of valuable information at the seminar, including the names of attorneys who regularly handled these types of cases. One attorney in particular impressed me—Donnie Lee Booker. In his early thirties, Booker was a senior associate with one of the premier plaintiff firms in Atlanta. He had handled several RICO cases and had gotten favorable verdicts in all of them. During the lunch break, I purposely sat at the table next to him and found out he would be in Conecuh the following Thursday for a deposition. I invited him to stop by the firm for a drink after he finished. I was delighted when he agreed. Barron was scheduled to try a will contest that day, a case in which there was no hope of settlement. At least he would be out of the way when Donnie Lee arrived.

Donnie Lee and Kelli got along very well. Both scotch drinkers, they were kindred spirits. And it was clear that Donnie Lee really liked Dixie. He couldn't keep his eyes off her. After about two rounds of drinks, the conversation finally came around to our potential RICO case. I outlined the facts and his eyes lit up. I could tell he was intrigued with the idea of bringing a major bank to its knees. "Hell," he said, "They'll even be able to pay the verdict when we get it."

Kelli and I glanced quickly at each other. It might have been a Freudian slip, but we'd both caught the importance of what he had said. He was in.

Around 6:30 p.m. Donnie Lee headed back to Atlanta. Kathy was at the hospital pulling the night shift for Rudy and Angela in order to give them a night away.

Swilling the Chivas Regal in her glass, Kelli smiled. "Mr. Booker is a nice young man. Smart lawyer too. I think it would be a good move if we associated him in our case against First Fidelity."

"That's why I wanted him here. I thought the same thing when I heard his presentation at the seminar in Atlanta. First, he has valuable experience that we need; second, his firm has the resources that we don't have; and third, we're in for one hell-of-a fight. But if we win, there will be plenty of money to go around."

"What do you mean, *if*?" she said. "It's *when* we win."

"You know, I'll bet his firm will loan him to us for the duration of this case. He could move in with one of us. We all have plenty of room. "

"Say, that's a great idea," she said.

"Kelli, can I tell you something just between us?"

"Sure. What?"

"Promise it stays here?"

"Yes, Jake. I promise. What is it?"

"It's Barron. I think he's trying to sabotage our case. Every time I turn around he's sandbagging me with some meaningless duty or case to handle.

"Look, I know I'm the new man on the block. I don't mind doing yeoman's duties, but as I calculate it, I've brought in more money than he has in the last two months. And really—to send me to a docket call in small claims court when we have only one case on the docket-his-is ridiculous. It killed my whole morning. We could have settled our $300,000 case a day earlier if I hadn't been fooling around with a docket call for a $300 collection debt. Hell, we shouldn't take those kinds of cases."

Kelli lowered her voice. "Being a member of a law firm is somewhat like being a member of a fraternity. You have to trust one another. When I took your case to Barron and Brook that Saturday, I was prepared for the worst. I was prepared to get shot down. We have a rule as law partners: a majority vote carries. I told you I figured Barron would be against it—the truth is he still thinks he's a blue-blood even though he makes his living from our mostly blue-collar clients."

"What are you talking about?" I asked.

"It's time for Barron to leave. Let's call it a dissolution of our partnership. More bluntly, I'm going to fire him."

"Oh, Kelli. Are you sure?"

"Jake, when Jack Owens died, I thought I couldn't make it on my own. As I told you before, I had no formal legal education and I thought I needed a prominent male attorney to lead the firm. Barron was at the right place at the right time.

"The ironic thing is that from the beginning, all of our clients have been mine. I've supported this firm for years.

Barron doesn't have many clients and he obviously won't even handle the ones he does have. He gives them all to you."

"I'd be willing to give them to you," I said. "I'll even give the Cochrans back to you." We both laughed.

"I knew I liked you the day you first walked in here. I saw that you were a fighter. You'll be a partner in this firm one day.

She poured another drink. "One more and we'll leave."

It was number four. "Are you all right?" I asked. "Can I drive you home?"

"No, I'm okay." I could tell something was weighing heavily on her mind and I didn't think it was the law practice.

She returned the decanter to the shelf in her credenza and turned to face me. "Let's just be prepared when we file this suit. We cannot afford to go off half cocked."

"We *will* be, Kelli. I promise. That's why I think Donnie Lee will be so valuable. Let's associate him."

"Okay. Do it," she said softly.

*****

I arrived at the firm early on Friday morning, about 7:30. Terri Beth was already at her typewriter. "You're here mighty early, boss," she said.

"Yeah, I've got a lot to do today."

"Boss, a Dr. Utz called you about fifteen minutes ago. You know him?"

"Yeah. Did he leave a number?"

I took the message Terri Beth handed me and went into my office and closed the door. I dialed the number and Dr. Utz answered.

"Mr. McDonald, I'm glad I caught you this early," he said. "Listen, my report went to the state fire marshal on Wednesday. The district attorney should have it by now. Did you say he's a friend of yours?"

"Yeah, we've known each other a while."

"The state fire marshal concurred with our findings and there's one more thing that you need to know. We analyzed soil samplings around the burned structure but the results weren't available at the time of my initial report.

"We found an accelerant that was used to speed up the burning. It's a not-so-common chemical compound that was used in the Vietnam War to destroy things in a hurry. We call them 'cindys.' They can burn through six inches of steel and quick."

My heart sped up. Was it possible that the people who'd burned Randy Perkins' condominium project had also set fire to Rudy Tolbert's house? "Thanks, Doc. Listen, if I send you a copy of another arson investigation, would it be possible for you to determine if there is any similarity in the accelerant used?"

"Sure, if there was proper examination of the evidence."

"Thanks. I'll get back to you." I hung up and buzzed Terri Beth.

"What do I have on my schedule for this morning?

"You've got a criminal plea in Superior Court."

"Find out if Don Pollard can see me before court."

"Sure."

In a matter of minutes, I was on my way to see the district attorney.

Pollard was always on a feisty ego trip on Friday mornings. Friday was plea day, the day when he was in complete control of the destiny of people's lives. He would send between thirty and fifty people to the state penitentiary for various violations of the law, including everything from auto theft to trafficking crack. He was like a Roman emperor in his chariot, parading his conquered foe before him.

"Good morning, Jake. Have any sterling clients you want to send to the state home for wayward boys? We're sending one of yours away this morning. I'm feeling generous. We'll knock two years off every sentence for a plea."

"Cut out the crap, Don. Have you seen the state fire marshal's report on Rudy Tolbert's fire?"

"Indeed, I have. I was going to call you later today."

"Don, I hired an expert to investigate the fire in full cooperation with the fire marshal's office. They both came to the same conclusion independently of each other. Nobody knows I hired Dr. Utz, and I'd like to keep it that way.

"He called me early this morning and said he had just completed the analysis of soil samples at the scene of the Tolbert fire. They show an accelerant was used. Listen to this. He said it was a peculiar chemical that they used in Vietnam.

He called them 'cindys'. Wasn't that the same thing Johnny Harbuck said was used in the Perkins fire?"

"Now that you mention it."

"I need a favor. Can we send the investigative report on the Perkins fire to Dr. Utz to see if he can find any similarities? Since my client is no longer a suspect, I believe it would be beneficial to the state's investigation. Here's his card".

"Jake, I don't have a problem with it, but I need to run it by Harbuck first. See you in court. Now how many years are we giving your client this morning?" He grinned and strutted out the door.

*****

Angel Tolbert's condition had stabilized and Rudy and Angela had found an apartment a block from their old home. With the money the firm had contributed, they were able to buy some furniture and new clothes and move out. Things were starting to look up for them. If we could just figure out who at Fidelity was responsible for the fire... I had a feeling Dr. Utz would do just that.

Five

Donnie Lee Booker was recently divorced so he could travel at will. The following week, he came down from Atlanta and we spent the whole day talking about the case and mapping out a strategy. His law firm had given him the go-ahead to move to Conecuh to work on our case if we could work out satisfactory financial arrangements.

We agreed to charge the clients a one-third contingency fee if the case went to trial or settled, and forty percent if it went up on appeal. We agreed to split the costs of litigation, with his firm fronting the money until the case was finished.

Brook had a rental house he had inherited from his mother. It was empty so he agreed that Donnie Lee could live there rent-free until the case was finished.

Donnie Lee suggested that we get all of the potential clients together in a meeting and explain exactly what we intended to do. We assigned Dixie to Donnie—she liked the intellectual challenge—and Donnie Lee had a good investigator and runner named Clint Moore. Clint would move in with Donnie Lee and help to recruit the necessary plaintiffs to create the class action.

The rest of the lawyers in the firm, excluding Barron, of course, agreed to take most of my caseload. Barron was intentionally excluded but he didn't know what was coming. I didn't relish what Kelli was about to do.

Donnie Lee was meticulous, methodical, and prepared. When it came to drafting pleadings, Donnie Lee was a wordsmith. His lawsuits spoke poetry. I nicknamed him the "Poet Laureate of the Plaintiffs Bar." He liked Dixie because both of them were cut from the same bolt of cloth. Donnie Lee brought a young paralegal with him from Atlanta whose sole job was to research the law and nothing else.

It was time to bring Terri Beth up to speed on what was going on. We took a two-hour lunch break and had lunch in a restaurant in the historic district. In a little corner room I outlined the when and why. She gasped at what was about to happen and the dangers that were fraught with this type litigation, but she said she could take it.

I thought so too. From the beginning, I had known that Terri Beth had an inner toughness. I guessed she had developed it when her husband had died in the plane crash, though she didn't show it on the outside. She would work exclusively on the case and would be the chief in charge of any and all other secretaries involved.

The meeting with the clients was scheduled for Wednesday morning at nine. Invited were Randy Perkins, Gene and Betty Cochran, Rudy Tolbert, and four other individuals whom Clint Moore had signed on as plaintiffs. Clint felt we could prove egregious cases of wrongful foreclosure with these plaintiffs as well. At the meeting the firm was represented by Donnie Lee Booker, Kelli, Dixie, Terri Beth, Donnie's paralegal, and me.

Donnie Lee took charge of the meeting, and through a series of charts, he outlined the various causes of action that each of the clients had. He was meticulous in his explanations. It was obvious to all that he had handled cases like this before. The most amazing thing, though, was that he was able to keep Betty Cochran in tow until he finished.

The clients were anxious about what they were up against. We would be going up against the most powerful institution in town and there would be great efforts by the defendants to dissuade their participation. They were warned not to discuss any aspect of their cases with anyone and to be prepared for a long, tedious, and expensive process.

After an hour of questions and answers by the prospective plaintiffs, each agreed to proceed based on a contingency fee contract that Donnie proposed. Everybody signed. There was a knock at the door and Neva brought in lunch, which had been catered by the Round Top Deli.

Six

Rube Wiseman was a worthless, low-life, scumbag, extortionist sonofabitch, who made his living trafficking in the foibles, failures, and weaknesses of other human beings. No foible or misdeed ever went unharvested. Rube turned everybody's misfortune into dollars for himself, and his favorite game was blackmail. He learned quickly the plaintiff attorneys' number one rule—go after the deep pockets. Don't waste your time pursuing "broke" targets.

The number one target in town was First Fidelity Bank and Trust. It had its good, its bad, and its ugly employees. With twenty-three hundred employees in its banking operation, it was a major employer in town.

Anthony Jacobs, the president of First Fidelity, understood the power of money and rather than put up with the blackmail games of Rube Wiseman, he found it was cheaper to make him one of their employees. Rube Wiseman was employed as a consultant to Special Operations at $5000 per month and in return he would overlook Jacobs' dalliances with young females who were not his wife. Jacobs couldn't resist young women with beautiful bodies.

Wiseman was adept at the extortion game with every major company and every prominent citizen in town, and First Fidelity prided itself in the politicians it owned as a result of Wiseman's ruthlessness.

It was a safe bet that there were a lot of people in Conecuh who were plotting his demise.

First Fidelity's vicious tentacles stretched all the way from the statehouse to the courthouse.

Rube Wiseman wasn't satisfied at making a good living in the extortion business. He was greedy. Those prominent citizens whose cases had been covered up became the victims of Wiseman on the side. He threatened to expose them unless they paid, and most did.

Dixie and Donnie Lee signed up fifteen plaintiffs to participate in the class action RICO case against First Fidelity Bank and Trust. The case was to be brought in four separate counts, based on: 1) wrongful foreclosure, 2) usury, 3) improperly applying payments on loans, and 4) violation of the Secondary Security Deed Act. There were numerous other minor allegations that supported the four main contentions.

Donnie Lee was meticulous and thorough. Every word in the 86-page complaint was carefully thought out, planned, and craftily worded. All the allegations were carefully researched and legal briefs were prepared and extensively researched by Dixie and Donnie Lee's paralegal. The final decision to be made was where we would file the suit, in federal or state court.

On Sunday afternoon we had a conference in Donnie Lee's Atlanta office. Kelli and I attended on behalf of our firm. Donnie Lee and two of his partners represented his group. Phil Pied and John Singer were partners of Donnie Lee's firm. They had a wealth of experience in class action cases. I was glad they were present.

I spoke first. I presented a background brief on each of our Superior Court judges and our U.S. District Court judge. This was comprised of public and private information gathered over the course of years. It was part of the data base system of the Georgia Trial Lawyer Association. It contained a statistical analysis of all the judge's rulings over the last seven years. I supplemented this information with my own opinions and background information on the various judges.

I pointed out to everyone that if we chose the Superior Court route that the cases were assigned on a rotational basis. I had a "sweetheart" in the clerk's office who would tell me which judge was up next in the rotation so we could time our filing to get the judge we wanted.

The U.S. District Court route was a different story. Federal civil cases are on a faster track and discovery times are shorter. The judges were less subject to political influence and were generally prima donnas. The good news was that the jury would be selected from twenty-three different counties, which would diminish the influence of First Fidelity over the jury panel.

The U.S. District Court judge was not in the pocket of First Fidelity. His rulings were fairly well balanced between plaintiffs and defendants. But, he had something that scared Phil and John. His brother was vice president of a bank. Federal court was out.

We turned to our Superior Court choices. We had four. Judge Lamar Braxton had a reputation that was known throughout the state. He was tough, knew the law, would move the case along; but if he didn't like our side of the case, the battle would be formidable.

The second judge was Mitchell L. Hollis. Hollis had previously had been a district attorney. He got convictions. It was feared that he would prosecute criminal cases from the bench but this proved to be untrue. In fact, he proved to be a jurist who bent over backwards to be fair, and turned out to be more popular as a judge than as a district attorney. The main negative that disturbed us about Hollis was that he had worked as a claims adjuster before he became an attorney.

The third judge was Fredrick Benton. Benton was the youngest of the four judges. Elevated to the Superior Court bench from a lower court, he was a former prosecutor. I never had any bitter cases with Judge Benton. He was a no-no from the beginning. His family was well connected in banking circles.

The fourth judge, Carol Randall, had been elected to the bench. Growing up in a family of intellectuals, she had been number one in her law school class at Duke University. After law school she was offered an associate's position at a local legal aid society and had patiently worked her way through the legal system, convincing opposing attorneys that her poor clients needed a break. Her kindness, honesty, sincerity, and perseverance landed her the head position at the Legal Aid Society. She had run in a special election against three other opponents, and won without a runoff. First Fidelity had funneled money into a fund to defeat her.

It was 6:30 Sunday night. Our consensus pick was Judge Randall. It was agreed that Donnie Lee's firm would do a thorough background check on Carol Randall before we filed our suit, and we all adjourned to the Abbey, a popular restaurant. It was a pleasant relief from all the stress of the previous week.

Kelli and I left the Abbey at 8:30 p.m., and began the two-hour trip home. After a few drinks she was in a talkative mood. "Jake, before we file this suit I'm going to have to cut Barron loose. We don't need his disruptions while we're in the middle of a big legal battle."

"What do you think his reaction will be?" I asked.

"That's what bothers me, Jake. I don't know. Your guess is as good as mine. I'm going to start the process rolling tomorrow. I'm having lunch with him."

"Good luck," I said.

*****

Anthony Jacobs, Robert Banks, and Ronald Sherman sat across the table staring at Roberto Costellano and Carlos de Salvo. Banks and Sherman were vice-presidents of First Fidelity and ran most of the commercial lending. They had been cut in on the Costellano money-laundering scheme years ago. They were both caught in a web from which there was no way out. The only exit from the trap was death. They were paid well for their work, earning far in excess of what bank presidents earned at other banks.

Roberto Costellano was the patriarch of one of the largest crime families in the country. Carlos de Salvo was his up and coming Don and his heir apparent. Costellano was a man who played no games. He had personally killed eleven people who wouldn't play his game. Their meetings with First Fidelity were always held out of town, primarily in Chicago. Never in Conecuh. When Costellano called a meeting, Jacobs and his lackeys arrived promptly.

A swarthy man of Sicilian descent, Costellano spoke with a heavy Italian accent. "Gentlemen, our reports show that we put out only two million dollars last month. What's the problem? Don't you boys have any real estate projects in Georgia? If you boys can't put the money out, then we will be forced to terminate our relationship and do business elsewhere with somebody that can. You understand what I mean."

Jacobs, Banks, and Sherman nodded in agreement. Jacobs spoke up. "Roberto, we should be able to double that amount next month. We have targeted several businesses that need refinancing."

"Get with it, boys."

Banks spoke up. "We've been having some trouble with some legal matters."

"Like so?" asked Costellano.

"We've got a case that is on appeal. Some young smart-ass attorney has caused us a lot of trouble. If he wins, then the bank will be in trouble in a big way."

Carlos smiled. "Do you think this smart-ass attorney needs persuading?"

"Not just yet. Let's see what the Appeals Court does first."

"Looks like we made more money on fires than we did on loans last month." Costellano grinned. "Our boys do nice work. I think that that slimy shit Rube Wiseman is getting too big for his britches. Maybe we need to reel him in a little."

"Hold off a while," Jacobs said. "I've got a plan for Wiseman that could be very beneficial for us all."

"Okay. Just don't let him go too far," said Costellano. "At some point in time we're going to have to take him out."

The bankers were glad to leave the meeting. Double martinis in the frequent flyers lounge at O'Hare helped wash away the unpleasantness of the meeting with Costellano.

*****

Kelli and Barron rode down the expressway towards Paula's Place. Paula's was an eatery on the outskirts of Conecuh some seven miles out of town. It was a place the locals liked to go because the food was good, the prices were reasonable, and the waitresses were friendly. Kelli selected Paula's because it would take a while to get there. She had rehearsed her speech many times and wanted to get it out before the meal was served.

Barron spoke up. "How's the First Fidelity case coming?" he asked.

"We're about ready to file suit," Kelli said.

"I think you're making a big mistake. The bank isn't going to roll over and settle. They're going to fight you until hell freezes over. They'll probably bankrupt the firm. You ought to send this case somewhere else."

"Barron, I'm not here to talk about the First Fidelity case. What I want to talk about is much more serious than that."

"What are you talking about?"

"Our relationship. We've practiced law together for four years and I don't think it's going anywhere. We seem to be going in different directions. You don't seem to care for the family practice. You're better at handling insurance defense work, which we rarely do. To put it bluntly, without wasting a lot of words, it's time to call it quits."

"Kelli, I'm shocked," Barron said. "I had no idea you were thinking this way. What brought this on?"

"Nothing in particular, Barron. It has been accumulating over the years."

"Look. I'll do better, I promise. I am willing to help with the First Fidelity case."

"Come on, Barron. You've hated this case from the day it came in. You don't have your heart in it," said Kelli. "Bottom line, Barron, I want to dissolve our partnership. I'll be fair with you money-wise so long as we don't have to litigate with each other."

"Hell, Kelli, I'm not going to do that. We're friends."

"Let's get the accountants to evaluate the business and I'll buy you out, or you can buy me out, whichever you prefer," said Kelli.

"What about the other members of the firm?"

"I imagine Brook will stay with me. Jake too. I don't know about Phillip and Parnell."

They ate lunch in silence. Both had the daily special, though neither remembered what it was. Kelli would have preferred a liquid lunch of extra dry martinis at the country club.

On the way back to the office Barron seemed resigned to what was really happening. His pipe dream was about to end. Once again he would have to return to representing insurance companies in subrogation cases. "How quickly can we get it over with?" he asked.

"I don't know. Let's call Fred when we get back. You know how accountants are."

"There are a few personal cases I would like to take with me. These are long time clients. There are just a few estates and some collection work."

"No problem," said Kelli.

*****

Donnie Lee's firm checked out Judge Randall's background with a fine tooth comb. She had graduated at the top of her class, summa cum laude. She was a Phi Beta Kappa. She had little social life in college or law school and met her husband three months after graduating from law school. They were married four months later and her first child was born exactly nine months later.

Upon graduation from law school she had applied for employment at many law firms. Female attorneys had been horribly discriminated against in those days, and every law firm turned her down except the legal aid society. Carol Randall took her job seriously. She put up real fights with loan sharks and dishonest used car dealers, and all the others who preyed upon the poor.

Sometimes she had faced formidable odds, but she had one member of the bar she could always turn to—Kelli Ferguson. If the case had money potential, Carol Randall sent it to Kelli. In return, Kelli handled hundreds of divorces for poor women for free.

The untimely death of a superior court judge left a vacancy on the bench to be filled by the governor, Zeb Moyd. Governor Moyd's first act after reading the obituary was to call Anthony Jacobs, his heaviest contributor and a fellow Democrat.

Governor Moyd intended to appoint Gerald Bonds, who was owed many favors because of his loyalty. Jacobs agreed. The deal was cut. Bonds was appointed with great fanfare.

When qualifying opened nine months later for Judge Bonds' seat, the first candidate to qualify was Carol Randall. Anthony Jacobs was furious. He quickly assembled a campaign committee of the wealthiest and most prominent citizens in town to serve on Judge Bonds' reelection committee. All the power brokers lined up behind Bonds. All the other voters lined up behind Randall. Anthony Jacobs and his moneyed influence peddlers were stunned on election day. Judge Randall was the first female to win an election as superior court judge. She carried two- thirds of the vote in a landslide. Anthony Jacobs was not accustomed to losing elections, or anything else.

Seven

I was on the phone when Kelli and Barron returned from lunch. She stuck her head in the door and gave me the thumbs up sign and winked. "Can you join me in my office tonight around 5p.m?" she asked.

I nodded in the affirmative. I was dying to know what had happened.

The afternoon was filled with appointments with one client after another. Someone must have put out the word that we were doing a fire sale on divorces. I talked with six clients all of whom wanted to get rid of their spouses. At 5:30 the last client left Kelli's office. Baron left around five to tell his wife the bad news. Phillip and Parnell had gone to a young lawyers' club cookout. Brook was at the golf course.

Neva was still pounding away at the typewriter when Kelli appeared in my doorway. "Would you like to join us, Neva?" Kelli asked. "You don't mind if she joins us do you, Jake? Neva is one of us. She knows everything. I only want to tell today's events once."

Kelli fixed herself a scotch and water. Kelli related the events surrounding her luncheon appointment with Barron. She said Barron had agreed to leave peacefully without a fight. Her eyes welled with tears. "I don't know if I did the right thing or not."

"Of course you did," Neva and I said almost in unison.

"You're my closest friends," she said to us. After discussing a few of our more innocuous cases and a couple more drinks Kelli decided to go home.

"You okay?" I asked.

"Yeah."

"Please drive carefully," I said.

I heard Kelli's car speed down the driveway. I prayed she would make it home okay.

There was a century of silence. Then Neva looked at me and I looked at her.

"Neva, Kelli is under a lot of pressure. This thing with Barron is having its effect on her. And now we're going to take on the biggest sonofabitch in town."

Neva and I fixed another drink. This was the first heart-to-heart talk I'd ever had with her.

She had a certain look in her eye. Then she asked me, "What do you think about Mrs. F.? What do you really think about her?"

"What is this? A spy mission?" I asked.

"No, Jake I'm serious. I'll tell you what she thinks about you. I promise I won't tell, I swear."

"You promise?"

"I promise."

"She's one hell of a lady. She is one of the most enthusiastic, energetic women I've ever known. She's loyal, and a ferocious fighter. She's striking. She's ego driven, and fearless. She's also self-conscious about her lack of formal education. She needs a strong male figure in her life. And she drinks too much. How did I do?"

"Jake, you just got an A in Psychology 101."

"Now I'm interested in your knowledge, Mrs. Gullihorn," I said.

"Jake, Mrs. F. has a crush on you. She's madly in love with you. She tells me these things unsolicited. I hope she doesn't talk in her sleep. Jake, I don't know what type of relationship you and Kelli have—it's none of my business— but please be careful. A lot of people could get hurt, including the people who work in this firm. I'll put it very bluntly. One afternoon when you weren't here, she had too many drinks, and she told me that she wanted to get you in bed."

Neva and I cleared away the bar. I appreciated her honesty. We left together out the back door. She stopped and said, "Look, maybe I shouldn't have said all that, but you need to know."

"Thanks."

We left. This was a wrinkle I hadn't expected.

*****

Ford Ashton had been one of my first clients. Kelli had handled a divorce and adoption for his wife years ago. He was a newscaster, the anchor at one of the local stations. He was also an entrepreneur who owned and operated the most popular nightclub in town, Rooster's, which was one of the first corporations I formed. Ashton knew the city well. He had started his journalism career as a police beat reporter and worked his way up to anchor. He was streetwise, and knew the who, what, when, where, why, and the for how much of Conecuh. He knew exactly who was doing what to whom and for how much. We trusted each other. I fed him the inside poop on the legal community and he kept me informed of what was happening on the street.

It was agreed between us and Donnie Lee Booker's firm that we would leak the story to Ford Ashton right before we filed it. We would commence the war with a surprise attack on the enemy. Donnie Lee and Dixie worked late into the night putting the finishing touches on the lawsuit. Every single paragraph and allegation in the complaint had been thoroughly researched, documented, and dissected. Legal briefs backed everything up. Donnie Lee had done his homework.

I called Ford Ashton after his six o'clock news program at home. "Ford," I said, "I've got a blockbuster that's going to hit the street tomorrow. Can you meet me at my office at eight a.m.?"

He said, "What is it?"

"I'll tell you in the morning. It's going to shake up the town. You'll get the exclusive."

I arrived at the office at seven a.m. and entered the back door quietly. Terri Beth's car was parked in the parking lot. She was standing over the telephone with a metal object in her hand. I couldn't see what it was. When the door slammed, she jumped and quickly put the object into her pocketbook. "Oh, my God, you scared the hell out of me, Jake," she said. "What are you doing here so early?"

"It's going to be a big day, Terri Beth. It's D-Day with the bank. Do we have plenty of coffee? Ford Ashton will be here at eight o'clock."

My mind wandered back to what I had seen Terri Beth do only moments before. Surely she wasn't doing anything dishonest. She didn't need money. Her references had checked out. I wondered what she had been doing. I was tempted to sneak a peek into her pocketbook. No, I decided. Terri Beth was a loyal soul mate of mine.

Donnie Lee and Dixie arrived next. "Looks like you guys were burning the midnight oil last night," I said.

"Yep. We finished about eleven. Our suit is about as tightly drawn as we could make it. I don't think they'll throw us out on a motion for judgment on the pleadings. Have you talked to Ashton?" he asked.

"Yeah. He'll be here in about half an hour."

Ford Ashton arrived promptly at eight o'clock. He was wearing a checkered sport coat and khaki trousers. Terri Beth took charge of the coffee.

"Ford, I want you to meet Donnie Lee Booker. He's an Atlanta attorney and he's been working with us."

"Hi, Ford," said Donnie Lee. "I've heard a lot of good things about you."

"Not from Jake McDonald," laughed Ford. "Tell me, you guys, what's going on?"

I handed him a copy of the lawsuit. "We're going to file this around ten this morning. You're the first to know about it."

The complaint was an eighty-six page document, was styled as a Complaint for Damages and a class action RICO case involving four basic counts. It named First Fidelity Bank and Trust and all its subsidiaries and affiliates as defendants, together with Southern Finance of Georgia, Inc., and each of their bankers and financial officers individually as co-conspirators and defendants.

Ford Ashton sipped his coffee slowly as he read through the complaint. Twenty minutes later he looked up. "Whew!" he whistled. "My God, can you prove all this stuff?"

"Every damn bit of it," I exclaimed.

"Where did you come up with this?"

"Ford, you've been around this town for a long time. You know what's going on. First Fidelity has its tentacles into everything. They own every politician. Every major business is in their pocket. They stomp on the little guy with impunity. It's time somebody broke up their tea party."

"Well, you're certainly going to mess up Anthony Jacobs' morning. King, Golden and Bonner should send you a Christmas present for creating their lawyer's relief and retirement program. Jake, the word on the street is that their firm is having cash flow problems. Did you know that?"

"No, I didn't."

"You know how secretaries are. A couple of their girls were in the club a few nights ago. My son Wendell was tending bar and he overheard them talking about some heated arguments the partners were having over money. Rumor has it they're going to let some of their lawyers go. Look, can I have a copy of the suit?" he asked. "It will be the lead story on the evening news."

"I have an autographed copy just for you," I said. "Let me file it first."

"What judge are you selecting?" he asked.

I grinned. "Ford, you know they're assigned on a rotational basis."

"Bullshit. I know better than that. You've selected the judge and I'm interested in knowing who you chose."

"You'll see," I said.

"Look, can we get an interview for the news? How about you and Donnie Lee and Kelli?"

"Okay. Let me get my makeup lady lined up."

Promptly at ten o'clock Donnie Lee and I arrived at the clerk's office. On a prearranged signal from Sue Bass, the deputy clerk, and our "sweetheart" in the clerk's office, I stepped forward with fifteen copies of the lawsuit. We paid the $229 filing fee. She stamped the copies filed, put a time on the filing stamp and initialed each copy. It took her another hour to prepare the summonses for the service copies. "This is assigned to Judge Carol Randall," she winked, as if I didn't already know.

"Sue, we would like to get service on these defendants as soon as possible. Do you mind if we personally deliver the service copies to the sheriff's office?" I asked.

"No, not at all," she replied.

We left the clerk's office with what was surely forty or fifty pounds of paper. Ford Ashton was standing in the hallway. I handed him a copy of the suit. "Have at it, chief," I said.

He rushed off. "I'll call you later in the day for the interview," he said.

Buster Blakeley was the deputy sheriff on desk duty. It was his job to log in all the filings from the Superior Court and to assign deputies to serve all papers filed in the Superior Court. "What in the world!" he exclaimed.

"Just a little lawsuit we're filing, Buster." I winked at Donnie Lee.

"First Fidelity Bank and Trust! You're suing them?"

"Looks like it, Buster."

Kelli arrived late that morning. She had been at the beauty parlor. She was attired in a conservative navy blue dress suit, and white blouse. A red, white and blue scarf was arranged around her neck. She had dressed for the big day.

*****

Five deputy sheriffs' cars went off in all directions to serve the suits. Anthony Jacobs was an easy one to serve. His office was right down the street from the sheriff's office, three blocks away. Jacobs was in a meeting in the bank's boardroom when the deputy arrived. Judy Curry, Jacobs's thirty-year-old secretary, greeted the officer. She was his personal secretary, and it was known in the bank that she took many out-of-town trips with Jacobs. She made a high salary. "Can I help you?" she asked.

"Yes, ma'am," Buster replied. "We've got some legal papers to serve on Mr. Jacobs."

"Can it wait?" she said. "He's in an important meeting." She tried to intimidate Buster with her charm.

"I'm afraid not, ma'am. This is a summons from the Superior Court."

"Just a minute." She left the room and entered the boardroom.

Anthony Jacobs was agitated as she handed him a note. "Just a minute, gentlemen. I'll be right back." He excused himself and went into the anteroom.

"Mr. Jacobs, I'm Deputy Buster Blakeley of the sheriff's office and I have some papers to serve on you."

Jacob's turned white when he was handed the lawsuit. His face turned crimson red as he read through the complaint. "Get Brad King on the phone immediately. Tell him to get over here now!"

Deputy Blakeley went from floor to floor in the bank, serving the other officers who had been named as defendants. Robert Banks and Ronald Sherman were in Robert's office when the deputy sheriff arrived. They sat stunned and spoke not a word as they read the allegations accusing them of conspiracy to commit racketeering activity. This was the first time either one of them had been sued personally.

The word spread quickly around the courthouse. It was the lunchtime talk for the courthouse crowd. The story quickly hit the news media. They all wanted a copy of the suit. The clerk's office had to set up a special copying machine to make copies at $.25 per page.

Promptly at 11:30 a.m. Ford Ashton appeared at our office with his television crew. He was dressed differently from earlier in the day. He was wearing a navy blue suit, a white shirt, and a red power tie. He looked like an attorney going to court.

We all assembled in the library. Present were Donnie Lee and one of his Atlanta partners who had also signed the suit, Kelli, and myself. Donnie Lee was our spokesman. If anybody asked technical questions, he would handle it. The interview went well. We knew Ashton would not sandbag us. At 1:30 p.m. the other news media requested interviews. The other two television stations had reporters present. There were four radio stations represented as well as reporters from AP and the *Atlanta Constitution.*

The local paper was represented by Karl Stein. Stein was a sleaze bag police beat reporter who was paid under the table by First Fidelity to cause trouble for its enemies. He had blackmail goods on everybody, including his own boss, the editor of the newspaper. Donnie Lee had been previously warned about Stein, so he refused to make eye contact with him, and he avoided answering any of Stein's questions. The interview lasted about thirty minutes. The reporters rushed off to meet their deadlines.

Judy Curry had one of Bradford King's associates hand him a note during the deposition that was going on in his conference room. It read, "Brad, I need to see you immediately. It's an extreme emergency of the utmost importance. Anthony Jacobs."

King was visibly shaken. He immediately took a break from the deposition and called the bank. He was put through immediately to Jacobs.

"Brad, have you heard what those bastards have done?"

"No. What are you talking about?"

"That Barrett, Ferguson and Thomas firm has filed a multi-million dollar lawsuit against us for fraud, usury, and racketeering under the RICO statute. I need to see you immediately."

"Tony, I'm almost through here. I'll be over shortly. Calm down."

"Calm down? Hell, these bastards are going to pay for this crap."

Bradford King cut his depositions short and headed to the bank. He knew that the inevitable had happened. He had heard it would be only a matter of time before some smart plaintiff's firm put two and two together, and figured out there was a pattern in First Fidelity's insidious conduct. He hoped that his law firm would not be caught up in the bank's crooked legal entanglements. He secretly prayed that he could milk enough

116

attorneys' fees out of the bank to pull his own firm out of its financial problems. Maybe this was the miracle he needed. If he could squeeze a $100,000 retainer out of the bank up front, he would be able to get the creditors off his back, pay the back salaries to the attorneys, and he wouldn't have to lay off anyone. He was determined to make it work.

Anthony Jacobs was furiously pacing around his office when Bradford King arrived. "Look at this crap." He tossed the suit towards King. King read the lawsuit. He knew instantly that this was no nuisance case meant to extort money from the bank. The plaintiff lawyers had done their homework. The bank was in deep trouble.

*****

The consensus was that the television interview went as well as could be expected. We had not had any hostile questions from the reporters, and Karl Stein hadn't time to do his dirty work.

We set up a command post in the library so we could watch the news report on a portable TV. The newscast began, "A multimillion dollar law suit was filed today against the largest bank in Conecuh. Fraud and conspiracy are alleged. More details in a moment." We got a full ten minutes on the evening news. Ford Ashton did a good job portraying our lawsuit in a light most favorable to us. The phones rang off the hook from plaintiff firms all over the state offering their assistance.

After the news Kelli asked me to join her in her office so we could, in her words, "talk about a lot of things." Everyone had gone except Kelli and me. She closed the door and got out the ice bucket. She poured herself a scotch and water.

"Jake," she said, "During all the hullabaloo over the suit, Barron and I reached an agreement. We agreed to let Fred help us put a value on the practice and I agreed to buy him out. He will go quietly."

"What about the lawsuit?" I asked.

"He agreed to make no public comments and not to interfere in any way. It will be made part of the agreement."

"Kelli, we've got to be especially careful while this suit is pending. The defense team will be watching us like hawks. Loose lips sink ships. I think we need to hire a guard for the office at night."

"Do you really think they would try something?" she asked.

"Absolutely!"

"Okay."

We immediately contacted a local security service and they committed to having a guard on the premises by eight. I volunteered to stay and wait.

*****

I heard Kelli's car as she pulled out of the driveway, and called Kathy and apprised her of the situation with the security guards. She said, "Did you see yourself on TV? It's all over the news. Our phone has been ringing off the hook. A Karl Stein called," she said.

"Turn the answering machine on. I don't want to talk with him."

The security guard arrived at 7:45 p.m. and set up his command post behind the office building. I went home.

Kathy had prepared a surprise for me—a candle light dinner of beef Wellington and a fine bottle of cabernet sauvignon. I could tell she was in a romantic mood. It had been so long since we had had a romantic evening together. I had come home every night and fallen into bed. The lawsuit had finally been filed.

I glanced at the clock. It was two a.m. Kathy was asleep. (The next thing I knew the phone was ringing.) "Damn it. Probably some divorce client."

She moaned and moved slightly.

"Hello," I said softly.

"Jake?"

"Kelli. Damn, do you know what time it is?" I asked.

"Hell yeah, it's two a.m. Listen, I just got a call from the police department. Somebody tried to break into our office tonight."

"You're kidding me," I said.

"No. The guard we hired fired a shot at him. They want one of us to come down."

"Look, I'll go. Stay there and I'll meet you early in the morning. I woke up Kathy. "I've got to go to the office. Someone tried to break in and the police need to see me."

"Damn," she said.

I got up, dressed, and drove to the office. There were two squad cars with lights flashing and the security guard. Apparently the burglar had tried to get through the side window and the guard surprised him and tried to stop him. The intruder pulled what looked like a gun and the guard got off a shot.

Kathy was wide-awake when I returned. "What's going on?" she asked.

I went over the details.

"Oh, Jake, it's that lawsuit, isn't it?"

"Maybe, sweetheart."

*****

I dragged into the office around 8:30 a.m., half-asleep. It had been a long night. I hoped I would be able to make it through the day.

"Good morning, boss," said Terri Beth. She was always pleasant and always smiling. "I understand we had some excitement around here last night."

"Well, it wasn't exactly the shoot out at the OK Corral, but our security guard almost got him a thug."

Juanita buzzed me on the intercom. "Jake, the district attorney's office is on line one and Gene Cochran is on line two."

"I'll take line one. Tell the Cochrans I'm out of the office." They were the last people I wanted to talk to this early in the morning.

I gulped down a cup of coffee and picked up line one. It was Don Pollard. "Jake, I understand you guys keep so much money over there that even the common cat burglars want some of it."

"You smart ass," I said.

"Jake, on a serious note, I have something in my office which might be of interest to you. What are you doing in the next fifteen minutes?"

"I'll be right over," I said.

Pollard's office was the usual scene of a rat race of assistant district attorneys running around with arms full of files on their way to court, but his appearance was the same as always. His tie was pulled down, his collar was unbuttoned at the top, and the sleeves on his rumpled shirt were rolled up. He looked more like a blue-collar sweatshop steward at the textile mill rather than the successful district attorney he was.

He shut the door behind me. "Coffee?"

"No, thank you."

He grinned. "It's nice to know a celebrity. Every time I turn on the television I see your damn face telling some reporter what bastards First Fidelity Bank and Trust are. Wow! You guys have a set of brass ones filing that suit," he said. "If you win it, I'll come work for you."

"Not *if*." I said. "When."

"Look, I just got the final report from the state fire marshal's office. The accelerant used in the Perkins fire and the Tolbert fire are the same, just as we suspected. It was a compound used in Vietnam to disable tanks and armored personnel carriers. In fact, the state fire marshal was able to trace the compound down to the specific lot and manufacturer. It was stolen from an ordnance depot at Fort Bragg, North Carolina.

"Jake, these fires were set by professionals. The type of accelerant that was used links them. There are two other links: one, both victims were your clients and two, First Fidelity held the mortgages on both of them. This isn't a coincidence.

His face grew solemn. "I don't know if we'll ever catch the sons of bitches that torched your clients, but I'm telling you as a friend, look out. Suing First Fidelity, in my opinion, was not a smart thing to do. But that's your decision. You're the lawyer. These bastards are going to play hardball with you. They're ruthless and they will do anything to win. I would advise you to keep a few security guards around your office. If you or Kathy need any help in the way of protection from my office, I'll be glad to set up some of our plainclothes folks to watch out for you. Good luck."

I left the district attorney's office convinced more than ever that First Fidelity was behind the fires. We would follow Don's advice.

*****

Delta Flight 1029 arrived at the Conecuh Municipal Airport promptly at 9:45 a.m. Alberto de Salvo deplaned the small jet and moved quickly to the baggage pickup area. He grabbed one bag and caught a cab to the Rest Inn, a small hotel near the airport and checked in under the name of Frank Turner.

"Has an overnight package arrived for me?" he inquired.

"Yes, Mr. Turner. It came in thirty minutes ago."

He picked up the package and went quickly to his room. He refused the bellman's help, and carried his own bag. Tossing the bag in the corner of the room, he quickly ripped open the package. He removed a 9mm Glock semi-automatic, the serial number, of which had been filed off. Next he attached a silencer and popped an empty ammo clip into the base of the weapon. He pulled back the hammer and pulled the trigger. "Click." The weapon test-fired perfectly.

He loaded the clip with nine rounds and popped the magazine back into the base of the pistol.

*****

Ford Ashton's Rooster Club was packed. The band had just finished the first set, and the crowd was thinning out. People were lining up outside the restrooms and others were congregating outside to take in some fresh air.

A siren could be heard in the distance. Three major hospitals were located within two miles of Roosters, so sirens were a common event.

The Rest Inn was located in a shopping complex between Roosters and a multiplex theater. The sirens were getting closer. The red lights of an ambulance were visible from Roosters parking lot. The ambulance was coming straight towards the nightclub. It turned the corner at a high rate of speed and sped past Roosters, pulling to a stop in front of the hotel. Two attendants jumped out of the ambulance and hurriedly carried a stretcher into the front door of the hotel. Thirty seconds later a police car with flashing blue lights pulled in behind the ambulance.

"What's going on over there?" Ford Ashton asked the group that was standing in the parking lot.

"It looks like somebody had a heart attack."

Three minutes later an unmarked car with a blue revolving light on the dashboard wheeled into the parking lot behind the police car. Its tires squealed to a halt. Ford recognized one of the two men as Ron Bullock, a homicide detective with the Conecuh police department.

A large crowd had gathered in the parking lot. A dark blue Oldsmobile pulled up and Phil Stanley, the county coroner, emerged. Stanley, a former undertaker and now political hack, had a reputation as a hotshot at homicide scenes. The district attorney's office and the police department hated him. They said he was like a bull in a china shop at crime scenes.

Forty-five minutes later the ambulance attendants came out the front door of the hotel with a stretcher covered by a white sheet. It was obvious that there was a body under the sheet, probably a dead one. The ambulance sped away, its sirens wailing. The police cars, detectives' cars, and the coroner's automobile remained at the scene.

A news car from Ashton's TV station parked behind Roosters. Five minutes after the ambulance left, Dusky Sanchez, a reporter from the station, spotted Ford in the crowd and motioned for him to come over. "Ford, we've got a hell of a news story."

"What's going on?" asked Ford.

"It seems we've had a nasty murder. A man checked in this afternoon under the name of Frank Turner. They found him in his room with nine bullet holes in him. He was totally naked. It was a bloody mess."

The crowd started to drift back inside and the band started to play again. The police detectives were still on the scene as Rooster's was closing down for the night.

Ford stepped outside to get a breath of fresh air from all the cigarette smoke in Rooster's. Dusky Sanchez was still there. He approached Ford. "Ford, I just got word from one of the detectives that Frank Turner was an assumed name. The man came in on a flight early today, which originated in Chicago. The man received a package when he checked into the hotel. No one heard the shots. The police are checking his fingerprints against the FBI files."

*****

I walked down the driveway in my bathrobe to retrieve the morning newspaper. Kathy was preparing breakfast. The headline of the newspaper grabbed my attention. "Reputed Mobster Murdered In Local Hotel." The front-page story reported that a Chicago hood by the name of Alberto de Salvo had been shot nine times. No motive for the killing was apparent, and police had no information as to what de Salvo was doing in Conecuh. The story went on to report the past criminal history of de Salvo and the fact that he was a known hit man for the Costellano crime family. I shuddered and put down the paper.

Eight

Tom Dupree and his wife Kitty had been friends of ours for a long time and we had invited them over for a cookout at our new home. Tom and I had double dated in college and he had met his wife Kitty on a blind date that I had set up. Tom had gone to the Medical College of Georgia and was doing his internship at the Conecuh Medical Center in pathology. He supplemented his income as a deputy medical examiner and was present at most of the autopsies performed in the county. Though he thought what I did for a living was a rotten existence, I'd always thought that cutting open dead bodies had to be worse than handling divorce cases. Kitty was a registered nurse.

It was quite a respite to get away from lawyer types for an evening. Tom and I stood around the grill, cooking the steaks, and talking about our old hunting days. We were both avid bird hunters. Both of us would drive two hundred miles to hunt any kind of birds—ducks, quail, doves, pheasants, or turkeys—it didn't matter.

The girls were busy inside talking about decorating houses and the other things women talk about. Tom was intrigued with the lawsuit. He had always pulled for underdogs and wanted to know how we had gotten the goods on First Fidelity.

The conversation drifted to the de Salvo murder. "If I fall asleep on you, please forgive me. That damn coroner of ours woke me up at three this morning to do an autopsy ... Jake, it was a bloody mess. I dragged my ass down to the morgue at three in the morning to find a hit man for the mob that had more holes in him than Swiss cheese. He paused and looked at me conspiratorially. "Everything I tell you is in the strictest of confidence, okay?"

"Yeah, of course."

"The man was shot nine times. It was most unusual. Microscopic examination revealed that eight of the shots were from a 9mm weapon and the other shot was from a .357 magnum. It's unlikely that he shot himself and then somebody pumped rounds of a 9mm into him. You figure it out, Jake. Either the murderer used two weapons or there was more than one murderer. The evidence points to the fact that the .357 was fired first, but it was not the fatal wound."

The girls had everything on the table and the steaks were ready. "Jake, did you know that if you eat enough of these steaks that the cholesterol will clog up your arteries and you'll die? I'll show you some slides of clogged arteries after we eat."

Kitty shrieked. "Tom Dupree, we are going to send you home."

"That's all right, Kitty." I said. "I'll be glad to represent you for free in your divorce against your jerk husband. I believe he's a medical doctor, isn't he? You should get plenty of alimony. All you'll have to do is bat those pretty big brown eyes in front of the jury and let the tears roll down your cheeks. He'll pay and pay and pay."

Everybody laughed. The steaks were delicious.

Monday morning came much too soon. The newest lawyer in the firm was delegated the task of picking up the mail every morning at the post office and I was it. There was a notice from the post office that it was holding a package that was too large to fit in our box. I presented the ticket at the call window, and the postman handed me a package that weighed at least four pounds. The return address was that of the law firm of King, Golden and Bonner. They had paid $6.27 to mail us the thing. They could have had one of their many $14 per hour runners deliver it in person.

I arrived at the office around 8:30 a.m. Terri Beth was pounding away at the typewriter. "Good morning, boss," she smiled.

"Good morning, sunshine," I replied.

"How was your weekend?" she asked.

"Pretty good. We had some friends over Saturday night. People we haven't seen in a while. Medical types. He was one of the doctors who did the autopsy on that Mafia thug that was killed."

"Really?" she said.

"A real mess."

Terri Beth fixed me a cup of coffee—black with artificial sweetener. I opened the first installment of the many epistles that surely were to come from the Philistines. The package contained six motions filed by the bank's attorneys. Each one was supported by a legal brief. Their poor associates and secretaries must have worked all weekend. They wasted no time running the clock on legal fees at $250 to $300 per hour.

At this rate their law firm should not have any further cash flow problems. I hoped they would send us a thank you note.

Their first motion was one to dismiss the lawsuit for failure to state a claim upon which relief could be granted. This was a standard motion. It was always filed with every defensive pleading, and it was rarely granted.

The second motion was one to strike some of the language from our complaint because they alleged it was inflammatory and was intended to prejudice the jury. All lawsuits are intended to do that. What else was new?

The third motion was to seal the pleadings and discovery from the public and for a motion for a gag order. Obviously, they didn't want the public to know what big crooks they really were.

The fourth motion was to dismiss for lack of jurisdiction. They contended that since Southern Finance of Georgia, Inc. was incorporated in Delaware and its home office was in Delaware that we should have filed the suit there. This struck me as humorous. Southern Finance of Georgia, Inc. was a Yankee corporation?

The fifth motion was to remove our case to the federal court since Southern Finance of Georgia, Inc., was a Delaware corporation and because two of the defendants lived across the river in Alabama.

It was the final motion that caught my attention. It was a motion to have Judge Carol Randall recluse herself because of a close personal relationship with Kelli Ferguson. In my opinion this was the dumbest motion they could have filed.

Carol Randall had been friends with a lot of attorneys over many years. She treated our firm no better and no worse than any of the other law firms. It's one thing to sue the corporate giant and a major employer in town, but it's dumber to attack the judge who is going to try the case. It was in the sole discretion of the judge to grant or deny such motions, and it is dumber than hell to file an attack on the judge unless you can prove the judge personally sticks pins in voodoo dolls of all the lawyers in your firm on a daily basis. After reading the motion, maybe Judge Randall would pull out her needles.

Dixie and Donnie Lee arrived around eight. I noticed that they had been arriving about the same time every morning. They had spent a lot of time together. I suspected some of it had been intimate. I couldn't blame them – both were single and Dixie was a good-looking woman.

Dixie stuck her head in the door. "Good weekend?"

"Great, Dixie. How about yours?"

"Wonderful," she said.

I looked at Terri Beth and she looked at me. We didn't need to say a thing.

"Dixie, we received the first installment of legal billings on the First Fidelity case from the defense boys. Six motions. Most of it is the standard b.s., but take a look at the motion to get Judge Randall removed. I think they're nuts. That's your first assignment. Go get 'em, tiger!" I said.

"Where's Kelli?" I buzzed into Neva's office.

"She called in and said she would be coming in late this morning. She's been having a lot of stomach problems. No doubt it's all related to what's been going on around here lately."

I walked down the hall and there was Barron clearing out his desk. "Need some help, Barron?" I asked.

"No, I've about got it," he said.

"I'm sure going to miss you. No more dry wit around here."

"I'm sure you'll manage," he said. "Maybe we'll meet in the courtroom and we can exchange insults," He smiled, but it was tense.

"No thanks, Barron. I'm going to settle all my cases with you. You'd win hands down."

"How's the First Fidelity case coming?" he asked.

"They sent the first one hundred pounds of motions today."

"You know how defense attorneys are," he said. "They charge by the pound."

"What are you going to do?" I asked.

"I'm going to take a couple of weeks off and work on my boat in Florida. Then I'm opening a small office down the street. I have enough money, so I'm going to limit my practice to estates, wills, and small insurance defense. No major litigation. I've had enough of that. I'm going to leave that to you younger guys."

"Well, if we can help you, let us know. I'm sorry it didn't work out between you and Kelli."

"Me too," he said.

"Is Kim going with you, Barron?"

"Yeah," he said.

"Hey, don't take all of the good looking ones with you. Leave some for the rest of us." He nodded and I continued down the hall.

Dixie, Donnie Lee, and I spent most of the day working on the motions that First Fidelity's lawyers had filed. Most of it was standard stuff meant to slow down the wheels of justice and to run up their client's bill.

Sheila, Judge Randall's secretary, called and said the judge had scheduled the motion hearings for Monday, two weeks away at ten a.m. All of the legal research had already been done by Dixie and Donnie Lee and I felt comfortable we would prevail. I still couldn't figure out why they had taken the risk of attempting to remove Judge Randall with such a frontal assault.

Kelli was busy with divorce hearings all day. Brook was involved with a manslaughter trial. Phillip handled the bankruptcy hearings all day and Parnell was in small claims court.

The most important matter dealt with our motion to have the suit proceed as a class action. If granted, it would open the floodgates for everybody who had ever been screwed over by First Fidelity. The damages would be enormous.

It was five p.m. Kelli was seeing her last client. Juanita buzzed me on the intercom. "Mr. McDonald, there is a gentleman on line one. He won't give his name but he says he has some information you want."

"What the hell?" I mumbled.

"Mr. McDonald?"

"Yes," I said.

"Jake McDonald?"

"Yes. What can I do for you?"

"There's a plane leaving from the airport at seven o'clock in the morning. Its destination is the Turks and Caicos Islands. It pertains to your case."

"Who is this?" I asked.

"It's not important who this is. What is important is who is on that plane." I heard a click and then a dial tone.

What next? I wondered. I couldn't afford to be seen at the airport. I dialed the number of Stanton Parks at the college. Parks was an old fighter pilot in Vietnam. He had flown thirty-five combat missions and knew airplanes. He was a retired Army colonel and got his PhD in education, of all things. He was the head of the Education Department at the college.

Parks answered the phone.

"Stanton, Jake McDonald here."

"How are you, Jake? I've been seeing you on television and in the newspaper."

"Listen, Stanton, I need your help. I just received the strangest call from someone who wouldn't identify himself. He said somebody connected with my case was flying out of the airport to the Turks and Caicos Islands at seven in the morning. I need a favor. Can you do a little spy mission for me?"

"Sure," he said.

"I need somebody there that they wouldn't suspect. You know how to read flight plans."

"I hope I do," he interrupted. "Look, Jake. I have some of that secret photographic stuff we used in 'Nam. Maybe I could get some pictures."

"That's perfect, Stanton. You're a good man."

I joined Kelli in her office. Dixie and Donnie Lee were in the library working. Kelli had the ice bucket out and had fixed a drink. She was in a good mood. Her hearings had gone well that day. "How'd your day go?" she asked.

"Busier than hell. Whenever you guys are in court, every Tom, Dick and Harry comes in off the street to see us."

"Collect any good fees?" she asked.

"A few good ones. A couple of $1000 retainers on new divorces. I turned them over to Neva."

"She's good with handling clients. They came to see you anyway."

"Listen, I received the strangest call a few minutes ago. Somebody who wouldn't identify himself said there was a plane leaving for the Turks and Caicos Islands at seven in the morning and it pertained to the First Fidelity case. I put Stanton Parks on it. He's going to sneak out there in the morning and find out what's going on. He said he'd get some pictures."

"Hmm," she said. "That *is* strange, isn't it?"

It was 7:10 p.m. when Kelli and I left the office.

"Goodnight, you guys." Dixie and Donnie Lee were still working. "We're going to be here a while, Jake. We're getting prepared for the motion hearings."

"Good night."

I had driven two blocks down the street when I heard a loud crack. It sounded like a gun going off. I felt my left front tire go flat. It was a blowout. "Damn," I muttered. I pulled off the road and parked the car. I walked back to the office to call Kathy and Triple-A. I didn't feel like changing a tire in a coat and tie.

I walked through the back door and could see the library light was still on. I appeared in the doorway and Dixie and Donnie Lee were lying on the sofa. Her blouse was lying on the floor. I couldn't see Donnie Lee. He was lying on his back on the sofa and Dixie was straddling him.

Of all times for me to show up. I darted out the doorway and into my office, and picked up the phone. "Anybody here?" I shouted. I could hear them grope and scramble.

"Yeah, we're still here," Donnie Lee said.

"I blew a damn tire," I said. "I'm calling Triple-A." I called Kathy and told her what had happened. Then I called Triple-A. I walked out the back door and stopped at the library doorway. There they were like two innocent canaries. Dixie had on her glasses with her hair up on top of her head and she looked like a schoolteacher. They didn't suspect that I had seen them.

"You two have a good time. I'm going to see about my car."

When I got outside I burst out laughing. I had caught my legal assistant and a lawyer friend screwing in my library.

The Triple-A truck arrived about fifteen minutes later. The mechanic rolled the hydraulic jack under the frame of the left front wheel. He pumped the jack handle three times and then he stopped. He flashed his light underneath the car and rolled out quickly.

"What's the matter?" I asked.

"I don't know, but we're getting out of here fast. Get in the truck," he said.

I didn't ask any questions. I jumped into the cab of the tow truck and he took off immediately, leaving the jack under the car. He radioed the police department and requested the bomb squad.

"What the hell is going on?" I asked.

"There's a bomb attached to the front axle of your car. Something cut the inside of your front tire. If your tire hadn't blown, that bomb would have gone off."

The bomb squad arrived along with three other police cars. Dixie and Donnie Lee heard the commotion and drove down the street. They were stopped at a roadblock 1500 feet away from my car and saw me standing off to the side. "Are you all right?" they asked.

"Yeah. Just a little bomb. Nothing to really worry about."

"A bomb? Jake, you could have been killed!"

The bomb squad lieutenant walked up. "We disarmed the bomb, Mr. McDonald and we're going to tow your car in so the crime lab can go over it with a fine-toothed comb in the morning for evidence. We can arrange for a patrol officer to give you a lift home."

"That's all right," Donnie Lee spoke up. "We work with him. We'll give him a ride."

"Thanks, officer."

"Here's my card, Mr. McDonald. We'll talk with you in the morning."

Donnie Lee pulled into my driveway. Kathy ran out. "Jake, what's happened? Where's your car?"

"Let's go inside. You know Donnie Lee. He's our associate attorney from Atlanta. And you know Dixie."

"What's going on?"

"Some body tried to bomb my car."

"Oh, Jake!"

"I had a blowout two blocks from the office and the Triple-A man came out and jacked up the car and discovered the bomb. I'm glad I didn't try to change the tire myself. I might have been blown away."

After about an hour Donnie Lee and Dixie left. Kathy was visibly shaken. "Jake, it's that case. Your life isn't worth suing that bank."

"Sweetheart, that's the reason they need to be stopped. They threaten and intimidate everybody who gets in their way."

"Damn it, Jake. I don't want to be a rich young widow."

"Hey, if you were a rich young widow, then you would have a whole herd of studs lined up to marry you. You could have your choice."

"Somehow I don't find that a bit funny." She stormed out of the room and slammed the bedroom door.

I didn't want to press my luck by asking her to fix dinner. I made a couple of turkey sandwiches from leftovers. The bastards at the bank were playing hardball.

My mind kept going back to the conversation with the unknown individual on the phone. Who was he? Of what significance was it that a plane leaving for the Caribbean in the morning? Mentally exhausted, I fell asleep in the chair. At two a.m. I woke up, turned off the lights, eased into the bedroom, and managed to crawl into bed without waking Kathy.

The alarm clock went off way too early, but I jumped up, took a shower, and dressed. Kathy had breakfast ready. "Look," I said, "I'm sorry I acted so stupid last night. I only meant to break the tension."

"I know, Jake. I'm sorry. I love you. I'm just scared."

"This weekend I want to make a date with you, Kathy."

"Where are we going?" she asked.

"To the pistol range. I'm going to teach you how to shoot."

"Oh, Jake, I'm afraid of guns."

"It's time you learned to get over that fear."

I drove Kathy's car to the office and arrived right at seven a.m. My mind raced to the airport and Stanton Parks. I hoped he'd been successful.

Terri Beth arrived at the same time. "Did Kathy run you off, boss? You're at work too early for a lawyer."

"Almost, Terri Beth. I've had a rough night."

She fixed coffee while I related the events of the previous evening. "Kathy is scared to death. Don Pollard has offered me protection. I'm considering taking him up on it. . . . If Stanton Parks calls, find me no matter where I am. I need to talk to him as soon as possible. I need to find that bomb squad lieutenant and see if I can learn anything."

I finally got through to Lt. Chico of the Conecuh Police Department after a series of telephone run-arounds. "Mr. McDonald, we are dusting your car for prints now. Whoever placed that bomb under your car was not an amateur. The explosive device is one we haven't seen in quite a while. It was used in Vietnam. It's called a 'cindy'."

I was stunned.

*****

"Sunshine," I said to Terri Beth, "I need to tell you some things in the strictest of confidence. You can't even tell anybody in the firm."

She smiled. "I'm loyal to you, Jake. You know that."

"The bomb underneath my car and the accelerant that caused the fires at Randy Perkins' condo project and Rudy Tolbert's fire were the same. Terri Beth, do you know how to use a pistol?"

She was taken off guard. "Well, I, uh . . . I . . . well, I. . . . No," she said.

"Why don't you let me show you and Kathy how to shoot a pistol this Saturday? We're going to the pistol range."

"Okay…I guess I could."

We poured a second cup of coffee. No one else had arrived yet, and it was too early to call the district attorney's office or to try to reach Stanton Parks. "Can you keep a little secret?"

"What is it, Jake?" she asked cautiously.

"You know our little suspicions about Donnie Lee and Dixie?"

"Yeah?"

"Last night when my car broke down I walked back to the office to call Triple-A. I came in the back door and Donnie Lee and Dixie were still here. They didn't hear me. I started to go into the library, but Donnie Lee and Dixie were on the sofa. You could say they didn't have any clothes on. At least Dixie didn't."

"You're kidding me," she giggled.

"No. I went down the hall and made a big noise. I messed up what they were doing."

"You are a very bad boy," she laughed.

"Our love birds need to get themselves an apartment or something. What if Kelli or Barron had discovered them?"

"Heck, Barron might have enjoyed it, and Kelli would've wanted to join them."

Neva arrived. Dixie had already called her and told her about the bomb. "Jake, I understand that you had an exciting night."

"I could have used less excitement, Neva. Maybe I ought to be a real estate lawyer and check titles."

Donnie Lee and Dixie came in. "You all right, Jake?" they asked.

"Yeah. Except they still have my car impounded, and Kathy is scared to death."

Neva said Kelli would be coming in later, it seemed she was still having stomach problems.

"She needs to go to the doctor and get that checked out," I said.

At 11:00 a.m. Juanita buzzed the intercom. I was with Randy Perkins going over the progress of his case. "Sorry to interrupt you, Mr. McDonald, but the individual you were expecting is on line three."

I immediately picked up the phone. It was Stanton Parks. "Jake, can you join me for lunch? I think I've got what you want."

"Where?" I asked.

"How about the Steak and Ale. It's near the college. I'll see you there at noon."

I arrived at the Steak and Ale precisely on time and Parks was at the front door waiting for me. He had a brown envelope in his hand. We got a corner table and placed our order.

"What do you have?" I asked.

"Take a look at these pictures."

There were pictures of three men standing beside an airplane—a private Gulfstream jet. One man I clearly recognized as Anthony Jacobs. The other two I didn't recognize. They looked foreign, either Hispanic or Italian.

"Jake, these guys were acting awfully suspicious. They wasted no time getting on the plane and getting out of there. What's even more interesting is the flight plan. Their final

142

destination was the Turks and Caicos, with a stopover in the Grand Caymans. What does that tell you?"

"It tells me that Mr. Anthony Jacobs and his two friends have some business with off-shore banks."

"You're being too polite, Jake. We are talking about two of the largest money laundering capitals of the world."

"Stanton, you have stumbled on to something very important. We have to keep this on the Q-T. These boys play rough." I related the events of last night. Parks was excited. He was now part of a great detective thriller.

I was tempted to go straight to the feds, but I remembered what Don Pollard had told me. I needed to see Pollard immediately.

He saved me the phone call. I walked in the door from lunch and he was on the phone. I grabbed it and spoke before he had a chance. "Don, we need to get together."

"I know," he said. "I've got a bond revocation hearing in a few minutes. It won't take long. Come on over. Johnny Harbuck will be joining us."

Harbuck was there when I arrived. We went into Don's office and shut the door. "You had a rough evening yesterday, didn't you?" said Harbuck.

" Johnny, I wish I was a school teacher."

He opened the manila folder he had on his desk. Fifteen minutes later Pollard came in and got straight to the point. "Jake, that bomb they took off your car was put there by a pro. You are a lucky sonofabitch. One of the clamps they used had a sharp flange that cut into your tire. The GBI believes the bomb was installed at your house and not at your office."

My blood turned cold. I could never, ever tell Kathy.

"Jake, we found the same chemicals that we found in the two fires involving your clients. I think it's time you took our offer of protection."

"I've already thought about it. Do it. Kathy is scared to death anyway, and there's something else you need to know. Yesterday around five p.m. I got a call from a man who wouldn't identify himself. He said what I was looking for in my case would be leaving from the airport for the Turks and Caicos Islands at seven this morning. I have a friend who's an expert photographer who went over there. Here's what he saw." I handed them copies of the pictures.

"Whew," whistled Johnny. "Mr. Jacobs keeps some international company."

"I worked for the FBI for fifteen years. I know a Sicilian when I see one."

"Look at the flight plan. They had two stops. The first was Grand Cayman Island. The second was the Turks and Caicos Islands. The two dirty money laundering capitals of the world."

Johnny said, "We need to run these photos through the FBI identification unit in Washington. I'll check the plane's registration today. In the meantime, Jake, we'll put a plainclothes unit around your house. You won't know they're there. Just don't beat up Kathy, or run around on her, or have any wild parties, 'cause we'll know about them." I didn't feel much like laughing.

"Gentlemen," Don cleared his throat, "all this is in the strictest of confidence. Something big is going on here. I see a sinister pattern developing and I don't like it."

"Johnny, do you think you can help me get my car back? Kathy can't go anywhere because I'm having to use her car. We might have to come to your house for dinner."

He smiled. "I think I can handle that."

*****

Thank God for Fridays. I spent the morning winding down other cases, shifting some to Brook, Phillip, and Parnell. The plan was for Donnie Lee, Dixie, and me to go full time on First Fidelity until its completion. My morning was interrupted with an unannounced visit from the Cochran's. I had managed to put them off on Terri Beth as much as I could. I decided to talk with them and hopefully buy at least another week without their interruptions.

Betty was her usual self, always interrupting and butting into the conversation. She always seemed to have a new theory and a new tangent to go off on. I listened as patiently as I could until I finally had to cut her off. Gene always wanted assurances that we were going to win his "big case". I explained to them that their case was an integral part of a larger class action, and therefore the risks had been spread out. I told them that we had invested a lot of time and money in their case and we had associated the best attorneys we could find who were experts in the area.

I had pre-arranged with Terri Beth to interrupt me after thirty minutes to say that Judge Braxton was expecting me in his office in five minutes. This would give me an excuse to end what would otherwise be a long bull session with the Cochrans which served no purpose. Oh, how I feared the day when Brad King took their depositions. We would need to spend hours upon hours preparing Gene and Betty for that unwelcome event.

The Friday luncheon at the country club served as a pleasant break from the events of the past week. It seemed as if I hadn't seen the other lawyers in the firm in a month. Everybody was going in five different directions. The guys had had great successes in court. Even Parnell had won a $2500 verdict in small claims court.

After lunch I told Terri Beth I needed to run an errand and would be back in about an hour. I went to Johnson's Sporting Goods Store downtown and was met by a clean-cut young man. He had a short haircut and he looked like he had just gotten out of the military. "May I help you?" he asked.

"Yes. I'm looking to purchase a pistol for my wife and me."

"Do you know anything about weapons?" he asked.

"Yes. I've had quite a bit of experience. I'm looking for a smaller handgun for my wife, probably a .32 caliber semi-automatic and either a 9mm or a .357 magnum for me."

He showed me several, and I selected a Smith and Wesson .32 caliber semi-automatic for Kathy and a 9mm Glock for me, and bought four boxes of ammunition for each.

The next morning Kathy and I picked up Terri Beth at her apartment and drove to the pistol range on the edge of town. Terri Beth wore blue jeans, a pullover sweater, and a denim jacket. Kathy and Terri Beth always got along. They treated each other like a sisters.

I loaded the pistols and explained to them how they worked. I talked about their safety features and the basics of marksmanship. Kathy was apprehensive. She had never fired a pistol before and didn't relish the idea, but she went first. Her hand jerked upward as she flinched, and the noise scared her, but after about a dozen rounds she began to relax. She even hit the target several times.

Terri Beth didn't seem quite as apprehensive. She fired off several rounds and then turned to me and said, "Let me try the 9mm." She seemed to know how to use it. She fired five rounds. Three hit the black area of the target.

"I thought you said you had never fired a gun before," I said.

"I guess it's beginner's luck, Jake." There was a look of determination in her eyes.

We stayed at the range for two hours and by the time we were done, Kathy had overcome her fear of handguns. Terri Beth had never shown any fear. I thought this unusual for someone who claimed she had never fired a pistol before.

We left the range and had lunch together at a very popular barbecue restaurant in town. Both women seemed to have enjoyed the outing.

When we returned there was a message on the answering machine from Stanton Parks. "Jake, call me as soon as you can. I'm at home." I returned his call immediately.

"Jake, we got some more information for you. I can't discuss it over the phone. Why don't you and Kathy join Debra and me for dinner? We're grilling chickens. It'll give y'all a chance to see my farm."

"Just a minute. Let me check with Kathy."

I quickly explained to Kathy that Stanton and Debra had invited us to dinner. "You mean a whole day without having to cook?" she asked. "Let's go."

"Stanton, we're on. What time?"

"How about four? It'll give us time to go over what we need to talk about."

Stanton and Debra lived in a rural county north of us. It was a bedroom community where a lot of retirees were moving. It took us forty minutes to get there.

"Jake, how are you? I haven't seen your pretty bride since the wedding." Stanton gave Kathy a big hug.

Debra came out to greet us. She was Stanton's second wife and fifteen years younger than he was. I had handled the divorce between Stanton and his first wife. It was peaceful and uncontested. They had just outgrown each another.

Debra was evidently keeping him happy. He looked good, and so did she. They showed us around the farm. They had all kinds of animals—chickens, pigs, goats, and a horse or two.

"Sweetheart, why don't you show Kathy around the house? Jake and I have to talk business." Stanton ushered me into his office. It was part of a converted barn.

"I guess college professors have to have an office no matter where they live," I said.

"Need the tax write-off, Jake." Stanton joked in response and then grew serious.

"Jake, you know that I'm an old Army intelligence officer in addition to being a pilot."

"Army intelligence? That's an oxymoron, Stanton."

He smiled. "Anyway, I've been doing some additional snooping for you. After that plane took off the other morning, I paid the aircraft maintenance supervisor a C-note to get me the information off the instruments and logbook when the plane returned. The plane is registered to our old friends at First Fidelity.

The information he gave me is very interesting-the instrument readings and fuel log don't match up with the flight plan. The mechanic verified that the Gulfstream was carrying a full load of fuel.

If you had three passengers and the pilot, and a normal cargo, the plane had a range of the Turks and Caicos Islands. They would have had to land there to take on fuel. There is no way they could have flown to the Caymans without refueling. "Okay," I said, "so what's the problem?" The problem is that there's only one refueling station in the Turks and Caicos. I've flown in there many times. I checked with the guys at the airstrip. No plane with that ID number ever landed there or refueled. Something funny is going on."

*****

Don Pollard and Johnny Harbuck were working Saturday preparing for a murder trial, which was scheduled to begin Monday. The fax machine rang and began receiving a message. It was from the ID section of the Federal Bureau of Investigation in Washington, in reference to the photographs that Stanton had taken and Johnny had forwarded to the FBI. The message read: WE CANNOT RELEASE THE INFORMATION THAT YOU HAVE REQUESTED. THIS INFORMATION HAS BEEN BLOCKED FROM RELEASE BY THE DIRECTOR. The document was signed by the head of the head ID section.

"What the hell is going on?" exclaimed Don. "Johnny, we're in the middle of something much more serious than a couple of arson cases. I believe Jake has stepped in the big one."

*****

Donnie Lee and Dixie had just about completed their research and briefs on the defendant's motions. The motion hearings were two days away and we had decided that I would argue half of the motions and Donnie Lee would argue the others. This was the first of the many attacks that would surely come from the defense. King, Golden and Bonner were notorious for filing lots of paperwork.

We felt confident that Judge Randall would not dismiss our case at this stage. The worst that would happen was that she would strike some of the inflammatory wording in the complaint. The defense was hoping she would take the easy way out and remove the case to federal court. We figured this was the reasoning behind the motion to recluse.

Terri Beth arrived early to work as usual bearing the mail. I had delegated my lowly task of picking up the mail to her.

I had the usual requests from attorneys asking that a case be placed on the trial calendar, attorneys asking for leaves of absence, and a counter-offer in a divorce case. One piece of mail caught my attention. It was a postcard with a turtle farm on the front and was postmarked Grand Cayman Island. Someone had written across the front, "Your case is here." The postmark bore the date Anthony Jacobs and his friends had flown out of the Conecuh airport.

I showed the card to Donnie Lee and Kelli. They were as startled as I was. It was evident that there was a mole on the other side. Who or why we did not know. I wondered how we could coax whomever it was to come out of the closet.

*****

Hearing day came. Judge Randall was as straight-laced a judge as there could ever be. If she had any prejudices, she didn't show them from the bench.

The defendant's attorneys argued loud and long, advancing the usual arguments. Donnie Lee quickly dissected their arguments for what they were—a lot of hot air.

The last motion argued by King was the motion to have Judge Randall rescue herself. He started off apologetically, saying that he had no animosity towards Judge Randall and Kelli, and that he considered them as friends, but due to the long friendship between them, Judge Randall should step down out of an abundance of precaution to avoid any appearance of bias.

Judge Randall showed no emotion whatsoever as he argued. He cited several cases as legal authority. We couldn't read from her expression what she was thinking.

I countered his argument that if what he said were true then no judge could sit on any case, because judges had many friends in the bar. They were practicing attorneys before they became judges. I pointed out that we had tried many cases against King, Golden and Bonner before Judge Randall and she had ruled against us on many occasions.

Judge Randall denied the defense's motions without comment. "As to the motion to have me recluse myself," she said, "Mr. King, it is true that Kelli Ferguson and I have been good friends for years, just as I have been a friend of your law firm for years." She smiled at Kelli. "You have presented no evidence for me to step down in this case. Unless you have something further, then I'm going to deny your motions. Mr. McDonald and Mr. Booker, prepare an order for my signature denying each of the motions."

"Yes, your honor," I said.

She left the bench and the bank's attorneys gathered up their briefs and law books and quickly left the courtroom. Though they had lost the first skirmish, they would be back.

Kelli was delighted. She had finally sat across the table from Brad King and beaten the number-one defense attorney in town. This was a battle the defense had never expected to win, and was simply an exercise to test the waters and run up one hell of a legal fee.

I could see the word processors at King, Golden and Bonner running now—26 hours of lawyer time at $225 per hour—32 hours of paralegal time at $52 per hour and 17 hours of secretarial time at $23 per hour plus $326.50 in costs. Eight thousand, two hundred and thirty-one dollars billed to First Fidelity for four perfunctory motions pulled off boiler plate forms on a word processor. The briefs to support them had been prepared nine years earlier and had been filed in defense of every case ever handled by King, Golden and Bonner. Every plaintiff's lawyer had dozens of them in their files. The standard defensive pleadings had been prepared years ago. If the general public only knew the real truth about their legal fees ...

Interrogatories and depositions were next. The Georgia Legislature finally limited the farce of interrogatories, questions that one side can compel the other to answer in a lawsuit. Formerly, the number had been unlimited. The defense usually sent out hundreds to intimidate the poor under-financed plaintiff's attorney. The real reason was to run up a horrendous legal bill for their clients and to have an excuse to pass the case at the next docket call when the plaintiff hadn't had time to answer them.

The Legislature limited interrogatories to thirty for each side unless either side obtained a court order to extend. It was no surprise that we received a motion to extend the very next day. I wondered what King, Golden and Bonner P.C. billed its client for *this* freebie. Judge Randall quickly saw through the legal maneuverings and before I could file an answer, I received her order denying the motion.

Depositions were next. Most of our lay witnesses I was not concerned about. They would simply testify that their houses had been foreclosed upon because they couldn't make their payments to First Fidelity. Dixie had carefully selected the twenty-seven clients who had had their second mortgages foreclosed upon. It was important to establish in their depositions that they were not furnished a closing statement as required by the Secondary Security Deed Act.

The depositions that concerned me were those of Gene and Betty Cochran. It would take an act of Congress to stop Betty from talking too much. Donnie Lee, Dixie, Kelli, and I worked for many hours to tone her down.

We worked with Randy Perkins and Rudy Tolbert for nine hours preparing them for their depositions. Both had been sued before so they were familiar with the process. It was really a pleasure to work with the two of them.

Surprisingly, the discovery process moved very rapidly. We began to wonder if the defense team had a trick up their sleeves.

The case was passed at the first two docket calls. This was not unusual. Both sides agreed to pass the case. At the third docket call I intended to announce ready. We were the number three case on the docket.

The courtroom was full of attorneys on docket day, the first Monday in October. Judge Braxton entered the courtroom in his usual manner—in a black robe—promptly at nine a.m. He had hardly sat down when he began to call the docket. He wasted no time and was known for impatience with attorney's who were unprepared. His job was to set all of the cases for all the Superior Courts. Docket call in his courtroom was a traumatic event.

I rapidly rose to my feet when Judge Lamar Braxton called case number 85-1369CV—Perkins, Tolbert, Cochran et al., Plaintiffs vs. First Fidelity Bank and Trust, Southern Finance of Georgia, Inc. et al., Defendants. "Ready for the plaintiffs, your honor," I said confidently.

Brad King arose. "Ready for the defendants." I was shocked. The defense actually announced ready in a case for a change.

"Your honor," I spoke, "this is a class action suit that will require a special setting."

Judge Braxton quickly retorted, "Mr. McDonald, if you and Mr. King can agree on anything, then I'll gladly grant you a special setting. As a matter of fact, I'm going to order one if you agree to it or not. How long will this trial take?"

I looked at Brad King. He looked at me and grinned. "Well, Mr. King, how long do you anticipate this trial will take?" Judge Braxton asked impatiently.

"Two to four weeks your honor," King answered.

"Very well. I'll specially set the case for next Monday morning at nine a.m. You gentlemen will be ready."

I was stunned and so was Brad King. The judge had just called our bluffs. It was time for a full court press. We were the plaintiffs. We would go first. Sudden panic set in my stomach. We would enter combat with the king, First Fidelity Bank and Trust Company, beginning on Monday morning at nine.

Nine

I got off the elevator on the second floor of the courthouse. Sandy Robinson, the chief deputy clerk, sat behind her familiar desk. "Sandy, do you have a jury list for Judge Randall's civil cases for next week?"

"Yeah, sweetheart," she said, using the pet name she used for every lawyer she liked. Kelli was smart. She always took care of the courthouse crowd every year at Christmas time. Sandy liked Wild Turkey. Kelli provided a half-gallon every year. We had no trouble from Sandy.

"Here's the list. I've crossed through the ones that have called in wanting off jury duty. You know the ones—the cripples, the dead, the deaf." She laughed. "Friends of mine." Sandy was a blue hair herself, in her sixties. She knew everybody in the county.

I hit the office running. Seven days until D-Day and counting. I met Dixie at the front door and shoved the jury list in her face. "Here it is, chief. No breaks for a long while. Research this list like you've never researched one before. Give it to Carl, our private investigator down the street."

Donnie Lee and I spent the rest of the day together. Subpoenas had to be issued. Depositions had to be reviewed. Our clients had to be rehearsed. Opening and closing arguments had to be prepared.

Terri Beth was a jewel. She needed no instructions. She had been through the D-Day countdown before. She understood the short tempers, the long hours, and the total focus.

It was 5:30 p.m. Terri Beth and Neva set up bar in Kelli's office. They were pros. They knew what was coming. For the next week or so there would be no sleep, no rest; it would be an all-out assault.

Everybody was keyed up–Kelli, Donnie Lee, Dixie, Neva, Terri Beth, and me. A sense of relief became prevalent. It was the calm before the storm. The next week we were going to be in a pressure cooker.

Donnie Lee and Dixie left first. Terri Beth and I knew why. Kelli was drinking faster than usual. She began to get loose with the tongue. "When we win this big suit, then my partner Jake and I are going down to the Caribbean on a cruise together. I'll show him what an older woman can do for a younger man." I blushed.

Neva and Terri Beth picked up on it real quick. Neva was used to Kelli when she had had too much to drink. "Mrs. Ferguson, it's time to go," she said. She knew how to take charge. Neva convinced her to go.

We heard Kelli's car cruise down the driveway. "Jake," Terri Beth said, "you don't need to tell me what's coming next week. I've been through this before in Goldsboro. I just hope Kathy is prepared for it. Neva needs to keep Kelli away from the booze next week . . .. Jake, can we have a heart to heart talk right now?"

"Okay," I said. "It's your nickel."

"Jake, Kelli has more of an interest in you than just as a law partner. I think she has a very strong romantic interest in you."

I blushed. "What makes you think that?"

"I can see it all over her when she's around you.

"Jake, I shouldn't say this. I was deeply in love when I married John. I wanted to have babies and live on a North Carolina farm forever. I had found Camelot. Then there was a big explosion in the sky, and his plane evaporated. It was all over. I knew then I needed to have a backup plan in my life. I was on my last leg when I met you. I was so depressed when we met. I was ready to end it all."

"You don't mean it," I said.

"Yes. I was ready to commit suicide."

"But you're so beautiful and happy," I said.

"That's because you gave me hope."

The back door slammed. It was Neva coming back in. "Damn Kelli," she said. "She's so difficult when she gets drunk. She didn't want to leave. I had to force her to go home."

"W hat did you do?" I asked.

"Do you need for one of us to drive you home, Neva?" I asked.

"No, I'll be all right."

"I need Terri Beth to type a letter for me and we'll be leaving."

"I'll see you guys in the morning." She left.

We heard her car go around the building. I looked at Terri Beth.

The phone rang. It was Kathy. "Where are you?" she asked.

"I'm running late. Last minute trial preparations. I'll be home shortly."

"Terri Beth, we have to go."

Ten

Monday, nine a.m. "All rise," Deputy Sheriff Chester's voice boomed. Judge Randall moved quickly to the bench. A jurist of quick mind, she was very impatient with those who wasted her time, or lawyers who were unprepared. "Case number 85-1359CV, Perkins, Tolbert, Cochran et al., plaintiffs vs. First Fidelity Bank and Trust, Southern Finance of Georgia, Inc. et al, defendants." She called the case almost from memory.

"Ready for the plaintiffs." I quickly rose to my feet. My throat was dry and my adrenaline was pumping.

"Ready for the defendants, First Fidelity Bank and Trust," announced Brad King.

"Ready for Southern Finance of Georgia," boomed T. Miles Stanfield, the silk stocking attorney from Atlanta who specialized in defending financial institutions that were the frequent targets of plaintiffs.

"Gentlemen, do I understand that this case will take a minimum of three weeks to try, and possibly as long as six weeks?"

"Yes, your honor," said Donnie Lee.

"Subject to what the plaintiffs have to offer, that would be our assessment," said Brad King.

"Well, the court would like to be informed of any serious settlement negotiations. You gentlemen are aware that we have numerous cases on our docket this term of court and there are many lawyers anxious to get their cases tried."

"Yes, ma'am, your honor," I said.

"Yes, your honor," Brad King said. "At this time we see no possibility of a settlement."

"I understand the Ferguson firm always wants more money than you are willing to pay, Mr. King." Judge Randall laughed.

"Something like that, Judge."

"Mr. Bailiff, bring in the jury panel."

Civil cases in Georgia are tried before a jury of twelve. Each side gets six peremptory strikes out of a panel of twenty-four. All jurors are drawn at random from the voter registration list. The jury list that Sandy had given me from the clerk's office was unremarkable-mostly blue-collar workers with a smattering of retired military, and a few professionals. It was not a jury panel that would hurt us. We would use our strikes on the professionals and the Chamber of Commerce types that were tied into, friends of, or "owned" by First Fidelity.

The first twenty-four jurors paraded into the courtroom one at a time and took their seats in the first three rows of the courtroom. I made eye contact with each as they sat down. I had tried about twenty cases before juries in my first eighteen months of law practice and felt confident in selecting juries. This was the first jury panel that we had researched so thoroughly; the first time we had had a jury panel checked out by a private investigator.

I didn't know whether it was the stress of trial preparation, my lack of sleep, or my normal trial anxiety, but something was wrong. This jury panel was not right. Another sense told me that this jury would screw us to the wall. I don't know why I felt this way. This was a jury panel composed of three-quarters blue-collar workers—perfect against a bank.

And then I saw him sitting in the back of the courtroom. What interest did Rube Wiseman have in this case?

Jury selection moved quickly. It was obvious that both sides had done a thorough job researching the jury. We decided that I would do the voir dire and opening statement. Rapport with a jury came easily for me. Most of the questions in the voir dire examination had already been answered long before we arrived in the courtroom. I never understood voir dire anyway. Jurors are never going to answer embarrassing questions truthfully. That's why, in a big case, you hire an investigator like Carl. It was obvious that both sides had decided which jurors they would strike in advance.

Voir dire and jury selection took an hour and fifteen minutes. We must have set some sort of a record for a class action suit. I didn't want to tell Donnie Lee, Dixie or Kelli, but I didn't feel good about what was happening. Cases this big didn't move this quickly. Everything seemed too orchestrated and scripted. On paper we had the best jury we could hope for under the circumstances—seven blue collar types, a retired Army major, a construction foreman, a housewife whose husband worked for civil service, a high school librarian, an office copy machine salesman and a disabled carpenter drawing workers' compensation. The rest of the jury was composed of a young female day care worker, a receptionist at a textile mill, and a college professor who taught economics at the college. He worried me. The last two jurors were obviously captives of the defendants. One was a stockbroker in his twenties from Merrill Lynch and the other was a physical therapist in her thirties. Stock brokers and physical therapists normally are Republican types who think all plaintiffs are blood-sucking and greedy. Carl's research confirmed this. We hoped to persuade these two with the enormity of the defendant's egregious conduct. We prayed that neither would be selected as foreman.

My opening statement went well. It took an hour to outline our case. The defendants took forty-five minutes. Brad King presented the opening statement for all the defendants. He was well known in the community and did a good job, but I felt I had done a better job. For the first time I felt more positive about our case.

It was 12:30 p.m. and Judge Randall recessed for lunch. Donnie Lee, Dixie and Kelli were more optimistic about the jury than I was. Somehow I couldn't shake the feeling that the deck was stacked. It had gone too smoothly. And what was Rube Wiseman doing there?

The first week we hammered away with witness after witness, all plaintiffs, who testified that they had done business with the defendant First Fidelity Bank and Trust and had lost their homes in foreclosure. We decided to call Betty and Gene Cochran in the middle of our case, right after lunch. The jury

164

would be half-asleep and hopefully would miss half of what Betty had to say. If we didn't let her testify we would never hear the end of it.

When we put Betty on the stand, Dixie and I were sweating cold blood, but no problems occurred. Donnie Lee was a real pro. He quickly moved through Betty's direct testimony without a hitch. I feared what Brad King was about to do to her on cross-examination, but he took only a half hour. King had missed a grand opportunity to put our weakest witness through the meat grinder. I was relieved when he was finished. Brad King had scored a few minor points, but I was proud of Betty. She had performed much better than expected.

It was Friday afternoon and the jury was ready for the weekend. Promptly at five o'clock Judge Randall declared a recess. After giving the usual admonition not to discuss the case, she let the jury go. Donnie Lee, Kelli, Dixie, and I retired to Kelli's office. Everyone was excited over the week's events. Kelli could not believe that Betty had finally testified and had emerged from cross-examination relatively unscathed. I was silent. "What's the matter, Jake?" asked Kelli. "You look down."

"I don't know, Kelli. I just don't feel good. Something is wrong. This trial is not going well. The defense has something up their sleeves."

Terri Beth stuck her head in. "How'd it go, boss?" She was still at work.

"It went real well," said Kelli.

"Too good," I said.

"How did Betty do?"

"Super," said Donnie Lee.

"Yeah, I thought she and Brad King were going to have a love-in. Something's up," I said.

"Who do you know in Hell, boss?" asked Terri Beth.

"What?"

Terri Beth laughed. "Who do you know in Hell? You got a postcard today from Hell."

I looked at Donnie Lee and we instantly blurted out, "Cayman Islands." The town of Hell is located there.

"Let's see it, Terri Beth."

It was our secret pen pal again. Same handwriting. Same cryptic message. "Your case is here, not in the courtroom."

Kelli laughed. "Maybe we can send First Fidelity Guaranty and Trust and their lawyers there after we stomp them in court."

"Kelli, I think we need to turn this over to Don Pollard. Somebody is trying to screw with our case," I said.

"I agree," said Donnie Lee. "But it looks like it's coming from a friend and not a foe."

"It looks like I'm going to be camping out down here this weekend. Don Pollard works most weekends, so I'll go see him," I said.

"Kelli, you look pale," Dixie said. "Are you all right?"

"Yeah, but I'm really tired. I think I'll go on home. We'll stay in touch this weekend. I hope next week goes as well as this one did." Kelli rose to leave. Her hands were shaking.

"You want me to drive you home, Mrs. Ferguson?" asked Terri Beth.

"No, I'll be all right. Thanks though." Kelli left the room.

"She doesn't look too good," said Donnie Lee. "Did she have too much to drink?"

"I don't think so," I said. "Kelli knows how to hold her liquor. She only had two drinks. Maybe the trial has worn her out."

Eleven

Saturday morning. I called Don Pollard at his office. He was just leaving to take his kids on a camping trip. We agreed that Dixie would meet with him early Monday morning. He couldn't figure it out either. "Maybe the devil is on your side," he retorted.

"Hell, the devil is on the other side," I laughed.

Kathy had gone to Florida to visit her parents. She knew how uptight I could be during a jury trial. She had learned early on to stay out of my way during trial week.

It was noon, and I had done all I could do to prepare Monday's witnesses. They were as prepared as they could possibly be. I was hungry. Tabby's was a favorite luncheon spot and watering hole for the courthouse crowd. It was located only two blocks away. I decided to go there for lunch.

Robbie, everyone's favorite waitress, met me at the door. Petite, with curly blonde hair, her bubbly personality made up for an obvious lack of education. Everybody loved her. She probably made more money in tips than our legal secretaries did in salaries.

"How's my favorite lawyer doing?"

" Robbie, you say that to all the lawyers."

"Ain't so," she said.

"Is so," I said.

She laughed. "I like lawyers. If you were single I'd sink my hooks into you."

I blushed. "By yourself?"

"Yeah."

She ushered me to a table in the back corner. "This okay, counselor?"

"This is fine, Robbie. This is where I sit every time I come here."

"I know," she giggled. "Drink?"

"I'd love a glass of Chablis."

"Be back in a minute."

Two women in their late twenties seated next to me were engaged in a lively conversation. I thought I recognized one of them. When I heard one of them say "First Fidelity," my ears perked up. It was obvious that they were both into computers.

Robbie returned with my glass of wine. "Sorry it took so long, Jake. We're short staffed today." Turning to the next table she said, "You ladies doing okay?"

"One more round, I think," said the lady I thought I recognized. (Her eyes met mine.) "Hey! Don't I know you from somewhere? Yeah. You're the new lawyer at the Ferguson firm," she said. "I'm Sandy Merck in the jury pool manager's office."

"That's right. I knew I had seen you around the courthouse."

"This is my roommate, Sissy Phillips. She's a secretary at First Fidelity and Trust."

"Uh oh," I said.

Sissy laughed. "I know who you are. No hard feelings. I have nothing to do with litigation. Just don't win too big a verdict. I need to keep my job. Actually, I'm trying to get promoted to the computer programming department."

"So what does a computer programmer do?" I asked.

"We design systems so our bank branches can talk with one another by computers. Not very exciting, but necessary."

Sissy intrigued me even though she worked for the enemy. "Maybe my computer can talk to yours someday," I smiled.

"We can program any computer to talk to another computer if they speak the same language."

"I'm afraid I'm computer illiterate," I said. "I leave that to my secretary Terri Beth."

"Terri Beth Flynt?" asked Sissy.

"Yes," I said.

"Is she your secretary?"

"Yeah."

"I know her. We're both members of the PSI— Professional Secretaries International. She's a doll."

"I know. Don't try to hire her away. I'll kill you."

We laughed.

*****

Monday morning, second week of trial.

Donnie Lee and I held down the fort at the plaintiff's table. Dixie was meeting with Don Pollard. Neva told us that Kelli had called and would be in late. Apparently she had been

170

sick all weekend. I was worried. I felt she was hiding something from us.

This week was scheduled to be Dullsville. We would put on all of our expert witnesses. They were economists who would testify as to the future value of the plaintiffs' losses. We had four attorneys, experts in real estate law, who would testify as to how the bank and the loan sharks had subverted the law and screwed up foreclosing our clients' homes.

Expert witnesses will testify the way you want them to, as long as they are paid well. It always amazes me that you could hire the two foremost authorities in the country and they would swear under oath that the other side was absolutely wrong.

Our experts were well- prepared. What was to follow was a script to be acted out in front of the jury. We expected no surprises.

After a break, Dixie joined us. Don Pollard had agreed to try to get a lead on our secret informant. He didn't want to contact the FBI at this point because he felt they were not leveling with him. Kelli arrived shortly before we resumed. She was wearing heavy makeup and looked very pale. "Are you all right, Kelli?" I asked.

"A little weak, Jake. How's the case going?"

"It's movie time, Kelli. You know the script. I figure the experts can handle it through the rest of the week."

Our next seven witnesses came through without a hitch. They were all paid experts who had testified in court many times before. I often wondered if being an expert witness, and *answering* the questions, might not be a better life style than being a lawyer *asking* the questions.

It was Wednesday afternoon and we had gone through every question that could possibly be asked of an expert witness. The jury had heard every hypothetical question that the defense and we could pose. The jurors had received a Ph.D. in foreclosure law in the last three days. We sensed that they were bored to death. The time was near.

Judge Randall recessed early in the afternoon. I didn't know whether she was bored by all the canned expert testimony or whether she was trying to help us out. Kelli didn't join us for the usual post-game review. She went straight home from the courtroom. I began to worry more about her.

I cornered Neva as she was going out the back door. "Neva, what's going on with Kelli?" I asked.

"Jake, if I knew I'd tell you. I'm not keeping anything from you, but I don't think Kelli is leveling with me. I think she's sick. I mean, really sick, and isn't telling us everything. Hey, you know I'd tell you the truth." Tears were forming in her eyes. She kissed me on the cheek and quickly darted out the back door.

Donnie Lee, Dixie, and I stayed another two hours. It was almost seven o'clock. I called Kathy and told her I would be home late and not to worry. She was used to this by now.

"Folks," I said. "I believe, like my old contracts professor in law school used to say, 'It's time to put the chairs back in the wagon, boys, cause church is over.' I believe we need to wind our case up, and quickly. Let's close on a strong note and get on with it. This jury is bored, and we don't want to lose any points that we've already scored with them."

Dixie chimed in, "I agree. Let's put on Rudy Tolbert and his wife and let the jury cry a while. Let's bring in all their children and seat them on the front row."

"Dixie, do I detect that you may be turning into a cold blooded bitch that wants to practice law for money?" I teased.

"You're damn right," she shouted. She was feeling her oats.

We all agreed. We had presented our case about as well as we could. It was time to let the defense fire its shots.

"Dixie, get Rudy and his wife on the phone and tell them to be here at seven tomorrow morning, all dressed up with their kids. I want to rehearse their testimony one more time before we put them on."

"Right, Jake." Dixie left the room. I could hear her on the phone.

"Donnie Lee, do you think we've made out our case?" I asked.

"Jake, I don't know what else we can do. Judge Randall is on our side, and I don't think she will grant their motion for a directed verdict when they make it, but I don't want to piss her off by dragging this thing out."

"Okay, then, I agree, let's wrap it up with Rudy and Angela. If we can't get the jury to cry with them, then we need to start selling used cars."

"I agree. Let's do it."

Ford Ashton gave us the leadoff story on the six o'clock news. It was as favorable as we could have asked for-only better if we had written it ourselves.

Kathy had been a saint throughout the whole ordeal. I regretted that she had to suffer through the shenanigans that were created by the bank's surrogates. Win, lose or draw, this too would pass. I dreamed of lying on the beach in Saint Thomas with millions in my bank account.

My dreams were shattered. The phone rang. It was Betty. She wanted a blow-by-blow assessment of how I thought the case had gone so far. I lied to her. I told her Kathy was sick and I had to take her to the emergency room. Anything to get Betty off the phone.

Kathy put her arms around me. "May I guess who that was?"

"Betty," we said in unison.

"It could be worse," I said. "I could be an OB-GYN on call."

"Right on, big boy. Then I would be living in the Moors, driving a Mercedes 380, and a member of the country club."

"You're right," I said, "with a $150,000 debt to a medical college and no time to spend the millions."

"You don't have time to spend your much-less-than millions now," she laughed. "But I'll keep you anyway. Besides that, if you win this case you'll own a bank and we'll have plenty of money, right?"

"You're right, sweetheart." I pulled her close to me and looked deep into her eyes. I knew why I had married Kathy. I

174

don't know why she put up with this. "Maybe I should have been a bond lawyer. Boring, but they keep regular hours and they're all rich. They don't get calls at night from clients."

*****

Rudy Tolbert was the kind of client that every plaintiff lawyer dreamed of-down to earth, had suffered a horrendous loss, and was believable. We decided that I would take Rudy and Angela on direct examination. It was our last shot at giving our case a humanistic closing, and quite a contrast from the dull expert witnesses who had proceeded them.

I spent most of the morning developing Rudy's background for the jury. He was dressed in a pair of khaki trousers, brown lace-up shoes and a blue button-down oxford shirt. This was quite a contrast from the vast array of expert witnesses who had testified before. We hoped he and Angela would be our sympathy trump cards.

Rudy came across as an ordinary guy who was raised by cotton mill workers who had worked hard all their lives, and made just enough to get by. They were owned and employed by the textile mill barons who had owned the town for centuries. Rudy inherited his creativity from his mother, learning as a boy how to build things from her. He had flair for design and color combinations, and would have been a wonderful architect. On the other hand, a formal education might have stifled his creativity.

The historical preservation society ladies loved Rudy because he could resurrect the most hopeless lost causes when it came to restoring old houses. We introduced color slides of some of Rudy's projects in order to give the jury an idea of who Rudy Tolbert was.

Slowly we unfolded the case against First Fidelity and Southern Finance of Georgia. The jury was sympathetic. Judge Randall allowed us to present evidence that Rudy and Angela's house had burned down over the objection of Brad King. I introduced this testimony in order to show that the bank received all the insurance proceeds and didn't rebuild their home.

What happened next was unbelievable. T. Miles Stanfield, the silk stocking lawyer, rose to conduct the cross-examination of Rudy. He ripped into him like a bull in a china shop. "Isn't it true that you remodeled your lawyer's home?" he asked.

"Yes, sir," said Rudy. "That's the reason I hired him as my lawyer. He was willing to help me."

"And you would say anything, including telling a lie, to help your case."

"Objection, your honor," I said.

"Sustained," Judge Randall responded immediately.

This mean spirited cross-examination went on for the rest of the afternoon. Maybe I was missing something, but they taught us in law school not to attack a witness who was sympathetic to the jury, especially one who hadn't hurt your case. Rudy Tolbert represented the greatest threat to the

176

defendant's case. I had objected so many times and had been sustained so many times that I threw up my hands, rolled my eyes back into my head and sat down. The jury got the message.

Finally Judge Randall had had enough. She sent the jury out of the courtroom on a break. "I want counsel to remain in the courtroom for a few minutes." After the jury left Judge Randall asked the bailiff to lock the courtroom door.

"Gentlemen, I've been patient with both sides in this case. I suggest that we move it along. Mr. Stanfield, I'm not going to tell you how to conduct your case. You are an experienced lawyer. But you are pushing your cross-examination of this witness to the limit. Mr. McDonald has made twenty-seven objections. Twenty-five of those objections I have sustained. The jury is about fed up. Let's take a fifteen minute recess."

"Yes, your honor," he answered.

T. Miles Stanfield finished his cross-examination of Rudy at 4:45 p.m. "How long will your re-direct last, Mr. McDonald?" asked Judge Randall.

"Quite a while, your honor."

"Very well then, we will take a recess until nine o'clock in the morning." Judge Randall reminded the jury not to discuss the case with anyone or read any newspaper accounts or listen to any television accounts of the case.

Rudy was relieved to be off the stand. "I'm sorry I messed up, Jake," Rudy said.

"Hey, Rudy, you didn't mess up. You did fine. Stanfield was the one who messed up."

"What about tomorrow?" he asked.

"We'll put Angela on in the morning."

"Do we have to, Jake? She's scared to death."

"Hey, Rudy, if she does as well as you did, then we're going to give you both an Oscar," I said.

"Jake, do I have to testify?" asked Angela. Her voice quivered.

"Angela, you'll do fine. We will be real easy on you. If they get mean with you like they did Rudy, then the jury will eat them alive. Don't worry. You will do fine."

We all left the courthouse. We were all exhausted. I was worried about Kelli. Neva met me at the door. "How's Kelli?" I asked.

"Jake, I didn't want to upset you during the trial, but Kelli was admitted to the hospital today," she said.

"Hospital!" I exclaimed.

"She's okay. She's exhausted and she's dehydrated. She hasn't eaten in three days. They have her on an I.V. She's going to be okay," Neva said.

I stopped by the hospital on the way home. Kelli was in a private room and was hooked up to an I.V. and a heart monitor. The nurse was just leaving. "Jake McDonald, Kelli Ferguson's law partner. How is she?" I asked.

"She's asleep under sedation," the nurse said. "She was in bad shape when they brought her in. She was pretty dehydrated. We think she will recover okay with a few days rest and some nourishment."

"Could you tell her I came by and that we are pulling for her?" I asked.

"Sure," the nurse said. "My name is Janelle. I've been assigned to Mrs. Ferguson full time, so call me anytime you need me."

"Thanks," I said.

*****

"All rise," the bailiff's voice boomed out. The jury was seated in the jury box. Judge Randall assumed her place on the bench. "Mr. McDonald, you may proceed," she said.

"Your honor, we have concluded our direct examination of Mr. Tolbert and wish to call Angela Tolbert at this time."

Angela Tolbert was dressed in a plain, neatly pressed blue jumper. She came across to the jury as a housewife and a mother of four. She was obviously nervous. After a few preliminary questions she relaxed. She had a winsome personality and I prayed that Stanfield would attack her the way he did Rudy.

Angela was on direct examination for two and a half hours. "Ladies and gentlemen," Judge Randall said, "we haven't taken a break all morning and I believe it would be a good time to break for lunch. Please be back at one o'clock."

Donnie Lee and I agreed that we would rest our case after Angela's cross-examination. The defense would make its usual motion for a directed verdict, which we expected to be denied. It would force the defense to start its case right after lunch when the jury would be sleepy.

There was no way to digest food during the middle of a jury trial. It's no small wonder that trial lawyers suffer from digestive disorders. Donnie Lee was confident that the case was going well. I would feel better once Angela got off the stand.

"Loosen up, Jake. It's almost over," said Donnie Lee.

" I don't feel good, Donnie Lee," I said.

"Relax. After Angela's cross you can go home to your sweet bride. I have to earn my keep. I'm going to cross-examine the hell out of all those boring bank expert witnesses."

Stanfield's cross-examination of Angela was short and to the point. He understood how juries fell asleep after lunch, and expected us to call more of the twenty other witnesses on our witness list.

"Call your next witness, Mr. McDonald," Judge Randall said.

"The plaintiffs rest, your honor."

The defense attorneys were stunned.

"Mr. King, call your first witness," said Judge Randall.

"Your honor, may we approach the bench?" Brad King was obviously shaken. "Judge, we didn't anticipate the plaintiffs wrapping up their case so quickly. As a consequence, our witnesses are not here."

"Mr. King, I can't waste these jurors' time, nor the court's. If you are not ready to proceed, then what do you expect me to do? I can always direct a verdict for the plaintiff. I suppose you have a motion to make?"

"Yes, we do, your honor."

"How long will your motion take? I suppose it's the usual motion for a directed verdict?"

"Yes, your honor."

"Well, go ahead and make it for the record. However, I'm not inclined to grant it at this time. I think the plaintiffs have presented enough evidence to get their case to the jury."

The defense team spent forty-five minutes arguing the motion they knew they would lose while the jurors cooled their heels in the jury room. Donnie Lee handled the arguments for our side. As expected, Judge Randall denied Brad King's motion.

The defense begged a thirty-minute recess. Their law clerks and secretaries were running around the courthouse looking for any witness to testify. The one witness that we wanted on the stand was seated at their table throughout the trial—Anthony Jacobs, the president of Fidelity Bank and Trust. They no doubt were saving him for last.

Brad King called as his first witness the assistant vice-president in charge of Fidelity's foreclosure department. She was a kindly lady who had been with the bank for seventeen years. She had just been promoted to assistant vice president partly because banks were under tremendous pressure from the federal government to end their discrimination against minorities and women.

Brad King's direct examination was long and detailed. He was obviously stalling. The jury was bored to death.

The witness testified as to the procedures of the bank relative to real estate documents and foreclosure procedures. She offered nothing as to the specific cases that we had presented to the jury.

Donnie Lee was the consummate expert of human nature and cross-examination. He understood people and their likes and dislikes. He knew how to cut to the chase and cut through the bull. He was a master tactician.

It was 3:30 in the afternoon. Brad King had asked every question he could possibly ask of their poor witness. Two jurors had fallen asleep. "She's your witness, Mr. Booker," Brad King said.

Donnie Lee lulled them off guard. His cross-examination was polite and to the point. It lasted five minutes. "Call your next witness, Mr. King," said Judge Randall. Brad King was beside himself.

"Your honor, we had not anticipated presenting our case in chief this early."

Judge Randall was obviously agitated. "Mr. King, this court will not tolerate lawyers who are not prepared. These jurors have lives too. Their time is as valuable as yours and your clients'. We are going to recess until nine a.m. tomorrow morning. Be prepared to proceed, or this court will take appropriate action." Donnie Lee winked at me. He had scored more points from the bench than on cross-examination of the witness and he knew it. He was a master of strategy. I was glad he was on our side.

*****

Nine o'clock a.m. The jury marched through the doors of the jury room and took their places in the jury box. Donnie Lee, Dixie, and I were prepared for a long day ahead. Donnie Lee's job would be to cross-examine the long list of expected defense witnesses.

I glanced over towards the defense table. Brad King refused to make eye contact with me. Something was up. When one fails to make eye contact, it is a true sign of deception. The vibrations were bad. We were in a trial against the masters of deception.

Judge Randall came through the door behind her bench. "All rise," the bailiff's voice boomed out.

"Please be seated, ladies and gentlemen. Are all the jurors present, Mr. Bailiff?" the judge asked.

"Yes, your honor."

"Then let's proceed. Mr. King, call your next witness."

"If it please the court, your honor, the defense calls Anthony C. Jacobs."

I looked at Donnie Lee and then at Dixie. Why would the defense put Anthony Jacobs on the stand so early? Surely they would put all their expert witnesses on the stand first. We had been caught off guard. I did not like the feeling of uncertainty that arrived in my stomach.

Anthony Jacobs exuded charisma. He was a slightly balding man in his early fifties, six feet tall and dressed for success. He wore a custom tailored navy blue silk suit, and a red, white and blue tie. His Johnston and Murphy wing tipped shoes were highly shined. With the body language befitting that of a man of total confidence and in control, he truly looked the part of a CEO.

What Brad King did for the next two hours was unbelievable. His direct examination was a dissertation of Anthony Jacobs' history as president of First Fidelity Bank and Trust and the success of the bank in terms of its financial achievements over the last ten years. If I hadn't known any better I would have believed that we had stumbled into an annual stockholders' meeting.

King finally moved into areas relevant to the lawsuit. "Were you aware of any violation of any state or federal laws that took place in any of the real estate closings alleged in the plaintiff's complaint?" he asked.

"Absolutely not," Jacobs answered confidently.

"Are you aware of any officer, bank employee or closing agent who violated state or federal laws with regard to any real estate transactions, any loan transactions, or any other business dealings with your bank?"

"Absolutely not," Anthony Jacobs responded, again in absolute confidence.

"Your witness, Mr. Booker."

It was unbelievable. Everything we had planned, worked for, and orchestrated to this point was now before us. Anthony

Jacobs was about to be cross-examined under oath by Donnie Lee Booker, one of the most skilled trial attorneys in the state of Georgia.

Donnie Lee quickly rose to his feet. He was ready to draw blood. "Mr. Jacobs, how long have you been the president of First Fidelity Bank and Trust?"

"Fifteen years, Mr. Booker."

"And in those fifteen years how many real estate closings have you personally attended?"

"A lot, Mr. Booker."

"How many is a lot?"

"Well, I can't say exactly."

"Isn't it true that you have never attended a real estate closing, Mr. Jacobs?"

"No. That's not true."

"Isn't it true that your secretary, Sissy Phillips, has prepared all the closing documentation and has conducted all of your closings?"

"She's done a lot. I don't recall how many."

"Isn't it true, Mr. Jacobs, that you threatened to fire Miss Phillips because she gave a favorable deposition for my clients?"

"Absolutely not."

Brad King's face was turning red.

"Mr. Jacobs, isn't it true that you have been having an ongoing forced sexual relationship with Miss Phillips?"

Brad King shot up from his chair. "Objection, your honor. I move for a mistrial."

Judge Randall quickly banged her gavel. "Mr. Sheriff, please take the jury to the jury room." The jury retired quickly.

Judge Randall was agitated. "Gentlemen, what is going on here? Mr. Booker, please explain to this court how Mr. Jacobs' relationship, if any, with his secretary is relevant to the issues in this case."

"Your honor, I'm on cross-examination and I'm entitled to conduct a thorough cross-examination of this defendant. His sexual conduct with one of the witnesses in this case is important to show that Mr. Jacobs has a motive to lie."

Brad King rose quickly to his feet. "Your honor, it's obvious that counsel for the plaintiff is attempting to influence the jury, and his attack on my client is nothing more than a subterfuge and a smoke screen. I must insist on my motion for a mistrial."

Judge Randall was obviously agitated. "Gentlemen, I'm getting very impatient with both of you. I want you to stick to the issues in this case. Mr. Booker, get to your point. If you can't link Mr. Jacobs' alleged sexual misconduct with his secretary to the issues of this case then I might be inclined to grant Mr. King's motion for a mistrial. For the time being, I am denying his motion. Mr. Sheriff, bring the jury back in."

"Your honor, may we have a five minute recess before the jury comes back?"

"Yes. I think that is certainly in order."

I dragged Donnie Lee out into the hallway. "I don't know what is going on here, but I think you are screwing up. The defense has something up their sleeve that we don't know about. Judge Randall is agitated with your cross of Jacobs and his sexual antics with his secretary. It may be titillating, but it's not proving our case."

"Damn it, Jake, can't you see it? They're presenting Jacobs as a smooth, slick banker sonofabitch. He's a slime bag. That's what I'm trying to show to the jury. What he really is."

"Okay. You're the expert. Do what you feel is right. Just don't get us a mistrial. I don't want to retry this one." We returned to the courtroom.

The jury came back in. "Good afternoon, ladies and gentlemen of the jury. You are reminded that you should not consider anything the court says as leaning towards one side or the other. The court is totally impartial to both sides, and what I say should not be interpreted to favor one side or the other. Mr. Booker, please proceed with your cross-examination."

"Mr. Jacobs, you will admit that you do not personally attend all the real estate closings that are conducted in your bank."

"Of course, Mr. Booker. The bank officers in our real estate department attend most of the closings. As you well know, it is not customary for a bank president to attend real estate closings. Even though I think I hold an important position in my bank, I can't do everything."

The jury laughed. Anthony Jacobs was a man of immense influence in Conecuh. He also knew how to exude charm and gain rapport with the jury.

"So, you don't know whether or not your bank officer who attended the closings relative to this law suit provided a closing statement to our clients?"

"No sir, I would not know that. You would have to ask them."

Donnie Lee continued his cross-examination for another forty-five minutes. Judge Randall sensed that the jury had had enough for the day. It was 4:40 p.m. "Ladies and gentlemen of the jury, it's shortly before five o'clock. I'm going to let you go home early so you can hopefully beat the traffic. Please be advised that you are not to discuss this case with anyone and you are to return promptly at nine tomorrow morning."

Twelve

Donnie Lee, Dixie, and I retired to Kelli's office. Neva joined us. Kelli wasn't doing well. Neva was really worried. My head was spinning. Between worrying about Kelli and what was going on in the courtroom, I couldn't help thinking about Don Pollard's investigation. We were not in the middle of a civil case. We were fighting a band of murderers and arsonists. I wondered why I had taken this case.

Terri Beth joined us. "How's it going, guys?"

"I don't know, Sunshine. It's too slick for me. Old Donnie Lee is trying to get us a mistrial, but so far so good."

Donnie Lee laughed. "Jake, you are too nervous. I've tried a bunch of these type cases. The defense is just posturing. Don't worry about it. I'm not going to give them a mistrial. That would be the last gift I would give them."

Donnie Lee and Dixie left together. Terri Beth and I winked. "Terri Beth, how is Kelli doing?"

"Not good, boss. You need to go see her."

"Will you go with me?"

"You know I will."

I called Kathy and told her the events of the day. She was shaken over Kelli's condition. Terri Beth got on the phone and comforted her. Kathy understood Terri Beth's role in my life.

Catholic Hospital was located in the northwest area of Conecuh. It was the most modern of the three hospitals in Conecuh and was the preferred medical facility of the rich.

Kelli was in room 245. With an I.V. in her right arm, she was semi-alert and her skin was a pale yellow. It was obvious that she was sick— very sick. Terri Beth and I entered the room quietly. Kelli opened her eyes and smiled.

"How are you, good looking?" I teased her.

"I'm sure you're talking about Terri Beth," she said as she forced a smile.

"Well, now that you mention it, I'm surrounded by *two* good looking women. How are you, Kelli?"

"Fair, Jake, just fair. I'm hurting a whole lot, but I'm glad to see the both of you. It's so good to see you and Terri Beth."

Terri Beth gave Kelli a hug.

I related the day's events to Kelli and expressed my concerns to her. Though her body was very weak, her lawyer instincts were still sharp. "Jake, do you think Donnie Lee is doing a good job?"

"Kelli, his instincts scare me. He has been absolutely brilliant on cross-examination. What bothers me is that I believe he knows something that we don't. We know he and Dixie are sleeping together, but it obviously has not affected either of their performances in the courtroom."

"In the courtroom or in the bedroom?" Kelli shot back.

We both laughed. "God, I'm glad to see you laugh again," I retorted.

"We need to go forward," she said. "Please keep me informed. I hurt so much. I don't know how much longer I'll last."

"What?" I said. "Wait just a minute. You're not getting out of this place without an apology for that remark."

Kelli's eyes sparkled. The thought of Kelli dying had never crossed my mind before. It could not happen. Kelli Ferguson was bigger-than-life, she couldn't die.

The nurse rolled in the cart of bland hospital cuisine. I kissed Kelli on the cheek. "Take care, pretty lady," I said.

"Win the case," she said.

I left and headed for home. It had started to rain.

*****

Kathy was lying in bed watching television when I arrived. It was obvious that she was not feeling well. "How is Kelli?" she asked.

"Her spirits are good but her body is not."

"How's the case going?"

"About the same."

"What's that supposed to mean?"

"Hell if I know," I snapped back.

"Well, just be a jerk about it," she fired back.

"Hey, I'm sorry. I've got a lot on me right now." Tears began to roll down my cheeks. "Kathy, I love you. I'm sorry. For some strange reason I feel uneasy about the case. It's going too smoothly. Kelli is another story. Kathy, she's dying."

We both began to cry. "Kelli is one of my closest friends. She hired me as an attorney. You, Kelli, and Terri Beth are the closest friends I have."

Kathy began to smile in her teasing manner. "If something happened and I died, who would you marry? Kelli or Terri Beth?"

"You silly goose. What kind of question is that?"

"No, who would it be?" she asked.

"Terri Beth."

We both laughed in unison. "You better not," Kathy said.

"Kathy, I love you. You know that. Now, tomorrow, and forever." We fell asleep in each others' arms.

*****

Judge Randall seemed very relaxed as she assumed her position on the bench. The defense lawyers were as cocky as Donnie Lee. The jury was very attentive in anticipation of what was about to transpire.

"Mr. Booker, you may continue your cross-examination of Mr. Jacobs."

Donnie Lee stood and looked Judge Randall in the eye. Then he looked towards the jury and then back at Judge Randall. "No further questions, your honor."

"Very well, Mr. Booker. Mr. King, you may call your next witness."

Bradford King slowly rose, and in his deepest southern voice announced, "Your honor, the defense rests."

The silence was deafening. Was this it? Was this the case that was supposed to make us rich and allow us all to retire? Was this the case that we had worked on so hard for so long?

Something was going wrong and we were going downhill fast. What was going on?

Even Judge Randall was stunned. "Gentlemen, do you need a recess, or can we proceed with closing arguments?"

Bradford King arose immediately. "We are ready to proceed, your honor."

"We need a short recess, your honor," said Donnie Lee.

"Very well. We'll take a lunch break until 1:30 p.m. Court is adjourned."

Donnie Lee, Dixie, and I quickly retreated to the deli across from the courthouse. We took a table in one of the private rooms in the back. The waitress poured a round of iced tea and we ordered quickly. I didn't have much of an appetite. "Donnie Lee, what's happening here? They're up to something."

"I can't figure it out either, Jake. Surely that can't be their complete defense."

"What about closing, Donnie Lee? Do you think we need to stall for more time?"

"No. I've been prepared to give this closing argument for months. Let's get on with it. I don't know what they can say in closing that will surprise us."

"Okay, but this is the strangest case I've ever tried. What is your reading on the jury?"

"I don't know. Normally I have a good reading by now. But I don't know. The lady in the blue dress on the front row and the guy in the checkered sport coat are on our side. The others, I don't know."

At 1:15 p.m. we returned to the courtroom. Brad King and his entourage arrived five minutes later. Jack Bullard, the bailiff, said, "The judge would like to see y'all in her chambers."

Judge Randall was sitting behind her desk and was surrounded by open law books and the pile of written jury charges that both sides had provided to her. "Gentlemen and Dixie, I must commend you on the dispatch with which you have handled this case. However, I must say I am surprised. I had planned on at least two more weeks of trial. I'm willing to recess the jury and give you guys another day to prepare your closing arguments if you want it."

"That won't be necessary, Judge," Brad King interjected.

"What about you, Mr. Booker?"

"We are ready to proceed now, Judge," said Donnie Lee.

"Very well then, let's talk about the charges."

We spent the next hour wrangling over the various charges to the jury. Judge Randall went right down the middle. She was known as a firm but fair judge, and she was well-respected by the members of the bar.

At 2:30 p.m. Judge Randall entered the courtroom. "Mr. Bullard, bring in the jury."

After the jury was seated, she said, "Mr. Booker, you have the first opening argument."

"Your honor, the plaintiffs waive opening and reserve closing."

"Mr. King, that means you go first."

Brad King rose slowly and approached the jury. He was the master of persuasion. Insurance companies and banks paid well for his closing arguments. What his clients paid in his hefty, legal fees, they saved in defense verdicts many times over.

The closing argument he gave did not disappoint his corrupt client. He painted the picture of first Fidelity Bank and Trust as the premier provider of Conecuh. He painted the picture of the many wonderful projects First Fidelity was involved with in the community, the many people it had employed, all the money it provided to charity. He left no stone un-turned. I was surprised that Donnie Lee didn't object to this ridiculous tripe. However, I always hated lawyers who objected during my closing arguments. Donnie Lee would get his chance. If the jury knew the truth about Brad King's client they would throw up. I have always believed in the wisdom of juries.

Exactly one hour and thirty minutes later, at four o'clock, Brad King closed his brilliant argument on an emotional appeal. "Don't punish those who provide us with the most."

Judge Randall declared a ten-minute recess. This broke the tension. Donnie Lee was wound up as tight as a top. Good lawyers always are before their closing arguments. "Good luck, champ," I whispered to Donnie Lee as he arose to address the jury.

The body language of the jury was strange. They were operating off of a different page—not at all like that of a jury during closing arguments. I couldn't figure it out. Brad King had just made a brilliant argument. Surely someone on this jury was motivated one way or another. They either loved us or they hated us. I had never experienced this reaction from a jury before. Then it hit me. If First Fidelity Bank and Trust was controlled by the mob, killed people, and burned the houses of our clients, why would they stop at doing whatever it took to win this case? It was so obvious. This jury was bought. I felt sick.

Donnie Lee was the master of persuasion. He knew what to say, how to breathe, how close to stand to the jury, how to use the right glances, the exact inflection of his voice. A more brilliant closing argument could not have been delivered. The lady in the blue dress connected with Donnie Lee. Tears flowed down her cheeks as he talked about Rudy and his family and how they lost their home to the fire. The man in the checkered sport coat was ours from the beginning. Donnie Lee was well prepared. I don't believe we could get a better closer. If he had been a baseball player any major league baseball team would have been proud to have him on their team.

Donnie Lee's closing argument lasted exactly one hour—thirty minutes less than Brad King's. It was all over except for Judge Randall's charge to the jury. This was merely a script. We all knew what she would say to the jury and what our objections to her charge would be. In one hour the case would be in the hands of the jury.

Judge Randall gave the jury a thirty-minute recess. Both sides adjourned into her chambers. Everybody was suddenly relaxed. We knew the baby was about to be delivered to the jury.

"Pardon me, gentlemen, but I haven't eaten all day. While you lawyers were having your leisurely luncheon at the country club I was working on the charges to the jury." She munched on a package of peanut butter crackers. We all laughed. Our disagreements over the court's charge to the jury were pre-tried in Judge Randall's chamber. Any objections would be entered as a matter of record. After the jury went out to deliberate, the objections to her charges were mere formalities to be entered on the trial record.

Judge Randall's charge lasted forty-five minutes, the average time for a charge to the jury in a civil case. It was 4:45 p.m. The jury went out. We knew we would not get a verdict that day, but at least the trial was over. It would be up to the jury to punish First Fidelity Bank and Trust for the rape, pillage, and plunder of the citizens of Conecuh.

At 6:00 p.m. Judge Randall called the jury back in and asked them if they were making any progress. They acknowledged that they were. She dismissed them for the day and admonished them once again not to discuss the case with anyone, and to be back at nine o'clock in the morning.

It was the first time in months that I finally had the monkey off my back. I made a quick call to Kathy. I told her the events of the day and that I wanted to make a stop by the hospital to see Kelli before I came home.

Donnie Lee and Dixie left together, no doubt to celebrate the end of a successful trial. Terri Beth was pounding away at her typewriter.

"Don't you ever quit typing?" I asked.

"Not as long as you're my boss," she laughed. "Let me fix you a drink. You deserve one."

"Okay, Sunshine. I can't stay long. I need to see Kelli before the visiting hours are over."

"I've been around enough trial lawyers to know when things aren't right." Terri Beth poured us both a stiff drink. "I know the trial has gone according to the game plan, but I sense you're not happy with the way it's going."

"Terri Beth, I believe this jury has been bought . The case has been too pat. Brad King is too cocky, and this jury has been acting strange from day one."

"It has happened before, Jake."

"These guys are totally ruthless."

I left to go see Kelli.

Kelli looked pale in her lacy green nightgown. She smiled as I entered her room. "Hello, sweetheart," she said.

"Hello, Kelli. How are you feeling?"

"Just so-so, Jake. How did the case go today?"

"We got it to the jury. Donnie Lee was great in closing." I didn't tell her my real feelings about the jury. "Kelli, I have three favorite ladies in my life—you, Kathy and Terri Beth. I won't tell you in what order."

"Jake, I had better be at least number two, and if Kathy isn't number one, then I'm going to represent her for free in divorce court when I get out of here. I won't leave you with a dime." We both laughed.

"Jake, please hold my hand. I need for you to be close to me right now."

"Kelli, tell me the truth. I need to know. What do the doctors say?"

She began to cry. "Jake, I've got pancreatic cancer. I don't have much longer. Maybe six months at the most." The tears began to flow. Mine mixed with hers. I laid my cheek on her chest. God, I couldn't bear the thought of losing my hero.

"Jake, Kathy, Terri Beth and I have one common trait. We all have a strong sense of intuition. And I have a strong perception that our case is not going well. Please, tell me the truth."

The tears began to flow down my cheeks. My face lay on Kelli's chest.

"The case has gone according to the game plan. Donnie Lee has done an excellent job. It's just been too perfect. That's the problem. Kelli, I believe these crooks have somehow bought this jury."

*****

The jury assembled promptly at nine a.m. They seemed very rested and relaxed. After some preliminary instructions Judge Randall dispatched them to the jury room to deliberate. Normally I would hang around the courtroom until the jury had reached its verdict. This is the one time in a trial lawyer's life that he or she surrenders total control. It was in the hands of the jury. I left Donnie Lee and Dixie at the courthouse and returned to the office.

Terri Beth had scheduled a full morning of appointments. It was a pleasure to get away from the courtroom for a change. Somehow, listening to women with domestic problems was a welcome change.

Time went by. The routine office tasks dragged on. It was 4:45 p.m. Still no word from our jury. I expected it would take a while. A quick verdict was a sure sign that it was a defendant's verdict. I truly felt that we had the winning side of the case. But I still had that gnawing sensation in my stomach that this jury had been bought by First Fidelity and their mob bosses.

I called Judge Randall's office. "Beth, this is Jake. Any word?"

"No, Jake, the judge is about ready to let them go for the day." Beth was a sweet soul, a dedicated, loyal employee. She never lied. She had no vices.

"Okay, Beth. Let me know if anything happens."

"You know I will. Donnie Lee and Dixie are over here holding down the fort."

"Okay, Beth. Have a good night."

I had just ushered out my last client for the day, a poor couple that was going through a tough financial crises. I had hoped that I could save their marriage. The phone rang. Terri Beth answered the phone. "Yes. Yes. You're kidding me. We'll be right over." Terri Beth hung up the phone. Her face was white. She barely got the words out of her mouth. "We have a verdict."

"My God, Terri Beth, it's too soon."

"I know, Jake." We hugged.

"It's against us."

"Jake, be an optimist. Whatever it is, it isn't our last case. Let's go find out."

The flight up the elevator to the eleventh floor of the courthouse seemed like an eternity. Donnie Lee and Dixie were waiting for us. They were both ashen and looked exhausted. Brad King and his team were moving into the courtroom. The tension was enormous. We had to wait ten minutes for the court reporter who had been dismissed for the day. She finally arrived.

Judge Randall put on her black robe and took her seat on the bench. "Mr. Bailiff, please bring the jury in."

"All rise." The jury moved quickly into the jury box. They looked battered and worn. Whatever the verdict, it was one that had been deliberated long and hard.

There was no eye contact from any of the jurors. This was not a good sign. The man in the checkered sport coat looked down towards the floor. This was a very bad sign. The lady in the dark blue dress was crying. I knew it was against us.

"Ladies and gentlemen of the jury, have you reached a verdict?" asked Judge Randall.

"Yes, we have, your honor."

"Would you please hand it to Mr. Booker so he may publish it."

"Yes, ma'am." The foreman looked uneasy.

I didn't need to hear it. I knew what it was. The bloodsuckers of the First Fidelity Bank and Trust and their mob bosses had bought off the jury.

Donnie Lee paused and read the verdict slowly. "We the jury find for the defendants, this the twenty-seventh day of October, 2002. J. B. Smith, Foreman."

Donnie Lee collapsed in his seat. A shout came from the defense table. Anthony Jacobs' smile was cocky and arrogant. Rube Wiseman laughed quietly.

Dixie had the presence of mind to ask that the jury be polled. They all agreed that it was their unanimous verdict. Donnie Lee was visibly shaken. He was seated at the plaintiff's table and was visibly crying as the jurors left the courtroom. Dixie was trying to comfort him. I was so weak I couldn't stand. Terri Beth was in shock.

If you represent the defendant and you lose a verdict, you can always appeal the case, sometimes forever. But when you represent the plaintiff and lose, your choices are limited.

I hugged Donnie Lee and Dixie as we packed up our papers and law books. I hated the thought of telling Kathy and Kelli the verdict. Kathy would be deeply hurt but would get over it. She would also be glad it was over. Kelli, I wasn't so sure. It would probably kill her.

I decided to go home and forego my nightly visit to the hospital. I hoped Kelli would not watch the nightly news.

Kathy knew the verdict. As I drove up the driveway she was there to greet me. We were both crying. "Kathy, I love you. But this jury was bought. I'm convinced of that."

The two drinks I poured before dinner turned into three and then four. I was getting sick on an empty stomach. I went to bed drunk without eating. I heard the phone ringing-Kathy was on the phone for a long time, but I did not want to talk to anyone. All I could think of was getting away from it all and going fishing. My father and I had a place called Lake Philema ten miles outside of my South Georgia home. I loved to fish for bream and perch. My head was spinning around and around. I finally fell asleep.

I glanced at the clock. It was nine a.m. Never before had I slept this late. Kathy was rubbing my back. "My God, is this a nightmare?"

"No," she smiled, "just a bad verdict and a hangover. Maybe I can have you back now. Here's some aspirin. You tried to drown your verdict in bourbon last night. You don't need to do that, Jake. I love you too much. You need to get some food in you . . . . Ford Ashton called last night and again this morning. He wants you to call him as soon as you can. He thinks you got screwed."

Kathy stood. "And, sweetheart, Terri Beth called about nine last night. She's greatly concerned about you. She says you haven't been eating very well lately. She also says that Kelli has taken a turn for the worse. She's concerned that the verdict might have had an adverse affect on her. . . . Jake, Terri Beth is such a sweetheart. I feel like she's my sister."

"What I need right now is a couple of aspirin."

The phone rang. Kathy answered it. It was Ford Ashton. "Just a minute, Ford. Here he is."

"Jake, Ford here. Look, I'm not calling about your reaction to the verdict. I'm sure you got screwed. I need to see you as soon as I can. I don't want anyone to see us together."

"What if we meet in the parking lot of the hospital, say around ten? I've got to tell Kelli the bad news."

"How's she doing, Jake?"

"Not so good, Ford. Please don't tell anyone, but she hasn't got long. She has pancreatic cancer."

"Oh, no!"

I arrived at Catholic Hospital shortly before ten and Ford was already there. We exchanged pleasantries and he got right to the point. "Jake, late yesterday afternoon I was having coffee at Sandy's. I was in the back corner. No one could see I was there. There was a man and lady in the booth next to me. They were talking about your trial. From what I heard, they were on the jury. They were both very angry. She kept saying, 'How can they get away with this?' He said, 'But we were outvoted.' She said, 'It was supposed to be unanimous. I would never vote for the defendants. We should go to the judge.' 'We can't. You know what the foreman said. We will pay the price if we don't go along.'"

Ford looked me in the eye. "Jake, you got screwed. The verdict was not unanimous."

"My God! Do you know who they were?" I asked.

"I don't know their names, but he was wearing a checkered sport jacket and she was wearing a dark blue dress."

"I knew it, damn it. I knew it. This jury was rigged. Thanks, Ford."

"Please don't reveal your source, Jake. I can do you more good if I remain anonymous."

*****

Now I had the dubious honor of telling Kelli the bad news. I entered her room. The lights were dim and Kelli was semi-conscious. Her skin had a pale yellow tint to it. She looked weak, but she recognized me.

"Hello, good looking," I said.

She smiled. "Hello, Jake. How's my favorite law partner?"

"Oh, so-so," I said.

She had that sudden look of terror in her eyes. She knew what I was about to tell her. "Jake, what's the matter? Have we gotten a verdict?"

"I'm afraid so, Kelli."

"Oh, no! Let's have it."

"For the defendants. A goose egg."

"Oh, no." She began to cry.

"Kelli, it was rigged." I related the events of the morning and my meeting with Ford Ashton.

"Jake, I told you from the beginning that First Fidelity owned and controlled everything in Conecuh. We must file a motion for a new trial immediately."

"Hold on, Kelli. Maybe we have one more bite of the apple. We must approach this very carefully. You know the jury can't impeach it's own verdict."

"But Jake, this is a fraud." Kelli was showing her old fiery spirit again.

A nurse entered the room. She began to take Kelli's blood pressure and temperature. "It's a little up this morning, Mrs. Ferguson," she said. "Have you eaten today?"

"I'm not hungry."

"Mrs. Ferguson, you have to eat. If you don't, the doc is going to order an I.V.. You don't want that."

"Get her, Miss Susie," I teased the nurse. Her name tag indicated that her name was Susan Grantham. "I have to go, Kelli. There are two things I'm going to do. Number one is to get you out of here, and number two is to get a new trial."

"Jake, don't ever give up. You hear me? We'll win."

"Damn right," I said. "And don't you ever give up. You're coming out of here too, and soon."

"I don't know, Jake. Every day I feel I'm getting weaker."

"Kelli, I'll make a deal with you. I'll get us a new trial if you'll tell me you are going to walk out of here."
"Jake, what I am about to ask may sound strange coming from me, but I feel the need to pray. Will you pray with me?"

"Of course I will, Kelli."

206

"Jake, it's a very special prayer that I learned years ago that I have tried to live by all of my life." We joined hands and bowed our heads in prayer:

"Lord, make me a channel of thy peace,

that where there is hatred, I may bring love;

that where there is wrong, I may bring the spirit of

forgiveness; that where there is discord, I may bring

harmony;   that where there is error, I may bring truth;

that where there is doubt, I may bring faith; that where

there is despair, I may bring hope; that where there are

shadows, I may bring light; that where there is sadness, I

may bring joy. Lord, grant that I may seek rather to

comfort, than to be comforted; to understand, than to be

understood; to love, than to be loved.

For it is by self-forgetting that one finds.

It is by forgiving that one is forgiven.

It is by dying that one awakens to Eternal Life.

I kissed her on the cheek and walked out.

*****

I pulled into the parking lot of the office. I dreaded what was waiting inside. Terri Beth was busy at her typewriter. "Hey, boss. Good to see you." She gave me a hug.

"Terri Beth, I need a lot of space today."

"I don't know why. You haven't had enough stress lately."

207

"Can you get hold of Donnie Lee and Dixie? We all need to have a meeting as soon as you can set it up. I need you there too."

She brought me a cup of coffee.

The day was spent returning telephone calls from fellow trial lawyers expressing their condolences. I revealed to no one my conversation with Ford Ashton. I talked with two new clients. One was a new divorce case. The couple just wanted out. No contest. No custody fight. An easy one for a change. The other one was a new estate. It was good to get back into the old routine again.

At 5:30 p.m. we all assembled in the law library—Donnie Lee, Dixie, Brook, Terri Beth, and me. "Ladies and gentlemen, we didn't lose our case. We were screwed, cheated, stolen from, and bamboozled." I outlined my meeting with Ford Ashton earlier that morning.

"God damn it!" Brook shouted. "We need to get these bastards disbarred."

"Hold on, Brook. We can't prove they had anything to do with it. So far, it's just the twelve members of the jury. We can't prove First Fidelity had anything to do with it either."

Donnie Lee stood. "Hey, until this moment I thought I had blown it. Thank you, Jake. I'm mad as hell. It's time to go to war. All out war. If they can play dirty, so can we."

"Wait a minute, Donnie Lee. We're not the crooks. They are. We can play fair and win. We can do everything legally, and win honestly. Let's do it right. Let's not get in the gutter with these scum bags. ."

Terri Beth caught my eye. She smiled. I knew she was with me.

Donnie Lee said he needed to get back to Atlanta for a few days. He wanted his firm's permission to work on a new strategy. We all agreed. He was a master of strategy.

*****

I pulled into my driveway. She was crying. She met me at the car, totally overcome. She wrapped her arms around me and sobbed.

"God, babe, what is it?" I asked.

"She didn't make it, Jake. Kelli is dead."

"What?"

"The hospital called. She just gave out. She's gone."

We collapsed on the driveway together.

Kelli was called away before she was able to keep her promise to me. If her body had not given out, there was no doubt that she would have kept her promise. I had held out for my hero. Her body was gone, but her spirit was not. My life was suddenly changed. I was determined to keep my promise to her.

The telephone rang. It was Terri Beth. "Kathy, Terri Beth. God, we lost our warrior."

"I know."

"What can I do? Would it be inappropriate if I came over?"

"No, Terri Beth. You know it wouldn't."

Thirty minutes later Terri Beth arrived. Terri Beth and Kathy embraced. She hugged me. We all cried.

"Terri Beth is my sister." Terri Beth and Kathy embraced. Loophole, our old wonderful Schnauzer, curled up at our feet and let out a moan.

We spent the rest of the night telling stories of Kelli, her triumphs and her screw-ups, and how much we all had loved her.

*****

It was seven a.m. The phone was ringing off the hook. I picked up the receiver.

"Jake, Ford Ashton. I just heard the news about Kelli."

"Ford, it's been a rough night, to say the least."

"She was a great lady. You know she handled the adoption of our child."

"Yes, I know, Ford."

"How do you want me to handle it, news-wise?"

"You don't need to do anything special. You always tell the truth. Do whatever you feel is appropriate. I loved the lady. She was my hero. The only thing you can do is let the public know that she always fought for her clients."

"Hey, we have always appreciated what your firm has meant to us. Thanks, Jake."

Funerals are always miserable. The quicker you can get through them, the better. Juanita and Terri Beth handled all the details. The funeral was held at Saint Joseph's Catholic Church; Kelli had not been devout Catholic in the sense that she had practiced all the tenets of the Catholic faith. She couldn't. A family lawyer, she had to work through too many compromises. But she had been a spiritual woman. She believed in God, and that God always worked through people for good.

I cried throughout the whole funeral. True human goodness somehow comes through this whole miserable experiment known as life.

Barron offered to give the eulogy. At first, I didn't know how to respond to his offer. Here was the man who'd been fired by the very woman he wanted to eulogize. At the funeral, Barron was a gentleman and one fine human being. I only wished we had had him on our team during the trial. Maybe the result would have been different.

Barron was the most eloquent human being alive. (I caught myself thinking that even Donnie Lee could have taken lessons from him.)

Thirteen

I was due a vacation. I took the next two weeks off, strictly for fishing. The first week I intended to go to my parents' home and spend a week on Lake Philema, the second I would spend in Destin, Florida, catching red snapper and basking in the Florida sunshine. Kathy loved my parents and they loved her. However, she left the sunshine of Florida strictly to me. She would spend that week with her parents.

Our old fishing boat was fifteen years old. It was just as we had left it when I was in the sixth grade. I could still smell the Tampa Nugget cigars that my father used to smoke when we were on the way to Lake Philema. Some of the old fishing spots were still there, but a lot of them were gone. I felt sad that so many of my childhood memories had disappeared.

It was a good day. I got really excited when I caught the first bream. In less than three hours I had caught thirty. I was excited about getting home to show Kathy the macho fisherman I was.

Fishing on Lake Philema is the greatest therapy a man could ever receive. It was the only thing that could have possibly gotten my mind off the bad verdict and the myriad of problems at the office. My mind wandered back to the trial. Then my mind wandered back 15 years to a time when my father and I were fishing and we got stuck in a ditch less than a mile from the spot where I was fishing.

It began to rain and I started back. The rain was really coming down by the time I got home. Kathy and my mother were on the front porch when I drove into the driveway.

"Well, Mr. Macho, how did you do?" Kathy asked.

"Enough to feed *me*, your highness. I don't know what you will eat. I assume you can eat grits."

"You'd better do better than that, big boy, or you had best be headed to the Piggly Wiggly." She opened the cooler. "At least I know that if my husband can't win trials he can catch fish." She stopped. "Hey, I didn't mean that." She started to cry.

I began to laugh. "Hey, I'm a damn good fisherman. For that remark you are sentenced to clean and eat fish for the next two weeks. Besides, I haven't thought about the law practice all day. I may quit being a lawyer and become a fisherman for life. Look what happened to Peter. He met Jesus while he was fishing."

"You ain't no Peter, sweetheart. I just hope you know Jesus. I'll help you clean these fish. Let's get started."

*****

The first week over, I left for Destin, the seaside fishing town near Pensacola. I spent the next four days catching fish—snapper, trigger fish, amberjack, dolphin, and shark. Kathy suggested that I should turn the sharks loose out of professional courtesy. We both had a sick sense of humor.

The next three days were spent on the beach reading all the books I had wanted to read but never had the time. No telephones. Plenty of suntan lotion and the most wonderful sea breezes in the world. To walk on the beach at night and feel the sea breeze and hear the waves crash on the beach is the most wonderful experience in the world. I dreaded having to once again walk in the front door of Ferguson, Thomas and McDonald.

Terri Beth and I made an agreement before I left for Florida. If it weren't an emergency, she would shield me, and would not tell anyone where I was spending my vacation.

The telephone rang. Kathy answered it and turned toward me with a questioning look, "It's Terri Beth."

"Jake, I know our agreement, but I couldn't wait to give you some good news. Donnie Lee has affidavits from the two jurors. They are willing to cooperate. Donnie Lee and Don Pollard have been talking, and Don is willing to take it to a grand jury. He believes he has a case for jury tampering and obstruction of justice. He wants to see you when you get back. He laughed when I wouldn't give him your number. He said he could issue me a subpoena. I told him to go ahead, that I would go to jail first. He laughed for ten minutes on the phone, and then he said any lady who would go to jail for Jake McDonald deserves a medal, and offered to hire me. I told him I already had the best boss in the world."

"Terri Beth, remind me to give you a raise when I get back."

"I will. You can bet on that."

214

"What else is happening?"

"Just the usual stuff—divorces, bankruptcies, shootings, and stabbings. Brook took in a good damage suit—a logging truck killed a young hospital intern."

"I hope we represent the intern's widow?"

"We do. There's plenty of insurance. Are we still the merchants of misery?"

"I'm afraid so, Sunshine. I'll see you bright and early Monday morning."

*****

My vacation was over. The problems that awaited me in the office were not. Terri Beth had not skipped a beat. My desk was completely organized, the phone messages were laid out in order of importance. She was busy at her typewriter, and a hot cup of coffee was sitting in the middle of my desk.

She heard me come in and jumped up. "Good morning, boss."

"Good morning, Sunshine."

She gave me a big hug. "Welcome back. How was your vacation?" she asked.

"Not long enough, Sunshine."

"That's okay. I lined up plenty of business while you were gone. At least you won't go broke."

"Take it slow. I'm still trying to get over the slow, easy, and wonderful beach life. Did you put Betty and Bill to sleep while I was gone?"

"No," she laughed. "But I told them the appeal would take ten years and not to call us until the year 2010."

"Good for you. That was worth the whole trip."

"Don Pollard said to call him as soon as you got back. We really got to know each other while you were gone."

"And just how well did you get to know him, might I ask?"

She laughed. "Damn, boss, he propositioned me, he bought me drinks, he seduced me, and he offered me a salary of $100,000 plus benefits if I would come to work for him."

"Tell me, Terri Beth, before I call his wife. Did you accept his offer, and did he pay you the $100,000 in cash?

"You are so bad. I would never ever leave you and you know it. You are so jealous."

"You're damn right I am. I want to see you typing away at that typewriter when you are 85 years old, gray, have no teeth, and weigh 250 pounds. Do you know how long it takes to find a secretary who can type a hundred words per minute with only three errors?"

"Two errors. I only made two errors."

I called Don Pollard's office. He was on the other line, but his secretary said she would slip him a note, and that he really wanted to talk with me. Thirty seconds passed and Don came on the line. "Hello, Jake. How are you? I'm glad you are so rich you can afford to gallivant around the world on a vacation."

"You overpaid government goldbricker," I laughed. "And if you try to hire my secretary away again, I'm going to sue you."

"Jake, you better latch on to that Terri Beth. She's the best thing you'll ever have."

"You are right," I said. "What's up?"

"I want you to come see me after work, or better still, let me come see you, in your office, say around 5:30. By then I'll have half your clients and the rest of the bar association's clients in jail."

"Okay, you mean bastard, I'll see you at 5:30 in my office."

The day was spent catching up. It was fun being busy again. All day I wondered what Don was going to tell me. I asked Terri Beth to stay around, along with Brook.

Exactly at 5:30 p.m. Don appeared at the door. I could never truly guess what was on his mind. He was a tough prosecutor, and I told him as long as he was in office we would be able to keep our fees in criminal cases high. I had fought some mean, tough courtroom battles with him. Some I lost. Some I won. One thing you could always say about Don Pollard was that he was honest. No cheap shots in the courtroom. His word was good.

Terri Beth opened the door. Don entered and gave her a hug.

"Hey, I thought you came over here to see *me*, not date my secretary."

"I did, Jake, but she smells better than you do."

"Right, and I'm going to represent your wife Cynthia for free. I've got the pictures and tape recordings."

"And I'll turn loose some of our best jailhouse customers over at the county jail to take care of you. For a few cigarettes you'll be history."

"Come on in, Don. Look, I want Terri Beth here. I trust her explicitly. If anything happens to me, I want all the witnesses I can get. You understand?"

"Absolutely, Jake. Besides that, she'll be a better looking witness on the stand."

"If you want her to leave, I'll understand."

"No, Jake. I came over here to level with you. You may be in grave danger. I don't mean to scare you, and I don't mean to tread lightly on this either. The FBI notified our office two days ago that there's been a lot of telephone traffic between the Costellano crime family and Conecuh. There's been a lot of communication with low-level street punks—pimps, gamblers, crack dealers, you know the types. We don't know what to think of it, but the feds intercepted a conversation through a wiretap. I don't mean to scare you, but they mentioned you."

I felt the blood drain from my face. "What did they say?"

"Jake, the feds don't tell us all, but they told us to offer you, in their words 'the utmost immediate protection,' or that they would. Jake, you and Donnie Lee have stirred up hell. This is not simply a case of a bank screwing people over. We are talking about a major criminal case involving a dangerous crime family. I'm not sure my office is equipped to handle it. I think we need to at least involve the GBI, and even the feds. In the meantime, I'm willing to set up a surveillance unit around your law firm and your house. I don't know how Kathy will take it. Maybe you need to send her to her mother's or something until this thing blows over."

"Kathy will be scared out of her wits. What do I tell her?"

"Just tell her that some crazy lunatic your firm sued in a divorce has threatened to kill all the members of your firm and that she needs to go to Florida until it all blows over. Downplay it as much as you can Jake, but this is serious business."

*****

It was dark outside. Brook had gone home. Don was just leaving. Terri Beth lingered behind. She knew I needed her at this moment. "Boss, I think I know you as well as anybody, you are a courageous man, but this time I can tell you're scared. I can see it in your eyes."

"You're right. My stomach is in knots. I wish now that we had never taken that case. I should be like Billy Packard down the street, checking real estate titles and closing loans. I'm sure he sleeps well at night."

"Boss, you would never be happy if you were not in the middle of a fight all the time. I don't know what to tell you other than to trust Don Pollard to handle it," she said.

"I know, Terri Beth, but sometimes I get so tired of this day-to-day crap that you have to put up with practicing law—

representing clients and pressuring people to pay legal fees they can't afford."

What Don Pollard had told me an hour earlier continued to gnaw at me. I knew I was dealing with bad people. They had beaten us in the courtroom and I didn't know how to extricate myself from this mess.

*****

I headed down Cox Boulevard towards 17th Avenue. Two pump trucks with sirens blaring flew past me. The smell of smoke was pungent in the air. I saw a fireball glowing in the direction of my house. My pulse raced. A million thoughts ran through my head as I pulled around the corner. I was totally numb. My whole life was disappearing before me in flames. My God, where was Kathy? Everything I loved and everything I owned was in that house.

I crashed my Buick Skylark against the curb, threw open the door, and darted towards my house. The smoke was thick and suffocating, and the heat was intense.

"Stop! You can't go in there!" a voice yelled out from somewhere behind me.

I turned in panic. "I live here.. This is my home. I've got to find my wife."

The fireman grabbed me around the neck and pulled me to the ground. I began to cry—I didn't know whether it was from the sting of the flames or the sudden sorrow that overcame me. Where was Kathy? *Oh God, I prayed. Please let her be out shopping somewhere.*

It was Rudy Tolbert. "Jake, my God, is that you?" he asked. "We got here as fast as we could. Where's Kathy?" Rudy asked.

It was then that it hit me. Kathy was inside that flaming inferno. I began to sob uncontrollably when Angela appeared out of nowhere. She put her arms around me and began to pray in her sweet unsophisticated way. Kathy loved Angela and often talked about how Angela had tremendous faith and believed that all things would turn out for good in the end. I had often wondered if people like Rudy and Angela were not better off than educated professional yuppies like Kathy and me. They had less money and education, but far more faith.

An ambulance arrived and my heart sank. A blast of water knocked down the front wall of the house and I saw four firemen with gas masks rush through the flaming inferno carrying a stretcher.

The firemen quickly loaded the stretcher onto the waiting ambulance. I began to scream, "Who is it? Who's in that ambulance?" I ran towards the ambulance.

A paramedic wrestled me to the ground. "It's going to be all right, buddy. We're going to take care of them."

"Who is it? My wife was in there."

"We don't know yet, but whoever it is is going to be all right, I promise you."

"Mr. McDonald? Are you Jake McDonald?"

"Yes, I am."

"Do you live here?"

"Yes, sir," I replied.

"Can you come with me to my squad car?"

I complied robotically.

"Mr. McDonald, do you know who might have been in the house?"

I turned white. "Sir, only my wife and my dog, and I don't know who else. God knows, I hope she wasn't in there."

"Calm down, Mr. McDonald. The paramedics pulled an unidentified victim out of there. We don't know whether it was male or female."

I was totally numb.

It was then that I saw a pale shaggy coat in the distance and I ran for my dog. He saw me and tried to run towards me. He tried to lick my hand, but his face and tongue were burned. I picked him up and held him in my arms, I felt the breath leave him, and I burst into tears. Loophole was dead and Kathy was nowhere to be found.

Rudy grabbed me by the shoulder and led me to his car. I don't remember the drive to the hospital to this day. All I remember is hearing Angela say over and over that everything would be all right.

The drive to the medical center seemed to take an eternity.

The elevator door opened onto the fourth floor. Nurses and interns were scurrying everywhere. The intercom blurted out, "Dr. Longstreet, ICU, code blue, stat. Dr. Longstreet, ICU, code blue, stat."

A tall figure with gray hair and a mustache came through the double doors that were labeled: INTENSIVE CARE UNIT, AUTHORIZED PERSONNEL ONLY. NO ADMITTANCE. Dressed in green medical garb, he was obviously a doctor. "Are you Mr. McDonald?" he asked.

"Yes, that's right. I'm Jake McDonald."

"Mr. McDonald, I'm afraid I have to be the bearer of bad news. The rescue unit brought in a female burn victim about forty-five minutes ago. It's your wife, Kathy."

I could hardly get the words out. "How is she?" I asked.

"Well, Mr. McDonald, I'm going to shoot straight with you. You're a lawyer, aren't you?"

"Yes, sir," I replied.

"I'm not going to sugar-coat it."

"I don't want that, sir," I said.

"Your wife has been badly burned, Mr. McDonald. She has first degree burns over more than half of her body. We've given her a lot of morphine, and she's not feeling any pain. But she's fighting for her very life. We must take every minute a minute at a time and if we get that far, then we'll take it hour by hour. Then we will fight for days, then weeks, and then months. But right now let's fight for one minute at a time. Mr. McDonald are you of a particular faith?"

"Yes, sir. Kathy and I are Methodists ."

"Would you care to join me in prayer?" He grabbed my hand. Rudy and Angela joined in. He prayed for Kathy and me, then turned and disappeared through the ICU doors.

Hours went by. I was empty. I realized that I hadn't eaten since lunch. I was hungry. Angela went to the snack bar in the hospital and brought back some chicken salad sandwiches and coffee. I hadn't even noticed she was gone.

Your real friends are the ones who are there with you in times of tragedy. One by one they began to arrive. Ford Ashton came through the door, and then Stanton Parks.

Don Pollard and his wife Cynthia arrived. They were both crying unabashedly. I embraced Cynthia and then Don. "Damn, Don," I said, "I need to get a picture of this for my clients—the district attorney with a heart." We both broke down.

*****

A warm hand touched my forehead. I sat up abruptly. I noticed the clock over the nurses' station. It was 11:35 p.m. I had been asleep for over two hours. A nurse stood over me. "Mr. McDonald, I'm Susan Baker, Dr. Longstreet's nurse. He would like to talk with you right away. Are you okay?"

"Yeah. I guess I just fell asleep."

"This way, please." She led me into a private office off the hallway.

Dr. Longstreet was waiting for me. The room was dimly lit. There was a pile of paperwork on the desk in front of him. He had a stethoscope around his neck. His eyes were swollen and puffy. "Mr. McDonald, please sit down," he said softly.

I slid into the overstuffed chair next to the sofa and we stared into each other's eyes. It seemed like an eternity before he spoke. "Mr. McDonald, I've been a doctor for twenty-two years. I entered this profession because I always wanted to help heal people. The greatest pleasure in my profession is to see people who are sick, lame, and hurt recover. I'm sure you get the same feeling when you win a case for your clients or help them solve their difficult problems. Mr. McDonald, we go through a lot of training in medical school but there's one course they don't teach you in medical school. It's the course on how to deliver bad news to a patient's family."

"Mr. McDonald, we did the best we could, but she was too far gone when she got here. Your wife died fifteen minutes ago."

"Oh, God, no! Please, God, no!" I screamed out.

Dr. Longstreet put his arms around me. "She had no pain when she left us and was unconscious the last hour of her life. She said to tell you that she loved you."

I collapsed into the chair and sobbed uncontrollably. The love of my life was dead at the age of twenty-four.

Fourteen

A pair of gentle hands rubbed my shoulders. I recognized Terri Beth's presence by the smell of her perfume. I turned to receive a tearful embrace.

"It's going to be all right. Kathy was a beautiful spirit, a beautiful woman. She's in heaven now with God and she's not suffering any more."

I sobbed as Terri Beth held me. Dr. Longstreet's nurse entered the room. "Mr. McDonald, Dr. Longstreet said to give you this if you'd like. It's Valium. It will help you sleep."

Everything became a big blur. I remember Don Pollard and Cynthia coming in. Then Ford Ashton and Debra and Stanton Parks but Rudy and Angela were the real angels. They took me to their home and put me in bed. I vaguely remember hearing the news account of the fire and Kathy's name before I drifted off into a deep sleep.

When I woke up, my head was pounding. Angela entered the room. "Jake, I brought you some breakfast. I didn't want to wake you. You needed some rest."

"What time is it?" I asked.

"It's 10:30, Jake."

"I need to call the office."

"I've already done that for you. Terri Beth and Dixie have taken care of notifying everybody. They told me to take care of you, and not let you worry about the details. They'll handle it, Jake. Regardless of the verdict in our case, I know we hired the right law firm. Your firm cares about people. That's what counts."

I choked down the eggs and bacon and toast. I was lost and out of touch with the world. I grabbed the telephone and dialed the office.

Juanita answered.

"Juanita, this is Jake. Is Terri Beth in?"

"Sure, Jake. Hang on a second."

"Good morning, boss. How do you feel?"

"Worse than the morning after the verdict came in."

"I know. Listen, I've notified everybody I think needed to be called. I used your Rolodex. I didn't think you would mind. Dixie and I are taking care of everything. We've notified your family and Kathy's. They're on the way. I didn't know you had so many wonderful relatives".

"Terri Beth, you're a sweetheart, do you know that?"

"Hey, I truly know how you feel. I've walked a mile in those moccasins." She began to cry.

"Sunshine, hang in there. You're the only strength I've got left. Who's taking care of the clients?"

"The other guys have been wonderful. You've got quite a following. I have never seen so many beautiful flowers in my whole life. I hope you'll let me keep some of the live ones to plant in my yard after the funeral, as a living reminder of Kathy."

"Sunshine, I just hope those flowers will be as radiant as your smile."

"And Kathy's love, boss."

I choked on my tears.

"On a very serious note, Jake. Don Pollard came over this morning. I've never before seen the look he had in his eye. It was the look of a cold-blooded killer."

I struggled to laugh. "That's the district attorney look. I see it every time he sends one of our clients off to the big house."

"No, Jake, Don was drop dead serious. He told me not to tell you this, but he already has the state fire marshal's office investigating the fire, and the GBI. He was really angry. He said if someone murdered Kathy he would make sure that they went to the electric chair before he died, and he wanted to personally be there to pull the switch."

The rest of the day was spent on the phone with my parents, Kathy's parents, and our close friends, and relatives. I didn't know what would happen when reality set in. I couldn't bear the thought of going to bed without Kathy by my side. I had last seen Kathy the morning of the fire, and I wanted to remember her as she had looked when I kissed her goodbye.

*****

A funeral is a numbing experience. I had attended too many of them. Kelli's funeral had torn my guts out. This one, to say goodbye to my soul mate and wife, would tear out my soul. I decided to try to be as mechanical as I could, to just somehow get through it. I was ushered to the front pew by one of the pallbearers. I don't remember much of anything else other than the tons of flowers and the hundreds of people that filled the pews. My parents and brother and sister and her parents and her sisters were all very comforting. I tried not to look any of them in the eye until it was all over-I feared I would collapse from the pain.

I held up throughout the funeral service until we stood to sing Kathy's favorite hymn, "How Great Thou Art." I couldn't do it. I caught a glimpse of Terri Beth out of the corner of my eye. She was bawling worse than me.

The ride back to the funeral home at the end of the service was sobering. For the first time in my life I was truly alone. I buried Kathy, the love of my life. My old companion and best friend since law school—Loophole, my dog—was dead. All of my earthly possessions were gone except for a photo of Kathy and me on my desk in the office. I prayed that there were negatives somewhere to reproduce the pictures I had lost.

A thousand things ran through my mind. I suddenly realized I had no clothes. What was I going to do for underwear? Of all the things to worry about in a moment like this. For the first time since I had started practicing law I really had empathy for my clients. I now truly understood what tragedy meant. Like Terri Beth said, this day I truly walked a mile in their moccasins.

All the people had gone. The funeral ritual was over. The ladies from the church had cleaned up all the dishes and had put away the food. I wanted some time alone. I wondered in what direction my life would take me. I loathed the thought of going back to the office. Kathy's death had ripped out my heart and soul. I no longer had the fire in the belly to practice law. I just wanted to find out who had killed my wife. Don Pollard and I would find out the truth.

I awoke early, showered, and put on my only suit. I called Terri Beth at home and told her I'd be coming in late, that I needed to go buy some new clothes.

It had been a long time since I had tried on new suits. Phil Olden fixed me up with a few suits that would get me by until I could restore my old wardrobe. I made it to the office at eleven and Terri Beth did everything she could to cheer me up, but I could not focus. My mind constantly wandered back to the fire and to Kathy. God, how I missed her.

I temporarily moved in with Phillip. He had a spare bedroom and was always gone anyway. He spent most of his time with his girlfriend, Judy

The days went by in a blur. Client after client. One hearing after another. The same old routine every day. I put in long hours as a distraction, returned to Phillip's apartment, ate and went to bed. God, I was too young to spend my life like this. My spirit was dying. Why had this happened to me?

Fifteen

It was a Friday, nine months after Kathy's funeral. I had made it through the week. I finished up at the office and went home. Before I left I called Bill Yarborough, my minister. He was in his office preparing his sermon for Sunday. "Bill, this is Jake."

"How are you, my friend? I was just thinking about you."

"I need to talk with you, Bill. I am so lonely."

"Do you need to see me now? Is everything all right?"

"I'm okay, Bill, I'll be in church Sunday. Can you see me then?"

"Absolutely. Hey, why don't you have lunch with Jean-Ann and me? It's fried chicken Sunday. You know she cooks the best."

"Thanks, Bill. I'd love that. I'll see you Sunday."

"Look, Jake, you don't need to wait until Sunday. If you need me, call any time. You have my number. Jake, are you okay?"

"Yeah, Bill, I'm okay."

"I'm praying for you. There are people out there who love you. Kathy is in heaven. She's in God's hands. Believe that."

Sunday morning, 11:00 a.m. and I was in church. It felt very strange being in a place where nine months earlier Kathy's funeral had taken place.

Bill Yarborough preached another dynamic and moving sermon. I looked forward to having lunch with him and Jean-Ann. I didn't look forward to unloading my feelings on Bill, even though he was used to it as a Methodist minister.

Bill and I talked while Jean-Ann fixed lunch. "Bill, you did another magnificent job today. You must be running for bishop."

Bill laughed. "No, Jake, when they promote you to bishop it means they are about to retire you. I've got too much to do before I retire. Like saving the souls of more lawyers for instance. I'm afraid the devil is getting more of them these days than the Lord." We both laughed.

Then Bill got very serious. "Jake, I've known you a long time, and quite frankly, something is seriously bothering you. Something as deep as Kathy's death. Talk to me, my friend."

"Bill, I wish I had never taken that case against First Fidelity. It wasn't for the money. It was the principle. You know me well enough to know I wouldn't file a frivolous suit to extort money out of a big bank. My clients were screwed."

Bill looked at me. "I know that Jake. First Fidelity has hurt some members of this church very badly. I can't reveal any names, of course, but I know you're telling the truth. The people who are in charge are money worshipers. You know what the Bible says. 'The love of money is the root of all evil.'"

I hit him with the bombshell. "Bill, I can't do it anymore. I've decided to quit practicing law."

"Dear God, Jake, what are you talking about?" Bill was dumbfounded.

"I've lost everything that means anything to me. Kathy is gone. I've let my clients down. I've lost all my meager possessions. My law partner died a miserable death. I've even lost my dog. But the worst is that I've lost my spirit. I've lost the fire in the belly to be a trial lawyer. It would be a disservice to my clients to put up a charade. They deserve better than that. Tomorrow morning I'm going to resign from the firm."

"Have you discussed this with anyone other than me?"

"No. I'm going to call Terri Beth, my secretary, this afternoon and tell her. She's my closest confidante next to you. She'll be heartbroken, but she won't have any trouble finding a job. She's the best legal secretary ever."

"Jake, what will you do for a living?"

"I don't know, but I'm going to find a change in scenery. Funny isn't it? Moving won't be a problem 'cause I don't have anything to move." I tried to laugh, but tears welled up in my eyes.

Jean-Ann came into the room. She saw I was upset. "Oh, sorry," she interrupted.

"It's okay," I said. "We were just finishing up."

"Lunch is ready, if you boys are hungry."

Jean-Ann had fixed a terrific lunch, but I wasn't very hungry. She finished putting the dishes in the dishwasher when she said, "Jake, you need to visit my Sunday school class, the New Seekers, sometime. I bet you would be a great teacher."

I looked at Bill.

He said, "We'll talk about that later, hon."

She seemed puzzled.

I had spent a pleasant two hours with Bill and Jean-Ann. I wondered if he were going to tell her what our conversation had been. I didn't care if Jean-Ann knew. Bill and Jean-Ann were close, and people I truly loved and believed in.

I dreaded what I had to do this afternoon. I didn't know how Terri Beth would take my decision to leave the firm. I could be shattering a bond of friendship that I had cherished since I first met her. Next to Kathy and Kelli, she had been my closest friend.

Finally, I picked up the receiver and dialed her number. "Hello, Terri Beth, this is Jake."

"Hi. What's up?"

"Terri Beth, I need to talk to you."

"Is everything okay?"

"I just need to talk, and soon."

"Okay. Where? How about the park next to Wolburn School?"

"Fine, I'll see you there in about thirty minutes."

I dreaded facing Terri Beth. I wished we could go off together and set up a small law practice in the hills of north Georgia and represent moon shiners and farmers.

Terri Beth met me near the playground of Wolburn School at the park where I jogged. She was wearing a tank top and a pair of tight blue jeans. Her dark hair was tied back in a pony tail. She looked happy, but what I was going to say would change her afternoon. "Let's go for a walk," I said.

"Okay, but I know you well enough to know that something heavy is about to fall."

234

"Kelli was my best friend next to Kathy. Then you came along and soon I had three best friends. I am a lucky man.

"When Kelli died, a part of me died with her. And then when Kathy…well…a lot of who I was and what I wanted to be disintegrated." I stopped to compose myself before starting again.

"Looking back at it all now, I know that taking on First Fidelity was a mistake. We should have gone about our business representing divorce clients, bankruptcies, and personal injury cases. This case killed Kelli and it killed Kathy. I not sure I can take any more.

"I think you know me well enough to know that I believe in my clients and I try to represent them with all my heart and soul. When we lose a case, I feel I somehow let them down. We let our clients down in the First Fidelity suit."

"That's not true, Jake. I have never seen a case that was better prepared. You and Donnie Lee and Dixie gave it everything you had. You know damn well that the jury was bought by First Fidelity."

I continued. "I went to church this morning—the first time in the nine months since Kathy's death. And I had a long talk with Bill Yarborough. He's one of God's best preachers and about as close a friend as you are. I unloaded my heart on him, and what I told him I am about to tell you.

"I need to get out of the way before more innocent people get hurt."

"Jake, what are you talking about?"

"Tomorrow morning I'm going to meet with the partners and I'm going to resign."

"Oh, Jake, you won't do any such thing," Terri Beth said. "You're a great lawyer. You've been through terrible trauma lately. Hey, it takes time to work through it. I've been there, remember? I lost my only true love and soul mate, remember? You came along and pulled me through it.

"I believe in you, Jake. The partners believe in you. You just need to take some time off and sort it all out. Hey, I'm with you all the way. I'll never leave you. I hope you'll be around forever. I love you, Jake." Terri Beth wrapped her arms around me.

Terri Beth pulled back. Her beautiful blue eyes met mine. We stared at each other for what seemed an eternity. The tears rolled down her cheeks.

Our lips moved closer together.

"Are y'all kissing?" a voice blurted out. Shocked, Terri Beth and I pulled apart. A little boy on a bicycle pulled up. We began to laugh.

"Why do you want to know?" Terri Beth asked.

"Because my momma said you are only supposed to kiss somebody when you are in love. Are y'all in love?"

"We just might be," said Terri Beth. "Now you run along."

He left. We both laughed out loud.

"Might be?" I asked.

Terri Beth looked up into my eyes. "Jake, think about your decision a long time," she said. "You're stressed out and

236

need some time off. I'm with you no matter what you decide, but I don't want you to destroy your career over one case. Nothing will bring Kathy back. This case can be won on appeal. Donnie Lee and Dixie are working on it right now."

"I'll think about it a long time. No matter what I decide to do, I'll love you always. I would never do anything to hurt you. You're the best friend I have, and I swear that if that kid hadn't showed up on the bike I probably would have . . . well, I don't know what I might have done."

"Jake McDonald, you are a naughty boy. But you never know. I just might have let you do what you were thinking about doing."

I laughed. "If I had done what I was thinking about I would no longer be practicing law anyway. If you're convicted of a sex crime, they take your law license."

*****

It was a long night. My thoughts drifted back to Kathy and the last day we spent together. I missed her sorely.

My thoughts drifted to Terri Beth and her comforting words. Why was I having these feelings?

And then there was the firm. Was I making the right decision to resign? Or was this a futile reaction to Kathy's death and the loss of the First Fidelity case? Everything told me I would somehow move through this. I could get through the First Fidelity case, make a decent living as a lawyer, and maybe become a good citizen in the community. Only Bill Yarborough and Terri Beth knew what I was thinking.

It was 1:30 a.m. It was time to get honest with myself. I laid it on the line. At 1:45 a.m. I decided that I could no longer be a hypocrite. No longer would I represent causes that I did not believe in. No longer would I represent frivolous cases that would create quick money and settlements with insurance companies for the quick kill. I would fight to the end for what was right. I would cut through the politics, the traditions, the money, the power structure, the appointed judges, and the good old boy politicians. I would have to cut through the impossible—everything impossible. I dreaded all of it. I was ready to quit. Nobody could defeat a hundred years of tradition. Not an upstart like me.

*****

It was Monday morning. I dreaded it. Neva had set up everything in the library. The partners had no idea what was coming.

"Well, Jake, you got us all here early on a Monday morning. What's this all about?" asked Brook.

I rose slowly. "You guys and Dixie are the best friends I have in my life. I say that because my very best friend died nine months ago.

"In the last twelve months, I've done my very best to support this law firm. I've worked hard to represent our clients. Sometimes we've won. Sometimes we've lost. I'd like to think

238

that the batting average in this firm is high. I know it is because I see a lot of people in our waiting room every day. These are the people who believe in us and pay our bills. Kelli would be proud of us. We still carry on her tradition. Take care of the clients first and they will take care of us, as she used to say.

"That's why I called this meeting. I feel that I have not been taking care of the clients. I have let everybody down. You guys have been carrying the load on your shoulders while I was pursuing a losing case that has cost our law firm a lot of money, respect, and prestige in this community. I also feel—"

I began to cry. "I also feel that it somehow cost Kelli and Kathy their lives. I bear full responsibility. And that's why I am resigning from the firm effective immediately."

Everyone sat stunned. Brook was the first to speak. "Damn it, Jake, You lose one lawsuit and you want to quit. I can't believe this. You're the best damn lawyer this town has seen in years. I was afraid you gathered us here to tell us that you were going to work for those King, Golden, Bonner jerks. You need to take some time off. We appreciate what you did. No other lawyer in this town has half the guts you have. You can't quit. We need you." Brook was speaking from his heart.

Dixie stood. Tears were flowing down her cheeks. "Jake, you're the best friend I ever had. When I didn't know where I was going, you were always there to give me a helping hand. Hey, you didn't let anybody down. If anything, we let you down."

Phillip was stunned. "Jake, you need to take some time off. This is not you. You have been under a lot of pressure. I don't know how you've taken all you have been through. Take some time off. Clear your mind and then come back. We need you."

I was truly moved. I almost caved in, but I did not. Kathy's death had been the final straw for me. "I love all of you. You know that. We've fought many battles together. I don't know what I'm going to do yet. No, I'm not going to work for another law firm. I would never work for another law firm."

Everyone was crying. I abruptly left the room and quickly went to my office and shut the door. I collapsed into my old red leather chair. I heard a quiet rapping at the door. "Jake, can I come in?" It was Terri Beth.

"Sure," I said.

She came in and locked the door. She sat down in front of me. "What's the verdict?"

"Terri Beth, they worked hard on me, but I quit." I began to cry.

"Jake McDonald, I would like to call you all kinds of names right now, but I really think that in your heart you believe in what you're doing."

"In the last few months, I've gone through the three worst days of my life. Kelli died, Kathy died, and now today I have quit the law firm, and I feel I'm losing you."

"Jake, you got two out of three correct. But you're wrong on the third one. You may quit this firm but you won't lose me." Terri Beth and I collapsed into each other's arms.

*****

The phone rang. Juanita said, "Mr. McDonald, there is a Mr. Robert Zimmerman on line one for you."

Robert Zimmerman? I only knew one Robert Zimmerman, and he was my big brother in Kappa Alpha, my college fraternity.

"Hello, is this Jake McDonald, the worst pledge of KA?"

"No, this is Leroy Knuckles of the IRS. Do you need an audit?"

"Jake, this is Robert. How are you?"

"Not so good, Robert."

"I know, Jake. Robin and I were at the funeral, but you were out of it. We decided not to bother you. Look, I need to talk to you. Robin and I would like for you to come to Atlanta and visit us for a weekend. Could you join us?"

"I don't know, Big Bob. I'm pretty down right now. I did something crazy today."

"What's that?"

"I resigned from my law firm."

"Jake, what the hell? . . . You're a damn good trial lawyer."

"Robert, look, I'll accept your invitation and I'll explain this weekend."

*****

Robert and Robin Zimmerman lived in an affluent north Atlanta neighborhood. He was the president of Southern Title Insurance Company. Robert and I were alike in every respect except he was more conservative than me. He liked the security of corporate America and I loved the adrenaline rush of being the trial lawyer.

I pulled into the driveway of the residence of Mr. and Mrs. Robert Zimmerman on West Paces Ferry Road in Atlanta. Robin was watering her flowers. She let out a shriek when I pulled into the driveway. She was a true southern lady from Montgomery, Alabama, and she gave me a bear hug as soon as I got out of my car.

"Can I sneak a kiss," I asked, "before Big Bob sees us?"

"You bet," she laughed. She smacked me on the lips.

Robert bounded out the front door. "Hey, I'm going to charge you with adultery." He laughed. "Jake, how are you? Come on in."

Robert, Robin, and I went inside. Their home was elegant. Robert and Robin were a couple with old south class and elegant taste.

"Jake, you don't know how much we have thought about you lately. We've seen all the reports of your lawsuit against that bank and then Kathy's death. Honest to God, we don't know how you have survived it all. On the other hand, I don't know how we survived college either—all those all-nighters before exams and all those fraternity parties. What is this I hear about you resigning from your law firm?"

242

We spent the next two hours talking about old times. "Big Bob, when Kathy died, my love for the practice of law died. I don't have it anymore. I don't know what I'm going to do."

"Where are you going from here?" Robert asked.

"I don't know, Robert. I need to do something different."

"Look I want to help you in any way I can. If you need help, I've got an opening in Fort Walton Beach, Florida. We need someone to run our title office there. Look, it's not trial work, but you'll receive a paycheck every month and we have full benefits. I won't fire you and you can go to the beach every day."

It was the perfect solution.

*****

In a matter of weeks, I had moved my life to Fort Walton Beach, Florida. Running titles in a laid-back beach town provided quite a contrast from the high-pressure law practice at Ferguson, Thomas and McDonald. The people were different. They shed all formality. Every day I went to work at the law firm in a coat and tie. Here you were out of uniform in a coat and tie.

It all went okay for a matter of months, but I soon learned I wasn't built for a laid-back life style. I had some very competent people in my office that loved what they did, but I did not. I found that I missed Terri Beth and called her every day. She had stayed with the law firm to fill in for Brook and Phillip and kept me informed of what was going on.

I wanted to hire her as my secretary and bring her to Florida, but I knew Southern Title would never pay her what she was worth. Besides, she would be bored to death, like me. Day after day the routine was the same. Check titles. Close loans. Details. Paper work. The money was good, but I was bored to death. I knew why I hadn't liked the property courses in law school. I wondered if I had not made a big mistake leaving the law firm.

I had just hung up the phone with Terri Beth when it rang again. It was Donnie Lee.

"How are you?" I asked.

"Not so good. We just got the opinion from the court of appeals. They denied our motion for a new trial. The vote was three to two. Those same old silk stocking judges voted against us. Their opinion was stupid. It had nothing to do with the law. They just hate plaintiff lawyers. Dixie thinks we need to file a motion for reconsideration. I disagree. I think we need to file a writ of certiorari directly to the Supreme Court. It's our last shot."

"I'm sorry you lost, Donnie Lee. What else is happening?"

"We've got a hot race for governor going on here. Thomas Burnett, the guy you clerked for in law school just might have a shot at being elected governor. He's running a real populist campaign. He is gaining in the polls every day and he just might make it."

"Wouldn't that be a hoot—a plaintiff lawyer as governor," I said.

Donnie Lee was quiet for a moment. "How are you doing?"

"The truth? I'm bored to death. I miss the courtroom. I miss you guys. I miss Terri Beth. Donnie Lee, I believe those bastards at First Fidelity murdered Kathy. I don't think I could ever come back."

The phone rang again. "Damn," I said. "Is this Grand Central Station around here?"

Jenny, our new receptionist at the title insurance company, buzzed in. "Mr. McDonald., there's a gentleman on line one who says he is a Don Pollard and needs to talk with you immediately. I told him you were very busy and I tried to take a number, but he was very persistent in talking with you."

"That's okay, Jenny. I'll take his call." I wanted to talk to Don, but I feared what he might have to say. I picked up the receiver.

"Is this the wimp lawyer who used to practice law in Conecuh, and after losing his first case quit and ran off to Florida to check titles?"

"I lost *two* cases, you smart ass, and neither one of them were to you."

"How *are* things in the sunshine state?" Don asked.

"Don't tell anybody up there, Don, but just between you and me, I'm bored out of my skull. I'm about ready to sell used cars or come work for you and get me a government paycheck."

"Hey, we've got a place for you, but you'll have to promise to bring Terri Beth with you."

"Mr. District Attorney, you had better keep your paws off her. You are a married man and I'll represent your wife Cynthia for free. I'm a widower and I'm not even allowed to date her yet."

He laughed. "Listen, Jake, this isn't a social call. I'm at a phone booth down the street from the courthouse and I'm about to ruin your afternoon.

"We had the state fire marshal's office on the scene the morning after your fire. I wanted to cover all the bases so I called in the GBI and hired your old friend, Dr. Utz, to conduct his own investigation. I was willing to pay him out of my office budget, but when he found out it was your wife and house, he refused to take a dime. I've received both the fire marshal's report and Dr. Utz's today at the same time. Let me read you the first sentence of Dr. Utz's report. In all caps. Quote, *'This is clearly a case of arson.'*"

My blood ran cold.

"Now, let me read you the *last* paragraph of the state fire marshal's report. 'All of the scientific evidence from our investigation clearly shows that an accelerant was used to start this fire. Chemical analysis shows that the most probable accelerant was a chemical compound widely used in the Vietnam conflict. It is our conclusion based upon the evidence that this is a clear case of arson.'"

I felt very weak.

"Jake, Kathy was murdered," Don shouted. "I'm going to find out who did this, my friend. And then I'm going to prosecute them, and then I'm going to convict them, and I promise you one thing, my friend. I will be there to personally pull the switch on the Georgia electric chair and watch the son of a bitch die.

I was crying and I could not respond.

"Jake, I'm sorry to bring you this bad news, but I felt you needed to know the truth. Kathy was a sweet lady. You are a decent human being. Y'all didn't deserve this."

"Do we need to call in the FBI?" I asked.

"Not just yet. I've kept Barksdale Clements apprised of the situation and he has advised me that the U.S. attorney's office is closely monitoring the situation. The FBI is conducting its own investigation into a closely collateral matter. He wouldn't say what. He was deeply moved by your loss. He couldn't believe that you quit practicing law and moved to Florida. Hey, I need to come to see you soon. You need to show me how to do some deep-sea fishing. You are in the best deep sea fishing spot in the world."

"Any time, Don. Please make it soon, and keep me informed."

"I will."

"Goodbye."

I was sick. "Jenny, something has come up and I'll be away for the rest of the afternoon."

"Are you all right, Mr. McDonald?"

"Yeah. I just need to take care of some personal business matters related with Kathy's estate. I'll see you sometime tomorrow."

I stopped by Big Mamma's liquor store on the way back to my condominium. I purchased a three-liter bottle of Jack Daniel. I felt the big mean coming on. It was Tuesday, but I intended to get drunk. I set up the grill on my balcony overlooking the Choctawhatchee Bay. The charter boats were just beginning to come in for the afternoon. They were always loaded with large catches of snapper, trigger fish, grouper, and amberjack. I would give anything right now to own a charter boat and get out of the boring stuff I was doing. I would volunteer to be a deckhand on a charter boat for free if I could get away from my miserable existence.

I had just finished off a porterhouse steak and about a pint of Jack Daniel when the phone rang. "Damn, I hope it's not somebody at the office with a title problem."

It was a familiar voice. "Hello, Mr. Title Jockey."

"This must be my partner in crime, Mr. Donnie Lee Booker."

"He was when I got up this morning. Jake, you sound like you have a cold."

"No, Donnie Lee. I'm three sheets to the wind. Stay off that booze. It's bad for you. I'm trying to drown some bad news I got today."

"I'm sorry. Let me give you some good news."

"Go ahead. I need all the good news I can get."

"Do you know what today is in Georgia?"

"It's November third, the same day as it is in Florida."

"Well, it might be, but it's election day here and your old boss Mr. Thomas M. Burnett has just been elected governor of the state of Georgia by fifty-five percent of the vote. Can you believe that?"

"You're kidding me. I knew I should have stayed with that firm. I could have been the Fish and Game Commissioner of Georgia—a free hunting and fishing license and everything."

He laughed. "You need to give him a call tomorrow after you both sober up and tell him to appoint some real plaintiff judges to the bench, and tell him to get rid of all those silk stocking clowns."

"Donnie Lee, I have no doubt he will do that. How is Dixie?"

"Jake, I hope this won't go anywhere else, but I'm in love. Dixie is so wonderful. I'm about ready to take the plunge."

"I've always known that, Donnie Lee, from the first time I caught y'all screwing in the library."

"What did you say?"

"Yeah, I saw y'all, about a year ago."

"You rat. How long were you there?"

"Long enough, about a minute.

" Jake. I'm going to kill you."

I laughed. "Hey, she's a beautiful woman, Donnie Lee. You couldn't find a better one. Marry her. Y'all deserve each other."

"Jake, what are you going to do? The word around here is that you're not happy being a title jockey."

"And I suppose that information was leaked to you by a young lady by the name of Ms. Terri Beth Flynt?"

"As a matter of fact, it was."

"Donnie Lee, I have been devastated this year. We lost the First Fidelity case, Kelli died and I lost Kathy. And today I just got the final blow, and the reason I'm getting drunk now. Don Pollard called. No one is to know this. Don had the state fire marshal's office and the GBI to investigate the fire. He also hired Dr. Utz to do an independent investigation. They all came to the same conclusion. The fire was arson. Donnie Lee, Kathy was murdered!"

There was total silence on the other end of the line.

" Jake, how long have you known this?"

"Only since this afternoon. Please don't tell anyone, especially Terri Beth. It might kill her. Let me tell her at the appropriate time. Donnie Lee, Don Pollard is livid. He says he's going to personally pull the switch on the killer. I'm going to be right beside him. I'm going to pull the switch twice. Once for killing my wife and once for killing my poor innocent dog."

"Jake, I know who did this."

"You don't have to say it, Donnie Lee. So do I. We just can't prove it yet."

"Yet," he said. "Let me turn the investigator at my law firm loose. He will find these murderers."

"Please coordinate everything through Don. I trust him. He has always shot straight with me."

"Okay, my friend. When are you coming home? We need you back."

"Gosh, I don't know. I don't think I would be much of a lawyer right now."

"Jake, you're kidding yourself. You're one hell of a lawyer, and you know it. You and Terri Beth are an awesome team."

"How is my favorite secretary?"

"She is as gorgeous as ever, but her spirits have been down since you left. Jake, she misses you so much. She talks about you every day. She wants you back."

Donnie Lee, I hurt so badly right now that I'm afraid if Terri Beth and I got together it might be a rebound thing after Kathy's death. But God knows I could fall in love with that woman. It's such a shame that her husband was killed in that plane crash. He was one lucky guy to be married to her. I wish he were still around to write a book on how he convinced her to marry him. I'd buy his book."

"So would I. Jake McDonald, we are going to somehow win this appeal. Then I want you to move back to Georgia and then we are going to win this case. We are going to win a big verdict and put these corrupt bankers out of business. We are going to collect every dime of the verdict plus interest, and then you and I are going to have a double wedding ceremony. I'll walk Dixie down the aisle and you'll walk Terri Beth down the aisle."

"Donnie Lee, I think you're drunker than I am. I'll call governor-elect Burnett in the morning. Good night."

I was wide-awake. It was eight a.m. and my head was throbbing. I crawled into the bathroom and reached for the aspirin bottle. Why did I do this to myself? Kathy would kill me if she saw me in this condition. I have to quit drinking. I was becoming an alcoholic. Was I powerless over alcohol?

I popped two aspirins and filled my coffee cup with a teaspoon of instant coffee and water. I popped it into the microwave and set the controls for two minutes. I sipped the hot coffee slowly. I needed to get some food in my stomach, but I couldn't bear the thought of cooking anything. I finished my cup of coffee, got dressed quickly, and headed to the Silver Dollar Pancake House. They served a generous helping of eggs, bacon, toast, grits, and coffee for $2.99. I ate there often. Sunny Weis was my favorite waitress. I often wondered why she worked as a waitress. She was a Ph.D. in the science of human nature. She was street smart.

"How's it going, Mr. McD? Looks like you were out partying last night."

"I wish, Sunny. I had to drink off some bad news."

"It couldn't be that bad, Mr. McD. That's no way to treat your body. You want the usual?"

"Yeah, sunny side up on the eggs."

I slipped outside and dropped three quarters in the *Atlanta Journal/Constitution* machine. I never figured out why the Silver Dollar had so many different newspaper machines from all over the United States. But I enjoyed buying a copy of a Georgia newspaper and keeping up with the news in my home state.

I was half-asleep and hung over, but two stories caught my immediate attention. The headline screamed out at me:

THOMAS BURNETT ELECTED GOVERNOR WITH 55% OF VOTE.

I smiled. At least I could say I worked for somebody who had achieved fame. Tom was a brilliant, hard-working lawyer who made his money in medical malpractice cases. I never knew what possessed him to go into politics. I guess the trial lawyers were getting beaten up so much in the legislature that they anointed him as their leader. I was surprised he was able to survive the onslaught of all the medical and insurance company money that was thrown against him. But, I believed he would be a good governor. I was proud of him. When my head cleared up, I would give him a call.

The second story that caught my attention was in the lower left-hand corner of the front page. The headline read:

JUSTICE GUYTON GUNN ADMITTED TO PIEDMONT HOSPITAL.

Justice Gunn was an appointee of the Bailey administration. He came from a silk stocking law firm in Atlanta and he had worked his way up the ladder to Chief Justice. He was a notorious defense attorney and had an obvious bias for the insurance industry.

It was 9:45 a.m. I called the office. "Jenny, this is Jake. I'll be coming in late this morning. I'm not feeling too well. Anything going on?"

"Not really, Mr. McDonald. Things are sort of slow this morning."

"Good," I said. "I'll get there when I can."

I went back to my condo. I showered and shaved. My head was beginning to clear. I called Governor-elect Thomas M. Burnett.

"Hello."

I was surprised that Tom answered the phone. "Is this Mr. Thomas M. Burnett?"

"Yes, it is."

"This is Ezra Higgins of the Federal Elections Commission and we are going to have to seek an injunction to freeze the election results in Georgia. Apparently the medical association and the insurance industry have discovered that you have been making too much money lately."

"Jake McDonald, I would recognize that voice anywhere. You can't fool me. How are you?"

"Congratulations, Mr. Governor."

"Hey, Jake, it has been a roller coaster ride. How are you doing?"

"Not so good, Tom." I related the events of the last year and the latest news I had received from Don Pollard. Tom had heard about my losses. "Jake, look, if you want to do something up here, come back to Georgia. I have a lot of appointments to make. I can get you any job you want in the state government."

"Tom, just appoint some of our kind of people to the Court of Appeals and Supreme Court."

"You can count on that, Jake."

*****

The next few weeks were slow and dull. I spent my evenings walking down the beach and wondering where I should go, and what course my life would take. I was not happy running a title plant. If only somehow I could shake this black cloud that was hovering over me, and I could get back into the courtroom where I would be happy again. I thought about taking the Florida bar exam. I couldn't bear the thought of studying for another bar examination.

I picked up the mail at the post office. There was a letter addressed to me from the Burnett Inauguration Committee. The stationary was embossed in gold foil and was expensive. Inside was an invitation to attend the inauguration of Governor-elect Thomas M. Burnett and two tickets to the inaugural ball on January eighth. Beneath the signature of the inaugural committee chairman was a handwritten note. "Jake, I hope you will join me for the celebration. I have enclosed an extra ticket for the ball just in case you have someone special you would like to invite. I would love to see you again. Thanks, Tom."

I was moved. Yes, there was someone special I would love to invite. I didn't know if she would go. It would be very awkward.

*****

255

I had always spent either Thanksgiving or Christmas with Kathy's parents or mine. I intended to go home for the Christmas holidays. It was a good time to get away from the title plant and just relax. There were always some high school classmates I enjoyed being with, and the dove hunting in South Georgia was the best anywhere in the world.

The smell of the morning dew of a South Georgia peanut field compares to nothing else. Wick Fields and Phil Anderson were my closest high school buddies. We had hunted together since we were ten. The doves were flying everywhere. I had forgotten what a good dove shoot was all about. We killed our limit by about one o'clock. We cleaned the birds, iced them down, and stopped by the Varsity Drive Inn for lunch. It was the hangout for all teenagers, the favorite make-out spot for every teenager who ever grew up in my hometown.

It was December 23rd. My mind wandered back to Kathy and how lonely this Christmas was going to be. This would be the first Christmas since our marriage that I had spent without her. I pulled into the driveway and my mother met me at the front door. "Jake, you just got a call from a Donnie Lee Booker. He said it was extremely urgent. He's called twice already. He wanted you to call him the minute you came in. Here's his number." I sat down at the phone table in the hallway. I dialed Donnie Lee's number.

"Hello, Donnie Lee Booker," the voice at the other end answered.

"Donnie Lee, Jake. What's up?"

"Jake! Where have you been? I've been trying to reach you all day."

"I've been out with some of my old high school buddies, killing God's little creatures."

"Jake, I hope you didn't kill too many of them, because God just moved over to our side."

"What are you talking about, Donnie Lee?"

"Jake, I just got an opinion from the Supreme Court. The Supreme Court just granted our writ for certiorari. They voted four to two in our favor. That old bastard Gunn was sick so he didn't vote. It wouldn't have made any difference. Jake, we have finally won a round."

"Thank God." I was shaking. "Where do we go from here?"

"Oral argument is set for February 14. Jake, we might have a chance at this. Dixie and I will get busy on the brief and oral argument."

"Donnie Lee, this is the best news I've heard in months. Do you need for me to do anything?"

"Not on the appeal, I want you to spend the next few weeks getting yourself mentally and physically prepared for the new trial. Jake, if we win an appeal you can't let us down. You must come back and try this case. Only you have the guts to do it."

I drove to a pay phone next to the Starlight Bowling Lanes. I didn't want my parents to overhear my conversation. I dialed Terri Beth's home number. The phone rang twice. She answered. "Hello?"

"Hello, sunshine."

"Jake, how are you?"

"Today I am wonderful, sweetheart. We were granted a writ of certiorari in the Supreme Court."

She squealed out loud. "Jake, I knew it! God, I prayed every night for this. We are going to win, Jake, believe me. We are going to win."

"We have a long way to go yet, sweetheart, but oral arguments are set for February 14th."

"Do you know what day that is, Jake?"

"I have no idea, Terri Beth."

"You un-romantic goose. It's Valentine's Day."

"I'm sorry, Terri Beth, but I haven't seen too much romance lately. Which reminds me of one of the reasons I'm calling you. Terri Beth, this is very awkward for me, so I hope you'll understand. I'm really embarrassed and I don't want to seem too forward or out of line. Terri Beth, Tom Burnett was my old boss back in law school. I was his law clerk and I managed his first campaign for the House of Representatives. He has invited me to the inauguration and sent me two tickets to the inaugural ball. I wonder if you would join me in Atlanta. Hell, Terri Beth, I don't know how to ask a woman for a date anymore."

She laughed out loud. "What's the matter, Jake McDonald? Do you actually think I would turn down an invitation to attend the inaugural ball for the governor of Georgia with a handsome lawyer? What if I were to say yes?"

I was silent. "You will go?"

"Silly, I'd love to."

"Does this mean that you will dance with me?"

She laughed. "I'll have to get a new evening gown. I'll get something that will show a little cleavage and drive you nuts."

"Terri Beth, you are wicked. You are totally corrupt."

"Jake, I'm proud of you. You are one terrific lawyer and the greatest friend I've ever had. You need to get back to practicing law here with us. If we win this case on appeal, will you come back?"

"We'll talk about it, sunshine. In the meantime I'm going to RSVP our reservation. I guess I need to check some books out of the library on what to do on a first date. It's been so long."

She laughed. "You don't need to do that, Jake. I'll give you a quick lesson. First, be your old sweet self. Second, don't step on my toes at the ball. "I'll call you again, sunshine. I'm really excited that you're going with me."

I decided that I would go home and tell my parents that I was taking my old secretary to the inauguration. I didn't want them to think I was dating too soon after Kathy's death. I walked into the den and the news was on the television. I caught the tale end of a story about Guyton Gunn, the chief justice of the Georgia Supreme Court. Apparently he had had a heart attack while he was sitting on the bench. The news reporter said that he had been admitted to the cardiac intensive care unit at Crawford W. Long Hospital and was in critical condition. Justice Gunn had been on the bench for decades. He was an appointee of Governor Bailey and was known to favor insurance companies and big business. He was defense-oriented to say the least. I didn't wish the man any harm, but maybe he would retire and let the plaintiffs win a case once in a while.

My mother was out Christmas shopping so I sat down and told my father about my plans to attend the inauguration. He asked me all about Terri Beth. He seemed excited that I was going out with someone. "Dad, I'm not marrying the lady. I'm just taking her to a dance. Kathy really liked her. I know you will too."

I left and drove downtown. An old James Bond movie, *Goldfinger*, was playing at the old Martin Theater. I hadn't been in there in years. I decided to go. Maybe it would take my mind off Kathy for a little while. The movie lasted a little over two hours. I decided to drive by the Varsity, my old teenage hangout. I stopped and got one of my boyhood favorites, a cherry Coke. Bill MacKay, the owner, always put plenty of cherry juice in his cherry Cokes.

When I arrived at home, my mother was still up. "And the funeral services will be held at Christ Episcopal Church on Piedmont Road."

"What was that?" I asked.

"Justice Gunn died this afternoon."

"What?"

"Yeah, it was a massive heart attack."

"That's too bad. I never liked the guy, but I hate to see him die. He always ruled against my firm."

"Tell me, Jake, who is this Terri Beth Flynt you're going to be taking to the inauguration?"

"She's just my former secretary, Mother."

"Well, she's more that just your secretary. Your father says she is real cute."

"Daddy, I'm going to sue you."

He laughed.

"Well, tell us, Jake, is she as pretty as Kathy?"

"Oh, Mother." I blushed. "You'll get to meet her one day. I'll bring her home. You'll like her, I promise."

*****

Atlanta traffic was terrible as usual. All the hotels were packed. "Where are we going to stay, Jake?"

"I rented the honeymoon suite at the Hilton," I laughed.

"Well, if that's the case then we had better arrange a quickie marriage. Before I sleep with you I want to make sure I'll have you on a permanent basis. No one-night stands."

I laughed. "No, sunshine, I got us two separate rooms. They don't even have connecting doors. I didn't want to push my luck with you."

"Shucks," she said. "I was getting excited about doing some sinning."

We both laughed.

We checked into the Hilton and there was a bottle of Dom Perignon in the champagne bucket. The note said, "We hope you and Terri Beth will enjoy this." It was signed, "The Firm." *Damn, I miss those guys.*

Terri Beth and I had dinner at Nicholi's on top of the hotel. It was famous for its revolving dining room and its cuisine. The meal was delicious. "Jake, I hope you'll like my dress. I bought it at Neiman Marcus two weeks ago."

"I can't wait to see you in it," I said. "I've got a little surprise for you after the ball. The firm sent it."

"What is it?"

"I'm not going to tell you. It's a surprise."

"Come on, just a hint."

"Well, don't drink too much champagne at the ball." I grinned.

Thomas M. Burnett had been sworn in as Georgia's forty-seventh governor at noon on the steps of the capitol. He would bring a different type of leadership to Georgia. Everyone predicted he would be a progressive governor. He had offered me a job as a law clerk in my junior year of law school and I wound up managing his first political campaign. We beat an incumbent for the state House of Representatives. He had been forever grateful for my efforts.

I knocked on Terri Beth's door.

"Just a minute," she said. She opened the door. "Surprise."

"Terri Beth, is that you? My God, you are drop-dead gorgeous." Her hair was up. She had on diamond earrings and a black silk dress with a plunging neckline. She was wearing black high heels and she smelled wonderful. I always loved her

262

perfume. "I don't think I'm going to let you out of my sight tonight. You should be required to get a license to go out in public looking that good."

"Help me with my coat, you silly goose. I want to see if you know how to dance."

I slipped her mink coat around her shoulders. It was a cold January night in Atlanta. I was proud to show off my beautiful date. I hoped I would run into some of my old lawyer friends. They would be jealous.

The reception line was long. Governor Burnett was dressed in long tails and a white tie. The first lady was wearing an elegant white evening gown. We approached and Tom recognized me immediately. "Hello, stranger. Jake McDonald, how have you been?"

"I think you know how I've been, Governor."

"I'm so sorry, Jake. I'm going to make sure the GBI catches the murderers. Please stick around for the reception. I've got some good news I want to share with you. Who is this gorgeous lady you have with you?"

"Terri Beth, please meet the new governor of Georgia, my friend Thomas M. Burnett. Governor, this is Ms. Terri Beth Flynt."

"How are you? I want to know how Jake McDonald convinced you to go out with him."

"He's real special to me, Mr. Governor. I used to be his secretary."

"Sweetie, you can come to work in the governor's office any time you want."

She grinned.

I recognized Gene Hemmings, an old classmate of mine from law school. "Gene, my friend, how are you?"

"Jake, McDonald, it's been over five years. Where are you practicing law?"

"I'm not, Gene. My wife died this year and I moved to Florida. I'm running a title insurance company."

"Oh, Jake, I'm sorry to hear that. Who is this lady with you?"

"Terri Beth, this is Gene Hemmings. Gene, this is Terri Beth Flynt from Conecuh." I could see Gene eyeing Terri Beth. Who couldn't notice such a beautiful creature?

The receiving line was winding down and the guests were beginning to spread out over the ballroom. The champagne was flowing. I felt good for the first time since the tragic fire. This was the way life was supposed to be. I wondered what Kathy would have looked like if she had been here with me. One must live in the present. There was no going back. Terri Beth was absolutely beautiful tonight. I remembered Kathy teasing me that night, saying if anything ever happened to her that Terri Beth would be her choice to replace her. Well, here I was.

Governor Burnett moved towards us. "Jake, could I talk to you for a second?"

"Sure, Mr. Governor."

"Jake, you know I'm going to have to fill the vacancy on the Supreme Court for Justice Gunn's seat. No, I'm not going to appoint you. He laughed. You're too young. Hang around. I might send you up there. Anyway, I'm going to nominate Adam Harris."

I grinned from ear to ear. *Thank you, God. We'll finally have a friend on the bench.*

"You must swear not to tell anybody. I don't want this leaked to the press. I want to make sure I have the confirmation votes lined up in the Senate. It won't be a problem. The Judiciary Chairman is a close friend of mine."

"Thank you, Mr. Governor," I said.

"What was that all about?" asked Terri Beth.

"Sweetheart, I swore not to tell, but if I get a kiss tonight my resistance will weaken."

The band began to play. "Come on, Mr. Attorney-at-law. Let's see if you know how to dance."

I pulled Terri Beth close to me and we glided across the dance floor. She was as graceful as a swan. Terri Beth knew how to dance. I prayed I wouldn't step on her feet. I would never hear the last of it. She was a good fast dancer too. She moved in a tantalizing and provocative fashion.

We danced until midnight. The band was playing "Georgia On My Mind" when we left.

"I have a surprise for you in the hotel room," I said.

"Oh, are you going to seduce me now?" she laughed.

"Maybe," I said.

We returned to my hotel room. The bottle of Dom Perignon was chilled to just the right temperature. "Here." I handed her the note.

"Oh, aren't they sweet?"

I placed two champagne glasses on the table and popped the cork. "I would like to propose a toast to the sweetest lady in my life right now."

"Oh, Jake. I would like to propose a toast to my secret lover with whom I'm deeply in love."

I blushed. We sipped the champagne.

"This is delicious," she said.

"It ought to be. It's a hundred dollars a bottle."

She almost choked. "I feel guilty drinking it," she said.

"Don't feel guilty. There's not an employee in that firm who has worked harder or who is more loyal than you, Terry Beth Flynt."

A tear rolled down her cheek. I kissed her.

"Jake, I meant what I said in my toast."

"Terri Beth, I meant what I said in mine."

Our lips came closer together. They met. My tongue went deep inside her mouth. Hers went deep inside mine. We were both aroused. We warmly embraced. She ran her hand between our legs. She knew I was ready for her. My hand moved across her breasts. They were full and firm. She began to unzip the back of her dress. Her dress fell off her shoulders. "Jake, I want you. Let's sleep together tonight. I need you, Jake."

I pulled back. "Terri Beth, I want you now more than anything in the world. You are so beautiful. But let me say something before we get carried away. I do hope you'll understand. Before she died Kathy and I were teasing each other, and I asked her who she would want me to marry if anything happened to her. She said, 'Terri Beth.'"

266

Terri Beth started to cry.

"And it happened, sunshine. She's dead."

We embraced. God, I wanted her. Maybe we should go to bed and make love all night. Maybe that's what I needed to get Kathy out of my mind.

"Sweetheart, I made a promise to myself on Kathy's death bed that I would never get involved with another woman until her killers were caught and put away. I feel that I would be cheating on her if I didn't keep my promise. It's not you, Terri Beth. It's me. God knows I love you. Terri Beth, there is no other woman in this world I would rather have than you. You are brilliant. You are beautiful. You are fun, and when we are married you will be what every man wants—a trophy wife."

"Did you say when we are married?" she asked.

"Did I say that?"

"Yes, you did." She gave me a passionate kiss.

"I guess it was a Freudian slip." I looked her in the eye. "But damn it. I meant it. That was not a marriage proposal. Let's just call it a pre-marriage proposal. Sort of a preemptive strike."

"Jake McDonald, you are so precious. I love you.

"Terri Beth, I need to get these issues resolved first. Then I'll do anything you want to do. If our relationship results in marriage I'll be the happiest man alive. If we can't make that commitment then I'm willing to live together. I need you in my life."

We poured another glass of champagne and lay down next to each other on the bed. She snuggled up next to me. The champagne took its toll. We both fell asleep.

*****

"My God, it's seven o'clock in the morning," Terri Beth exclaimed. "I've got to get out of here."

"Where are you going, sweetheart? I was just having sweet dreams about you."

"You can't see me like this, Jake. I'm a mess. Call me in about an hour. I need to get a shower." She looked back at me. "I enjoyed last night. I love you." She winked and left.

The trip back to Conecuh was very pleasant. Although Terri Beth and I had not had an intimate encounter, I felt that wonderful glow. She was to be the woman of my life. I was in love. I enjoyed her sitting next to me in the car. "Jake, I want you back in the law firm," she said. "I don't like working for anyone but you."

"Sweetheart, one day maybe I'll be working for you."

She sighed out loud. "Jake, I can't help it. I could never, ever replace Kathy, and I know how deep your loss is, but I do love you so much. Yes, I was teasing you last night, but nothing would mean more to me than to snuggle up next to you every night. I would love to make passionate love to you all the time."

I began to blush. "Terri Beth, don't turn me on. I'm trying to get us home." She snuggled next to me. God, was this really happening to me?

We arrived two hours later and we dropped Terri Beth's luggage off at her apartment. "Terri Beth, let's go pay a visit to the law firm. I'd like to see the guys again."

We pulled into the driveway. The place was the same. Terri Beth used her key as we entered the back door. "Hello, is anyone here?" she shouted.

Dixie stuck her head around the corner of the library. "Terri Beth, you're home. Jake, it's you." She threw her arms around me. It had been a long time since I had seen Dixie.

Donnie Lee came into the hallway. "Jake, how are you?"

"Pretty good for a title jockey. How are you?"

"You've lost some weight," he said.

"Yeah, no more of Kathy's home cooking, I guess."

"Come on in. We're working on the brief to the Supreme Court."

It was about five o'clock. The other lawyers and secretaries of the firm were glad to see us. It was like a class reunion. I was glad to be back with old friends.

 We've got a lot to talk about."

Dixie, Terri Beth, Donnie Lee, and I sat in Kelli's old office and exchanged war stories. Then the discussion turned serious. "Donnie Lee, what are our chances with the Supremes?" I asked.

"Fifty-fifty, Jake. Dixie just made an astonishing discovery today in the trial transcript. You won't believe this, but Anthony Jacobs was never put under oath. It was apparently a mistake on his lawyer's part, but nowhere does the record show that he was administered an oath. The case law is clear. No oath, and the testimony is not admissible, i.e., a new trial."

"Donnie Lee, surely this is a mistake on the court reporter's part. Maybe she just failed to enter it on the record."

"Nope, I had the court reporter replay the original tape back for me. Anthony Jacobs was not administered an oath. He would have lied under oath if one were administered. It's a very technical point, but it might give us a shot at a new trial. I believe our two jurors were pressured into consenting to a majority rather than a unanimous verdict. But you are familiar with the long line of legal precedent which says a juror can't impeach his own verdict. We'll argue this point, but I don't think we can win with this argument."

I was about to drop a bombshell and to break a promise I had made at the same time.

"I need to swear you all to complete secrecy. I am about to make your day."

"What is it, Jake?" Donnie Lee asked.

"Our old friend, Thomas M. Burnett, the new governor of Georgia, gave me my first job as a law clerk. I ran his first campaign for the state house. He trusts me like a brother, so I don't think he would mind me telling you what I'm about to tell you. If it leaks from this room it might be over. Terri Beth, do you remember when the governor pulled me off to the side at the reception?"

"Yeah, Jake, why?"

"Tom told me that he was going to appoint Adam Harris as the new Supreme Court justice to fill Justice Gunn's spot."

"Holy shit!" shouted Donnie Lee. "Oh, my God. Thank you, Lord." He hugged my neck.

Dixie began to cry. She hugged my neck.

"Hey, I'm getting jealous," said Terri Beth. She gave me a warm embrace.

"Jake, do you know what this does to our case?" asked Donnie Lee.

"Yeah. I hope it gives you a new trial, pal."

"It's *we*. *We* are going to try this case together and win it."

"I don't know, Donnie Lee. I lost more than just a case with this one. I lost my wife."

Terri Beth broke down and stormed out of the room.

"What's her problem, Jake?" he asked.

"She's real emotional right now, Donnie Lee. We became very close over the past few days. I think we are both in love."

Donnie Lee and Dixie looked at each other and grinned. "I knew it," Dixie said. "Double wedding."

"Double wedding," said Donnie Lee.

Terri Beth returned to the room. "I'm sorry, but I'm real sensitive right now."

"Hell, sunshine, Dixie has already picked out your wedding dress for you."

She gave Dixie a hug.

"Look, I've got to get going. Keep me posted on the brief. Oral arguments are scheduled for February 14th. I'll see what I can find out from the governor's office."

My ride back to Fort Walton was occupied with thoughts of the past few days and of Terri Beth. I fantasized about winning the First Fidelity suit and taking Terri Beth on a round-the-world honeymoon cruise. She was a beautiful lady. I was in love with her.

I had settled back into my old routine of checking titles and closing loans. It was the same old boring stuff day after day. There is one advantage to living on the Gulf coast. It's the beach. I took long walks every night down the sugar white beaches of Fort Walton and Destin. There is something about the sea breeze blowing against your face off the Gulf waters that calms your soul. I would stop by the water's edge and stare out into the Gulf waters. I would think of all my old clients, the many memories, Kathy, the fire, and my old dog Loophole, and I would cry. I had to move out of the past. I needed to somehow get back into the fight. My life was in the courtroom, not closing loans.

Always at the edge of my thoughts was Terri Beth. Some days I tried to block her out of my mind. More and more she was occupying my thoughts. Especially at night. God, I missed Terri Beth. I missed her perfume. I missed her touch. I missed her hugs. I laughed out loud. Hell, I didn't even know if she could cook.

The weeks rolled on. At five o'clock on the afternoon of February 14th, Donnie Lee called. He said that the argument before the Supreme Court went well. "Jake, you don't know what a difference Justice Harris means on the bench. He was polite. He had a sense of humor. And, for once, I felt empathy from a Supreme Court justice. I don't know. It could go either way. I just pray it goes our way."

"Hey, you did your best. When do you think you'll hear something?" I asked.

"Six weeks at the earliest," he said.

"Let's keep our fingers crossed."

"Jake, you need to give Dixie a special pat on the back. She argued the last five minutes of our allotted time. She was good. I'm not saying that because I'm in love with her, but she's turning into a good lawyer."

"Donnie Lee, you win this appeal and I will dance at your wedding."

"Dance at *our* wedding, Mr. McDonald."

"I don't know about that, Donnie Lee. I'm still in denial. Any word on the investigation?"

"Jake, I don't know what's up, but Don Pollard has had a grand jury tied up for two weeks solid."

"He's a good man, Donnie Lee. He's going to get Kathy's killer. How's my favorite secretary?"

"You need to get back here. She's love struck. She keeps a picture of the two of you at the inaugural ball behind her desk. You didn't tell me about how good she looked in that dress."

I laughed.

Terri Beth and I had kept in close contact throughout the ensuing weeks. She wanted me to come back. I resisted with every flimsy excuse I could think of. If I came back, I knew what would happen. I would have to break my promise to Kathy. More than winning the case against First Fidelity I wanted Kathy's killer on death row. Then I would let Terri Beth take my heart.

It was March 20th. I had just finished my two o'clock closing when the phone rang. Jenny said, "Mr. McDonald, Terri Beth is on line one." She knew Terri Beth's voice by now. They got along well.

"Mr. McDonald, this is someone who wants to be very special in your life."

"Listen, if this is a sexually harassing telephone call, I know who you are. I'm going to report you to the telephone company, then I'm going to sexually molest you and make love with you for at least twenty-four hours before I let you up for air."

She laughed. "I'm on my way."

"Sweetheart, what's up?"

"Jake, I hope you're not planning on going anywhere today."

"Why, sweetheart?"

"Jake, I'm serious now. Donnie Lee and Dixie are on their way down there. They left two hours ago. They need to see you. Don't leave."

"What's the problem, sunshine?"

"There's no problem. Just be available. I'll call you tomorrow." She hung up.

Terri Beth's call shook me up. At exactly five o'clock Donnie Lee and Dixie drove into the parking lot. Jenny was just leaving. "Mr. McDonald, there are some people here to see you. I think you know who they are."

"Jenny, send them on in."

Donnie Lee and Dixie rushed into my office. Before I could say a word Donnie Lee said, "Jake, have you got any ice?"

"Yeah, there's an ice maker down the hall."

Dixie got up and went down the hall. "What is going on?"

"I'll wait until Dixie gets back."

Several minutes later Dixie returned with a bucket of ice and some glasses. Donnie Lee pulled out a bottle of Jack Daniel and a bottle of Chivas Regal. He poured us all stiff drinks. "Jake, sit down."

"I don't know, Donnie Lee. I'm about to die in anticipation."

They both laughed.

"Jake McDonald, don't you ever say your friends let you down. We are your real friends." He reached inside his coat pocket and pulled out an envelope. It had a return address of the Supreme Court of Georgia. Atlanta, Georgia. "Take a sniff of this." He threw the envelope across my desk. I recognized the onion skin paper as an opinion from the Supreme Court. It was a thick opinion—about fifteen pages.

When you get an appellate opinion, lawyers always flip to the last page where they're told whether they won or lost. Affirmed or reversed. That's all that matters. I couldn't resist. I flipped to the last page of the opinion. The last sentence read in all caps. JUDGMENT REVERSED AND VACATED AND A NEW TRIAL IS ORDERED. JUSTICE ADAM A. HARRIS, JUDGE. DECISION FOUR TO THREE. SANDERS DISSENTING.

I was stunned. My whole body was suddenly numb. I screamed out loud, "We won, we won, we won!" I began to cry. I hugged Donnie Lee. Then I hugged Dixie. "You wonderful guys did it. Donnie Lee, I love you. I love you." I couldn't believe it.

"Jake, it was your governor buddy, Tom Burnett. It was Harris' vote that made the difference."

"I haven't read the opinion, of course. What was the deciding factor?"

"It was Dixie's argument, about Jacobs not being sworn."

I grabbed Dixie and gave her a big kiss on the lips.

"Hey, that's my girlfriend you're kissing. Get your own," Donnie Lee laughed. "Speaking of which, your sweetie said for you to call her as soon as we broke the news."

I dialed Terri Beth's number. "Hello, is this the most wonderful woman in the world? The lady that hangs the moon and makes the sun shine?"

"I'm sorry but you must have the wrong number." She laughed. "Oh, Jake, they must be there."

"They are indeed, along with the wonderful news that has been long anticipated."

"Does that mean that you'll now do what you promised in our last telephone conversation—sexually molest me and make love to me for at least twenty-four hours before you let me up for air?"

"Terri Beth, I would walk on water for you right now. This is one hell of a day."

The rest of the evening was spent in celebration. "Donnie Lee, do you have a place to stay tonight?" I asked.

"We'll find some place on the strip."

"You won't either. I've got a spare bedroom. Dixie can sleep there and you can sleep on the sofa."

"You crazy bastard, you know where I'll be sleeping tonight."

Dixie blushed. I laughed.

Donnie Lee got real quiet. "Jake, Dixie, Terri Beth, and the rest of the firm have had many long conversations of what we would do if this day ever came. I know you as well as anyone else in the firm, except for perhaps Terri Beth, and I have her proxy. We want you to come back home and try this case. We won't take no for an answer. That is unacceptable. We are going to handcuff you, chain you up, and take you back. You owe it to our clients."

I was deeply moved. "Donnie Lee, I don't know. I died when Kathy died." Dixie had gone to the bedroom to get ready for bed. Donnie Lee and I were alone.

"Jake, I want to tell you something. Just man to man. You brought me into this case and introduced me to that wonderful lady in the other room. I have never loved a woman more in my life. After this case is over, we are going to get married. It's all because of you that I found her. Jake, no matter how much you want it to happen, you can never bring Kathy back. She loved you because you were a fighter. Do this for her. She would want you to win this one. Don't let the people who killed her get away with this. Don Pollard is going to catch them and you know it. He won't stop until he sees them fry in the electric chair.

"Jake, we need you. You're the only person that can connect with the jury. The clients believe in you. Hell, we won this case the last time. We got screwed. The jury was rigged. We all know that. We must come back at them with a vengeance—a legal vengeance . . .. Jake, I'm going to give you some free advice, for whatever it's worth. There's a certain lady back in Conecuh who is madly in love with you. She worships the ground you walk on. I believe that you have the same feelings towards her. Jake, Terri Beth is a gorgeous woman. She's smart, she's beautiful, she's polished, and she would make a perfect wife. Come back and win this case. Do it for your clients and then marry her."

I laughed. "Find out if she can cook. If she can, I'll come back and marry her. Go ask her."

*****

278

It was Sunday morning. The phone rang. I glanced at the clock; it was seven a.m. Who was calling me at this time of the morning? "Hello?"

"Jake."

"Sunshine, what are you doing calling me at this time of the morning?"

"Jake, I just wanted to call you to tell you that I love you. And I also wanted to invite you to dinner to prove I really can cook."

I laughed out loud. "Somebody has gotten the word to you. I'm going to kill him."

"Jake, if that's the only reason left for you to come back, I'll enroll in the Cordon Bleu school in Paris."

"Sunshine, if you can cook a hamburger on a grill, I'll be back. If you burn it, we'll go to the Burger King. I'm probably stupid as hell, but I'm going to do this. I'm coming back. I must be honest with you. I'm doing this for three people and for three people only—Kathy, Kelli, and you."

She broke up over the phone. "Jake, do this for Kathy and Kelli, not me. I love you, but do it for them."

"Terri Beth, do me a favor. Call Donnie Lee and Dixie and tell them. I'll call them later, but you need to tell them first. Terri Beth, I've got a lot of decisions to make. I have to resign here. They're not going to like that. I don't have a place to live. I have to get relocated."

"You can live here, Jake. I have plenty of room."

"Sunshine, you know I would love nothing more than that, but I couldn't try this case with you in my bedroom. I couldn't concentrate. We're going to win this case and when we do I am going to insist that you cook a seven-course dinner for me, and then I'm going to get upon my knees and then . . . ."

*****

It was two o'clock p.m. The phone rang. "Jake, Donnie Lee."

"You guys don't waste any time, do you, pal?"

"We can't, Jake. Judge Randall has put our case on the fast track. All the discovery has been done and she wants us to try it and get it out of her court."

"Donnie Lee, I've got to get out of here. I've got to give two weeks notice and wind this operation down. They're not going to like it, but I'm going to move as fast as I can. I'm going to list my condo with a Realtor friend, but I don't have a place to live. Terri Beth wants me to move in with her. God knows I'd love that, Donnie Lee, but I'd never be able to concentrate. We've got to win the case. I love that woman, but let's win the case first. I'm going to need to be able to support her."

Donnie Lee laughed out loud. "Jake, I believe you are truly lovesick. Congratulations. I share the same feelings about Dixie. Jake, I've got a cabin on the backwater at Lake Harding. It's yours. Just tell me when you want to move in."

"Donnie Lee, are you sure? I can find a place in Conecuh."

"Jake, get back here. We've got a case to try."

Everything was happening so fast. My fraternity brother, Robert Zimmerman, the CEO of Southern Title Company, was not going to be happy. I had built our branch office into one of the top producers in the company. Hopefully, he could find someone to replace me quickly. I could not continue to be a real estate attorney. I loved the sting of the courtroom battle too much. God, how I wanted to get back into the courtroom.

Sixteen

This was the second time in just over a year that I felt that I was messing up my life. I had resigned my position at Southern Title Company, had packed my few remaining belongings in a U-Haul trailer, and I was headed back to Georgia to fight an iffy case on a contingency fee. Such was the life of the plaintiff's attorney. Sometimes I wondered what life would be like as a stall-fed, silk stocking, defense attorney who got a pay check from an insurance company whether he won or not. Such was not my lot in life. I was a gambler and a street fighter. I had to take this one to the end for the two people I loved most in my life. One was dead. The other one wanted to spend the rest of her life with me.

I pulled off the backwater country road where Donnie Lee's cabin was located. It was well off the beaten path. It was a perfect weekend retreat. Donnie Lee was out in the front yard burning brush. He waved as I pulled in the driveway. "Jake, how are you?"

"Donnie Lee, I am absolutely nuts, and I think you are too. Why couldn't we have been bond lawyers and worked for one of those big law firms on Peachtree Street in Atlanta?"

He laughed. "Because, Jake, once you have tasted blood you never go back. The silk stocking boys have never experienced the thrill of beating the crap out of an insurance company or a bank, because they have represented them all of their lives. Once you get the malaria in your blood as a plaintiff's lawyer, it's incurable."

Donnie Lee helped me move my belongings into the cabin. The river that flowed in front of the property reminded me of the Gulf of Mexico. I could tell I would be seeking its serenity just as I had on the Gulf of Mexico.

"Jake, as I see our case, we don't have too many surprises we can spring on the other side. I think they will bring on a few new expert witnesses. The first thing we need to do is get out a demand for their list of witnesses and then set up depositions for any new ones. I really don't know how we could have been better prepared than we were the last time. Let's review the trial transcript and see where we made any errors. We can use the transcript to help us better prepare our witnesses. I just hope Betty will do as well this time. She really surprised me. She was terrific on the stand."

"Donnie Lee, just don't give that woman my telephone number. Tell her I'm commuting from Florida and I'll show up at the trial." We both laughed.

"Jake, I believe the only place we screwed up last time was in the jury selection. We were killed from the git-go."

"Hey, we underestimated the power of First Fidelity to get to a jury. This isn't going to happen this time."

"What are your thoughts, Jake? What do you think we need to do?"

"Donnie Lee, I agree with your approach. I have a plan, as far as the jury is concerned. I need to work on it a while, then I'll run it by you."

"Okay, I'll leave you to get settled in. There is a sweet young lady that told me to have you call her as soon as possible." He left.

I immediately dialed Terri Beth's number. "Hello, sweetheart."

"Jake, you made it. How does it feel to be a Georgian again?"

"When can you see me?"

"Terri Beth, I need to finish moving in here and I probably won't be through until late tonight. I'll see you in the office bright and early tomorrow morning. Can I take you to dinner tomorrow night? I've got some things I need to discuss with you."

"You're on, good looking," she said.

"Hey, and by the way, do I get my old office back?"

"I don't know. You'll have to ask Brook. I went to work for Don Pollard. You've been gone too long."

"Tell that old government, gold bricker, that he might crave your body, but his wife Cynthia craves his paycheck, all of it, and I'm going to represent her for free."

"Jake, I'm teasing you. I would never do that. I am so in love with you that I would never hurt you—never. Yes, you can have your old office back. I've cleaned it every day since you left."

*****

I pulled into the back parking lot of the office. I couldn't believe it. There was my old parking place with my name "McDonald" painted on the sign. Maybe I was wanted back. I walked in the back door. "Surprise!" I was greeted by the whole office—Brook, Phillip, Donnie Lee, Dixie, Sarah, Neva, Juanita, and Terri Beth. I couldn't believe it. My eyes welled up. "I love you guys, but I came back upon only one condition—that I will never check a title again."

They all laughed.

"Jake, we didn't pick you up on waivers to check titles. You'd better still know how to try a case," Brook said in his booming voice. He gave me a bear hug. "Welcome back, Jake."

Terri Beth grabbed me by the hand and led me to my old office. It was really elegant. "Terri Beth, you didn't need to hire an expensive interior decorator to do all this. I don't need a fancy office."

"I did it for you, Jake."

"Terri Beth, how much did all this cost?" I asked.

"Jake, it's going to cost you a lot, a whole lot. I decorated it on my own six months ago. I knew you were coming back." She shut the door behind us. We looked deeply into each other's eyes. Our lips met. "God, sunshine, you don't know how much I've missed you."

"Jake, there is so much that I need to tell you, but I can't right now. Please just be with me. Don't ever leave me. I understand we can't share our true feelings in the office, but I need you."

"Hey, is our date still on for tonight?"

"I need to talk with you."

"Where do you want to go?"

"Is the George House okay?"

"You bet."

"Can we have the cozy room in the back?"

*****

I picked up Terri Beth at 7:30 p.m. at her apartment. She was radiant in a straight line navy blue dress. She had a beautiful scarf around her neck and was wearing dangling gold earrings. I didn't know how she could work all day and look so fresh and elegant at night. We went to the George House and were ushered into the back room by Crete, the head waiter. "Right this way, Mr. McDonald. We haven't seen you in quite a while.

"Sunshine, I have thought about you every day since the inauguration. You don't know how close I came to doing what we both wanted to do. Terri Beth, let me get this case behind us. I want Don Pollard to find Kathy's killers. Then I'll let my heart take me where it needs to go.

"Sweetie, I need to get real serious about this case. I'm now committed to winning it. This is part of the reason I need to talk to you. Do you remember a woman in the PSI by the name of Sissy Phillips?"

"Yes, why?"

"I met her at Tabby's. She was with a friend of mine from the jury pool manager's office. She worked in the computer department at First Fidelity. Later she called and wanted to hire me as her lawyer. She said there was someone in the bank who was putting pressure on her. Sexual pressure. She said one of the higher-ups was pressuring her to sleep with him, and intimated that her future at the bank depended on how well she performed, if you know what I mean."

"Oh, Jake, that's awful. What do you want me to do?"

"You're not going to believe this. And I want you to understand completely. My loyalty is completely to you. Terri Beth, I want you to set up a date between Sissy and me."

"What? Why?"

"Sweetheart, this is about business. I have no romantic interest in the woman. I need a meeting with her. She's single and I'm single. Believe me, it's for the good of the firm and for our good."

Terri Beth looked disappointed. "Can you tell me why, may I ask?" she said.

"No, not now. I'll explain later. You'll have to trust me."

"Jake, please tell me the truth. You don't have another woman in your life, do you?"

"Hell, no. Not now or ever. You are the one, sweetheart. Please believe that."

Terri Beth smiled.

"I need for you to set up this meeting as soon as possible. It has something to do with our case. I'll explain it later."

"I'm glad you called it a meeting and not a date. Sissy is a cute girl and I don't want you to get romantically involved with anyone else. I love you, and I'm jealous."

I grinned. "Will you do it?"

"Yes, but I want you to give me a blow-by-blow account. No hugging or kissing and you must take her home by 8:30."

I laughed. "My goodness, do I denote a streak of jealousy here? While I'm on my date with Sissy I hope you'll be in your cooking class at the college."

"How did you find out about that?"

*****

Terri Beth had done her job well. She had arranged a blind date between Sissy and me. She had told her that I had recently moved back to town and was looking for someone to date. She said that I had met her a long time ago and that I thought she was cute. Sissy was not aware of Terri Beth's and my relationship.

I picked her up at her apartment. Sissy was tall—five feet nine. She had dark hair, like Terri Beth. She was attractive and had been a secretary at First Fidelity for many years. She was the head of their computer department. I took her back to the George House. I had arranged for a private room in the back. I didn't want anyone to see us together, or anyone to overhear our conversation. I asked her what she wanted to drink and ordered her a scotch and water.

Crete was our waiter. I slipped him a twenty as we arrived. I told him I needed him to "take care of my date." He understood completely.

Sissy and I got along real well. She was obviously very intelligent and quite striking. We hit it off. After three scotch and waters, she began to loosen up. It was obvious that she was not happy at work.

"Jake, you don't know me very well, but I know you—at least I know your reputation. You have the reputation of being a fighter. You don't sell your clients out, and I wish I had known you when I was going through my divorce. That jerk Katz sold me out. Jake, can I confess something to you? This can go no further. I trust you. I really do. Do you know Robert Banks at the bank?"

"I'm afraid so," I said.

"Jake, Robert has been trying to get in my pants for years. Two weeks ago I was working late and Robert hit on me. I tried to get him to leave, but he insisted. I fought him off. Jake, he raped me. That goddamn pig raped me. I was afraid to go to the authorities. That bank has ways of 'eliminating' people, if you know what I mean. Jake, I'm scared. If I left them, I'd fear for my life."

"Sissy, can you trust me? I mean really trust me?"

"Jake, I need someone I can really trust. Please help me."

"Sissy, do you hate that damn bank? I mean, really hate them?"

"Jake, you're damn right I hate them."

"Sissy, will you do a little undercover work for me?"

"What do you mean?"

"Sissy, I was screwed in my trial against the bank. The jury was rigged. I just don't know how they did it, but I suspect that every member of the jury, with the exception of two, had connections with your bank. I need an insider who can do a little bit of intelligence work and keep me posted as to their shenanigans. Will you help me?"

She looked into my eyes. "Somehow I feel like Benedict Arnold, but Jake, I was raped by their vice president. After he finished his pleasure with me, he laughed in my face. Do you know what he said to me?"

"No. What?"

"He said, 'You wanted it, didn't you, bitch? You've always wanted it. Admit it. If you hang around me and give me what I want, you will go a long way in this bank.'" Sissy started to cry. "I hate him, Jake. Goddamn, I hate him. He raped me. Please help me. I'll do what you want me to do to take these bastards down."

I took Sissy home. I kissed her goodnight. She smiled. "Jake, I really want to see you again, but I'm scared. If the bank sees me with you, I would lose my job, or worse. We need to stay in touch. We need some way of communicating. What can we do?"

"Sissy, do you know the deli down the street from the bank? Let's meet there for lunch. We can sit at separate tables in the back. We can exchange messages via envelopes if necessary. I need to meet you there at noon on Monday. I'm going to give you a lot of names I want you to run through the computer system of the bank. Will you do that?"

"You know I will, Jake. You're a real hero."

I drove back to the cabin. I pulled the file of the old trial. I immediately went to the jury list. I wrote down all the names and typed them on my old Underwood typewriter that I had brought from Florida. It was late. Tomorrow was Saturday. I planned to sleep late.

At 8:00 a.m. the phone rang. Never a break. Who knew my number? It was Terri Beth. "Are you awake, lawyer McDonald?"

"Not really, your highness."

"What are you doing in bed?" she asked.

"Well, I'm just lying here in bed next to Sissy. I didn't think you would mind."

She screamed out loud. "You merciless bastard, I'm coming over to make sure you sing soprano in the boys' choir."

"Take it easy, Terri Beth. I'm teasing. I'm just trying to get your heart rate up. There's no one here but me. You are so jealous."

"Yes, I am. And there had better not be anyone else but you, unless it's me. How was your date?" she asked.

"Meeting, Terri Beth, meeting."

"You're getting better. How was your meeting?"

"The meeting went fine. Terri Beth, Sissy has been really hurt by the bank. I can't discuss it over the phone, but she has some female issues that you can help her with. Please stay close to her. She's a key in our case. You don't know all the details yet, but I'll tell you later. How was your cooking class?"

"Jake McDonald, I want to know who told you I was taking cooking lessons at the college. They are not cooking lessons. They are gourmet French chef classes. Who told you?"

"I will never reveal my secret sources, my dear. It's attorney-client privilege. If you do, in fact, perform well in the culinary area like you claim you are capable of, and I do want to see your grade in the course, then I might consider overlooking your other faults, like your good looks, your brilliance, your wit, your charm, your class, and your terrible jealousy."

"Jake McDonald, I just might not marry you."

"Who said I asked you?"

The phone was silent. "Oh, Jake, please don't ever say that again. I love you. You know that."

"Sweetheart, you know how I feel. You don't ever have to question that. Sissy is a looker, but she could never ever replace you. Believe that. I love you."

*****

I walked into the deli promptly at noon on Monday. By prearranged signal I took a table in the back. Sissy was seated at the table next to me. She got up to go to the rest room. She picked up the envelope at the edge of my table and stuffed it into her purse. Legal vengeance had begun.

I ate my turkey club sandwich as I glanced over towards her. She winked. Sissy was a pretty woman. I would love to see Don Pollard prosecute Robert Banks for raping her. She didn't deserve what Banks did to her. First Fidelity was totally corrupt. Their vice presidents were rapists and they were getting away with it.

In the next day's mail I received a thick envelope with no return address. I ripped it open. Inside was a ten-page computer printout. It was a loan computer spread sheet. I recognized the names on the printout. They were all jurors in our first trial. I couldn't believe what I was reading. I was looking at the loan history of ten of the twelve jurors in our trial. They all owed money to First Fidelity Bank and Trust. How did we miss this on voir dire?" It hit me. We didn't miss it on voir dire. These jurors had been approached. They had been intimidated and bought off. There was no doubt about it. Should I take this to the district attorney, or should I play it out until the civil trial was over? I didn't want to jeopardize Sissy's job, much less her life.

My heart was pounding out of my chest. I now knew that our first trial had been stolen from us. If I could only prove who killed Kathy. If I could prove the two were related, I might become a crazed terrorist and level that bank. I was angry. Very angry.

I waited until the office closed. I only wanted to tell those who needed to know—Donnie Lee, Dixie, and Terri Beth. When I showed them what I had, Donnie Lee went into orbit.

"God damn it, we need to take this to the U.S. Attorney. These bastards need to be indicted."

"Wait a minute, Donnie Lee. I didn't come back from Florida to prosecute a criminal case. Let's use our heads. First we beat the hell out of them in the civil case, and then we help put them in jail. Look, we've got a solid case based on the facts. The law is strongly on our side. We just need to get the right jury. The bank screwed us because they were far more sophisticated than we were in selecting the jury. They have all the computers and electronic resources. I think we need to be smarter than the enemy. We have an insider in the enemy's camp. We need to cultivate our resources and use guerilla warfare. Hell, they did it to us. It's about time that we fought smart."

Terri Beth spoke up. "Hey, our friend is a member of the PSI. Our annual banquet is Monday. I'm willing to do whatever it takes to get her full cooperation."

We laid out a plan.

Terri Beth and I went to the PSI banquet. We had agreed that we would spread out for intelligence- gathering purposes. Both of us agreed to pay particular attention to Sissy. Terri Beth was to approach her from the feminine side—as a friend, sympathetic and willing to help. I needed to gather intelligence on the enemy.

I saw Sissy in the corner. She saw me out of the corner of her eye and motioned me over. "Hello, Jake. I hope the information I gave you was useful."

"Excellent, Sissy. You are a real sweetheart. Listen, I don't want any spies that might be here tonight to make any connection between us, so I'll talk fast. Sissy, can you program things into the bank's computers?"

"Absolutely, Jake. I do it every day."

"So, if you programmed something into the bank's computers, whoever pulled it off the screen would have access throughout the bank's system."

"That's correct."

"The old GIGO rule still applies."

"That's right, Jake. Garbage In - Garbage Out."

"That's all I wanted to hear. Say, listen. You stay close to my secretary Terri Beth. She's my closest friend. I had to tell her what happened to you. I hope you don't mind. She's a person you can trust. Sissy, believe me, trust Terri Beth. Together we're going to bring these bastards down. Let's keep in touch. We're going to need your help. No one can know we are cooperating. If necessary, you can communicate through Terri Beth. If anyone questions you, you're talking about PSI business. You don't know how much we appreciate what you are doing for us. Sissy, we're going to get these bastards, believe me."

*****

Judge Randall had indeed put our case on the fast track. It was first on the docket. The trial was two weeks away. You could tell it was getting closer. The tension was increasing in the office. The last minute discovery had been completed. The only new witness the bank had was an expert witness who had been in banking for twenty-something years. He was a past president of the American Bankers Association. Donnie Lee got one of his partners to do the cross-examination of the expert. Donnie Lee's partner, L. W. "Zeke" McMurphy, was an expert in banking law. He cut the bank's expert no slack. He pinned him down on every point, including the fact that the bank was paying him $500 per hour for his testimony. Donnie Lee didn't think this witness would hurt us. We would make a big deal out of the fact that he was a "hired gun" for a big fee.

Neva returned from the clerk's office with the jury list. "Neva, could you make me about six copies of the jury list and take one down to Carl Schiff, our favorite PI?"

"I'll be glad to, Jake." Neva was such an efficient secretary. We kept her on after Kelli's death. She was as loyal as Terri Beth. We had given her a raise after Kelli's death. Neva was a healer and a consensus builder.

I got the copy of the jury list and scribbled a note to Sissy. "Sissy, please run these names through your computer and see if any of them are customers. Thanks. J." I sealed the note and the jury list in a plain envelope.

I handed the envelope to Terri Beth. "Sweetheart, how would you like to have a long lunch with Sissy?" I handed her two twenties. "Make sure she gets this envelope. And, Terri Beth, no one can know about this. That includes everybody in this firm. Do you know what I mean?"

"Jake, you're preaching to the choir when it comes to loyalty." She winked and left to make the telephone call to Sissy. Twenty minutes later she returned. "It's all set, Jake. I'm having lunch with Sissy at noon. Do I have permission to take a long lunch break?"

"Sweetie, you're on firm business. Take as long as you need."

"Jake, what's in the envelope?"

"Terri Beth, you don't need to know. Please don't open it. I trust you. Just say it's in the category of legal discovery."

"Jake, she isn't after you, is she?"

"Hell no, Terri Beth. You know me better than that. This is about the case. I'll tell you everything when it's over."

Terri Beth left for lunch with the envelope. If she only knew the importance of the contents of the envelope that she was carrying. I went to the YMCA for lunch. It had been along time since I had worked out with my old friends. I went through the aerobics routine and ran four and a half miles. I was glad to be back. Strenuous exercise always broke the tension.

Terri Beth returned at two, the same time I did. "How did it go, sunshine?" I asked.

"Just fine. We had a pleasant lunch. She really trusts you, and she said she would take care of your request. Jake, what's going on?"

"Believe me, Terri Beth. This is all about the case. What you did was very important."

"I understand what you're telling me, Jake. I just don't need to be left in the dark. We're too close."

"Terri Beth, just trust me on this."

Wednesday I received a plain envelope in the mail without a return address. I knew whom it was from. I shut the door of my office and immediately opened the envelope. It contained seventeen pages of computer printouts of seventeen different individuals on the jury list. Sissy was a hero. We would win this case for her. With her help we were going to win.

I called Carl Schiff. "Carl, how are you coming with the jury list?"

"Jake, we're doing just fine. We're using more sophisticated data bases since the last trial so we'll be able to give you a better profile of each juror."

"Thanks, Carl. Let me know when you have it done. I'd like to send you some names to work on first, if that's all right."

"Sure, Jake. Have Terri Beth call them to me."

It was Friday, two weeks before trial. I promised Terri Beth that I would take her out to someplace special if she would let me have tonight alone. I needed to clear my mind. She agreed. She said she needed to do some serious house cleaning and didn't need to deal with a cranky guy on Friday night. She was so cute. She knew how to resolve a fight before one developed. I only wished I could see more of her other than at the office. I was going to win this case.

The river that flowed in front of the cabin reminded me of the waves that crashed in front of my condo at Ft. Walton. Why was so much of my life tied up in this case? Why did I ever take this damn case? Why couldn't I be content handling the same old automobile wrecks and divorces that I used to handle? It was all on the line. I lost the case in front of a jury. I lost my law partner. I lost all my possessions including my house. I lost my old friend—my dog—and I lost the greatest love of my life; I lost my wife.

I had to make some serious decisions. The first decision I needed to make was if I were truly committed to winning this case, or should I bail out and turn it over to Donnie Lee. Then I needed to decide if I wanted to move back to Georgia and become a lawyer again. Lastly, I needed to decide what my future was to be with Terri Beth. I was glad that I had not slept with Terri Beth. If I had, I knew I would have lost all my objectivity. She was hypnotizing. If I knew her intimately, my decision-making ability would be totally blurred.

I loved being on this river. It was really like the gulf. The gulf cleared my head with its cleansing breezes. The river took on a life all of its own. A man cannot live with the paralysis of anger. I knew what the decision must be. I must win this case. I must represent my clients again as an attorney. I lost my wife. Now I was in love with another woman. I would marry her.

I woke up listening to the river. It was so peaceful. I wondered what the river sounded like in a rage. The book of Ecclesiastics in the Bible says, there is a time and a season for everything under the sun. A time to reap and time to sow.

Vanity of vanities. I have seen everything under the sun and all is vanity. I wondered why the Book of Ecclesiastics came into my mind. I guess it was the sound of the river.

I picked up the phone and dialed Terri Beth's number.

"Hello?" She was half-asleep. "Jake? What time is it?"

"It's eight o'clock, sunshine. Why are you still in bed?"

"I don't know. My lover hasn't woke me up yet. He's still asleep."

"You better not have a lover in your bed. I'm on my way over to kill him."

"Calm down, you silly goose. The only lover I sleep with is Bear."

"And just who in the hell is Bear?"

"Sweetheart, Bear will always be my lover. He's my Teddy bear. I have slept with him since I was three years old. And I intend to take him with me on my honeymoon if I'm so lucky as to have one. Speaking of lovers, when are you coming over tonight? I need to take a nap. I stayed up all night cleaning my apartment for you. I hope you appreciate it."

"I'll see you at eight."

"Oh, Jake, I'm cooking for you tonight, so go easy on me."

"I will, sweetheart. I'll bring the Rolaids."

*****

Terri Beth met me at the door.

"I brought you a surprise, sweetheart." I handed her a bottle of Dom Perignon.

"Oh, Jake, that's the expensive stuff. You shouldn't have done this."

" Do you know how to open it?"

She laughed. "That's what you're for, my dear."

She was dressed in a red T-shirt and a pair of tight jeans. "Damn, you look good."

She gave me a big hug. Our lips met. Our kiss was passionate. "Come on, let me show you around the apartment."

It was elegantly decorated. She was a lady of impeccable taste. "And here is where Bear and I sleep." We entered her bedroom.

"I want to see Bear."

She laughed. "Here he is." She picked up a large brown Teddy bear. "He sleeps with me every night."

"I'm jealous," I said. "I want to take his place."

"You'll never replace Bear, Jake. But he's willing to share."

"Share what?"

"I think you know exactly what I'm talking about." She laughed.

"Terri Beth, last night I sat down by the river. The river is so peaceful, it's a lot like the waves of the ocean. It has such a calming effect on the mind. I did a lot of thinking about a lot of different things. I thought about the case, and whether I should turn it over to Donnie Lee and get out of it. I was real hurt when we lost. I finally decided that I owed it to our clients, our firm, and to the people who have put a lot of faith in me to try this case and win it."

She smiled. "I'm proud of your decision," she said.

"I then thought about my relationship with the law firm. I was really hurt and disillusioned. That's why I quit. I learned something while I was in Florida. I learned that title work is the most boring work a lawyer can do. I belong in the courtroom. It's the only thing I know how to do, and the only thing I love."

"Jake, I've known that all along. I thought you made a mistake, but it was your decision, and I didn't want to interfere."

"Do you think the guys will be glad to have me back at the firm?"

"I know they will, Jake."

"Terri Beth, I want you to sit down. The next one is the big one."

"What is it, Jake?"

"Terri Beth, I thought about the fire and that horrible night. I have thought about it thousands of times. It was the worst thing that has ever happened in my life. Terri Beth, Kathy loved you very much. She trusted me with you. She was teasing me when she said that if anything ever happened to her that you would be her first choice. But she was serious. I was never able to tell her who my choice would be to replace me. I could never envision her with anyone but me. Somehow while I was sitting on the river last night verses from the book of Ecclesiastics kept running through my mind. I kept hearing, 'There is a reason, and a time, and a season.' It kept telling me that Kathy wanted me to put it all behind me. I believe that her spirit was reaching out to me. She was telling me there was a reason that she was taken away."

I started to cry. Terri Beth put her arms around me.

"Terri Beth, I thought about what I'm going to do after the trial. But I decided I didn't want the verdict to influence the decision that I made last night. I've only done what I'm now about to do once before in my life. I have made a decision."

"Jake, what is it?"

"Terri Beth, I love you."

"Oh, Jake."

"Terri Beth, will you marry me?"

She began to cry. "Oh, my God, Jake. I've laid awake for so many nights dreaming of hearing you say those words."

I switched to my lawyer mode. "Well, Ms. Flynt, you didn't answer my question. Please answer the question and then you may explain your answer. Will you or will you not marry me?"

"Mr. McDonald, I'm going to answer your question. You are the attorney, but you can't trick me. I'm going to answer your question, but I'm going to explain my answer first. Mr. McDonald, I love you with all my heart and with all of my soul. You are my soul mate. I want to be with you every hour of every day. I want to give myself totally to you. I want to be your wife. Is that a good enough explanation of the answer I'm about to give? My answer is yes. Yes, I will marry you."

We collapsed into each other's arms. "Oh, God, Terri Beth, I love you so much."

We collapsed onto the bed. We kissed passionately. My hand touched her breasts. They were throbbing. She pulled up her shirt. She was beautiful.

"Jake, take me, please take me. Give me everything, Jake."

"Terri Beth, we must stop. I know that neither of us are virgins, but I want you to be my virgin on our wedding night. I feel I owe that to Kathy. She is the one that would want it that way."

She jumped up. "Mr. McDonald, I tricked you. I got you to propose before you have ever tasted one of my meals." She laughed. "Come on, let's taste that champagne."

I opened the champagne. We sat staring at each other while we sipped the champagne. She said, "I can't believe this."

"What's that, sweetheart?"

"I'm looking at my future husband. Mrs. W. Lancaster McDonald. Terri Beth McDonald. I like the sound of that."

I smiled. "Ms. Flynt, would you care to give me your ring size? I sort of need to know."

"It's five and a half, my love."

"Terri Beth, I look forward to spending the rest of my life with you. I need to get this trial behind me. Then I want us to spend a lot of time together. I feel that I know you so well and yet I feel that I don't. We have never had a fight, but I need to know how to fight with you."

"Buster, you'll know it. I've been pissed at you, but I got over it. Jake, we don't need to fight, ever. You'll lose. God gave me all the good stuff."

I broke out in laughter. "Where did you come up with that?"

"Hey, that's good. . . . Terri Beth, I need your help with this trial."

"Jake, you know that I have been with you from the beginning. Whatever you need, I'm with you until the end. I now look at you as my husband."

"Terri Beth, I want you to have lunch with Sissy on Monday. I need for you to deliver another envelope."

"Jake, what's going on?"

"Terri Beth, you are my fiancee. I can assure you that I'm not doing anything illegal, but I want you to be out of the loop on this. This is an intelligence gathering matter that could really hurt Sissy if she were caught. Robert Banks raped Sissy, Terri Beth. This is her way of getting even. She can't go to the authorities. This is her legal vengeance. Please, sweetheart, trust me. This is critical to our case."

"Okay, my love. I'll do it."

Terri Beth and I spent a very pleasant evening together. I left. I wished we could have spent the night together. Later. The trial was one week away.

* * *

It was ten a.m. Sunday morning. I called Carl Schiff's home number. He answered.

"Carl, Jake McDonald. I'm sorry to call you at home on a Sunday morning."

"Hey, Jake, I know you well. No problem. What's up?"

"Carl, have you run the jury list through your sources?"

"Jake, I was going to mess up your ball game this afternoon anyway. Yes, I have. It's ready. You'll like it."

"Where can I meet you?"

"How about at Sandy's for lunch?"

"Your wife won't mind?"

"She'll be glad to get rid of me." He laughed.

I joined Carl at Sandy's He handed me an envelope. "Jake this is as comprehensive a report as we can run on individuals. Most of it is legal stuff. Some of it is, well, you know." He winked.

"Thanks, Carl."

We enjoyed lunch together.

*****

I spent the rest of the afternoon dissecting Carl's report. I sorted out all the jurors who owed money to First Fidelity or had any dealings with them. Then I analyzed all those jurors who had nothing to do with the bank. I separated them according to their prejudices, and according to all the personality profiles that the trial lawyers associations throughout the country had done for years. I pulled out my old

Underwood typewriter. I began to type. I spent the rest of the afternoon typing.

It was seven p.m. I truly believed that we were going to win, if what I had planned worked. I put a steak on the grill. Tomorrow would begin the countdown. We were on our way to victory. I kept thinking how wonderful it would be to be married to Terri Beth.

Monday morning Donnie Lee, Dixie, and I gathered in the library to map out our final plans for trial. Most of the hard work had been done at the last trial, so it was simply a matter of reviewing the trial transcript and making sure our witnesses were prepared for the final assault.

"How are we coming with the jury list, Jake?" Donnie Lee asked.

"I picked up the final report from Carl yesterday. He did a good job. I worked on it all day yesterday. Hopefully we'll do a better job in selecting the jury this time. We all know why we got screwed the last time. It won't happen again. We haven't heard from our old friends Bill and Betty in a while. Dixie, did you really tell them that I had moved out of the country?" We all laughed. "God, I hate having to prepare them for trial again. Let's get the copies of their testimony to them, and let them study it before they come in. I don't want them to deviate one bit. They really surprised me how well they did the last time. Let's set up the preparation schedule of the witnesses. Let's divide it up so we can get the work done in the time remaining."

It was 11:45 a.m. Terri Beth stuck her head in the door. "I'm going to lunch with our friend. You said you wanted me to deliver something to her."

"Here's an envelope I want you to give her. Tell her the instructions are on the inside. Have a nice lunch."

*****

Terri Beth joined Sissy at the back table of the deli. "Hi, Sissy. It's so good to see you again. Jake said to give you this. He said you would know what to do with it."

She smiled. "Thanks, Terri Beth. You don't know how much I appreciate Jake's and your support. I know he told you what that bastard Robert Banks did to me."

"Yes, he did, Sissy. God, we feel for you. Is there any way we can help you?"

"You don't know it, Terri Beth, but Jake just did. He told me not to discuss this matter with anyone."

"Sissy, he won't even discuss it with me. I'm his secretary, and as of Saturday I became his fiancee."

"Oh, Terri Beth, that's wonderful. When is the big day?"

"We don't know. We've got to get this trial behind us first."

After lunch Terri Beth returned to the firm and Sissy returned to the bank.

*****

It was 6:30 p.m. The bank officials were meeting with their lawyers at King, Golden and Bonner. Sissy locked the door to the computer room behind her and switched on her PC. She worked quickly. She used Robert Banks' access code. He had given that to her prior to raping her.

A secret glow came over her. She had completed her mission. It was 7:30 p.m. She shut off the power. Now she had to get out of the building without raising the suspicions of the security guard. She had a plan. She dialed a code on the telephone that would trigger an alarm on the eighth floor. It was a false signal that was used to test the security system, but maybe it would send the guard to the top of the building. She dialed the number. It worked. The alarm sounded. She waited outside the elevator. She saw the elevator go past her floor and on to the eighth floor, where it stopped. She quickly entered the other elevator and went to the ground floor and exited the building. It had worked.

She went to a pay phone at the Circle K a mile down the street and dialed a pre-arranged number. She let the phone ring two times and then hung up. She dialed the number again and let it ring three times and hung up again. She smiled as she drove back to her apartment.

*****

All the final trial preparations had been completed. All the witnesses were prepared. It was decided who would conduct the direct and cross-examinations of each witness. Donnie Lee would do the opening statement and I would do the closing argument. We set aside all day Friday to review the jury list and prepare for voir dire.

We all sat around the conference table with our stack of jury cards and the copies of the report from Carl Schiff. In a civil case each side has six strikes. We struck from the first twenty-four qualified jurors on the list. It was the deputy clerk's duty to type them on a jury list. The order in which they appeared on the jury list was very important. We were lucky. We only had five who would absolutely have to be struck. That left us with one spare strike. With any luck the bank's lawyers would strike some on our list. We all voted after much discussion as to how we would use our strikes, assuming the voir dire went well.

We adjourned for lunch at Sandy's. "What's going on with Don Pollard?" I asked.

Dixie said, "The talk at the courthouse is that he's got something big going on with the grand jury. Nobody knows what. He has armed deputy sheriffs posted at the door. It's been going on for three weeks now."

I took Terri Beth to dinner at a quiet seafood restaurant on the backwater near where I lived. This would be our last meeting alone until the trial was over. She knew what trial week was like, so she didn't put any pressure on me. We had a couple of glasses of wine and then the discussion turned to our marriage. She smiled.

"Sunshine, pick the date. I want this to be your wedding. When this trial is over let's sit down and work out the details. I love you."

"Jake, does anybody in the firm know that we're engaged?"

"Not yet, Terri Beth. I might wait until after the trial. I would like for you to visit some jewelry stores and look around for a while."

"For what?" she teased.

"I don't know. Maybe a bracelet or a necklace or some earrings. And while you're there would you verify your ring size again?"

"You silly goose."

I took her home, gave her a passionate kiss and a big hug and went back to the cabin. I practiced my closing argument several times. I wanted the jury to know the hell that our clients had been put through.

I sat down by the river. It was so peaceful. I wondered if river rats didn't have a better life than lawyers. The events of the past year went through my head like a rerun of an old "B" movie. I appreciated the love that Kathy had given me. My thoughts turned to my future life with Terri Beth. I felt true empathy for Sissy and I appreciated her help. I wanted her to get legal vengeance.

Seventeen

"All rise," the bailiff shouted out. Everyone in the courtroom rose. Judge Randall assumed her place on the bench.

"Please be seated, ladies and gentlemen. We call the case of Perkins, Tolbert, Cochran et al. vs. First Fidelity Bank and Trust and Southern Finance of Georgia et al. Mr. Booker?"

"The plaintiff announces ready, your honor."

"Mr. King."

"The defense is ready."

"Very well. Bailiff, will you escort the first panel of jurors in."

"Yes, your honor."

The first twelve jurors took their seats in the jury box. "As your name is called please answer," the deputy clerk said.

We had done our homework. The first twelve were in the exact order as appeared on our list. This process was repeated for the next twelve. We were lucky. No jurors had been excused by the clerk's office. We had been tracking this all week with the jury manager's office. It can have a disastrous effect on your jury if jurors are excused prior to trial.

The voir dire went according to the script with no surprises. Carl's research was paying off. We struck the first juror, number three. He was not really pro-bank, but we didn't trust his answers on voir dire. We had used our spare strike up front, hoping to draw the bank off guard. It worked.

Then the bizarre began to happen. The bank struck one of the jurors that we had targeted for one of our strikes. Then another. Then another. The bank was striking jurors that we knew had some affiliation with the bank, either as debtors or depositors, or who had a relative who worked for the bank.

"What the hell is going on here? This is too good to be true," whispered Donnie Lee. "Jake, do you know something that I don't?"

"Surprise, surprise, surprise, Donnie Lee. Its called legal vengeance." I winked. "Now let's try our case. What goes around comes around."

Donnie Lee made a powerful opening statement. The jury was moved. Brad King was shaken. He was not up to his usual performance.

The next week was a blur. One day rolled into the next one. Our witnesses performed like Oscar-winning actors and actresses. Bill and Betty were even better this time than last. They invoked the sympathy of the jury. Our last witness was Angela Tolbert. She was scared to death. Brad King made what I thought was a very bad tactical error. He attacked Angela so hard on the cross-examination that she broke down on the stand. Judge Randall had to call a fifteen-minute recess and had to admonish Brad King for badgering the witness. The jury was visibly angry. You could see it in their faces. We had gained more from Brad King's attack on Angela than we did from our direct examination of her.

It had been a week and a half. We decided that we had proved our case and it was time to rest. "Donnie Lee, you may have the honors," I said.

"Thank you, Jake . . .. Your honor, the plaintiffs rest."

Brad King rose. "Your honor, the defense has a matter to take up outside the presence of the jury."

"Very well. Let's recess for thirty minutes." She asked that the jurors return to their seats in thirty minutes. "The court is in recess."

Brad King made his expected motion for a directed verdict. It was the same argument he had made before. Judge Randall summarily denied it.

The defense called their expert witness, the banker who was the former president of the American Bankers Association. He was dressed like a typical banker in a three-piece navy blue pin-striped suit. Brad King took over a half an hour going through his credentials to qualify him as an expert witness. He was pompous and the jury was bored. Most of his direct testimony dealt with the technical aspects of banking and mortgage lending.

Zeke McMurphy, Donnie Lee's partner, took Dixie's place at the counsel table. I was glad we had Zeke on our side. He was a banking expert and he was well prepared to cross-examine this witness.

I don't think the jury comprehended all the banking jargon. I know I didn't. I was glad Zeke understood it. For over three hours the witness rambled on about the banking industry and how First Fidelity had done nothing wrong. Even Judge

Randall was bored. At one point she interrupted. "Mr. King, this is becoming very repetitious. Let's move it along." The jurors nodded in the affirmative.

Brad King finally concluded his direct examination. Judge Randall granted a thirty-minute recess. Then it was Zeke McMurphy's turn.

He immediately created rapport with the jury. "Mr. Zembrowski, you are from Philadelphia?"

"Yes, sir."

"Welcome to Conecuh, Georgia. We are so glad to have you here. We have never had the pleasure of having a man of your importance to testify in our court before."

The jury broke out in laughter. "Let's have order," boomed Deputy Taylor.

"Mr. Zembrowski, my questions won't take as long as Mr. King's because I don't think it will take that long to get to the truth."

"I was telling the truth, Mr. McMurphy."

"That's what we are here for, Mr. Zembrowski, to see if you are."

The jury liked Zeke. He was about to take this pompous ass down. "Mr. Zembrowski, now tell this jury, how many hours have you been on the stand?"

"It looks like three and a half, sir."

"How many hours have you been in Conecuh?"

"Two days, sir."

"And did you keep time records of how many hours you have spent working on the case for the bank?"

"Yes, sir."

"And what might that be?"

"Let's see. "So far it's a hundred thirty-seven."

"And the longer you're here the more hours you will add to that."

"Yes, sir, I'm an expert witness."

"And as an expert witness that means you expect to be paid for your testimony."

"I'm being paid to tell the truth."

"Well, what you are told and think is the truth. Please tell this jury how much you are being paid for your testimony."

He paused. "Let me review my notes."

"Come on, Mr. Zembrowski, you know the answer to that one."

"You're getting paid too, Mr. McMurphy."

"Yes, sir, but I'm the lawyer and not the witness. I'm being paid to ask the questions and you are being paid to answer them. Please answer the question."

The jury giggled.

"Five hundred dollars per hour."

There was a sigh from the courtroom.

"Five hundred dollars per hour. Let's see. . . . So far your bill is approximately $70,000.00 plus your expenses."

"I haven't added it up, but if you say so."

"Well, I want you to be truthful. That's what you said you wanted to be. Here's my calculator. Figure it up for the jury."

He calculated his bill. "Yes, sir, just over $70,000.00."

316

"That's more money than Rudy Tolbert's mortgage that First Fidelity tried to foreclose on, I guess. Well, let's see. The bank received $52,000.00 insurance proceeds from his fire. So you are receiving over $18,000 more for your testimony against him than your client, the bank, was paid from the insurance proceeds it received when his house burned down"

"If you say so."

"Mr. Zembrowski, have you ever met Mr. Tolbert?"

"No, sir."

"His wife, Angela?"

"No, sir."

"I didn't think so."

Zeke was one sly fox in the courtroom. He came across as a down-to-earth country lawyer. He was born and raised in Americus, Georgia, and even though he was an Atlanta lawyer, he never lost his touch with a jury. Methodically he dissected Zembrowski's testimony and he did it in an hour and a half, less than half the time of the direct examination. "No further questions, your honor." He took his place at the counsel table.

"Good job, Zeke," I whispered.

The remainder of the defense's case went according to the script. We were prepared. Dixie and I split up the duties of cross-examination of the string of bank witnesses. The real drama would be when they put on the president of First Fidelity Bank and Trust, Anthony Jacobs. Donnie Lee had been waiting for this moment since the lawsuit was filed.

Finally the moment arrived. "Your honor, the defense calls Anthony Jacobs," said Brad King. Anthony Jacobs was the most powerful man in Conecuh. He controlled politics and he controlled every major project in Conecuh. No one wanted to oppose him. And no one dared to cross-examine him except Donnie Lee Booker. Donnie Lee's idol was General George S. Patton, Jr. He told me he envisioned driving a tank up to the front door of First Fidelity Bank and Trust and raising the tank's gun to Jacobs' office and pulling the trigger. Donnie Lee had taken his deposition during the discovery phase of the case. Those two mixed like gasoline and water. After the first two minutes the sparks ignited. They hated each other's guts.

Brad King's direct examination followed the record of the first trial. They did not want to chance giving Donnie Lee any opportunity to show prior contradictory testimony. I thought Jacobs' testimony was convincing. He was brilliant and obviously well- schooled by his lawyers. Judge Randall recessed court until the next morning. This was an unexpected break for us.

Donnie Lee got a copy of Jacobs' testimony from the court reporter before he left the courtroom. No doubt he had a long night before him. Donnie Lee, Dixie, Zeke, Terri Beth, and I adjourned to Kelli's office. Zeke spoke first. "Hey, guys, I thought you said these guys were smart. How in the hell did they beat you the first time? They are putting on a dumb-ass case and the jury is with us."

"Zeke, the jury was rigged the first time," I said. "What do you think, Donnie Lee?"

"Jake, I'm scared it's going too well. I wonder what they have up their sleeve."

"Look, let's break up here and get to work," said Zeke. "Donnie Lee, don't piss the jury off. Just get Jacobs to lose his temper and you've got him. Jake, you come on with a powerful closing argument and then it's in the jury's hands."

"Dixie, how are we coming with the record? Do you see any grounds for appeal on their part yet?"

"Not a one, Jake. Judge Randall is protecting us on appeal. She has let in all their evidence and they didn't object to any of ours. So let's keep the record clean throughout the rest of the trial, and we'll have an appeal-proof record, assuming we can win this thing."

"Assuming? We are going to win," said Donnie Lee.

Everybody began to leave. Terri Beth stayed behind. We embraced. We gave each other a long slow kiss. For the first time in a long time, I felt I was kissing my wife and did not feel guilty. "How was your day, sunshine?"

"The routine, Jake." She giggled. "I did sneak out at lunch and I went by some jewelry stores. I tried on a lot of things like rings, and rings, and rings."

"Rings? And why would you do something like that?" I asked.

"Because it's been a long time since I was totally in love with a man and I want one."

"I hope he's me."

"He is."

We kissed again. "Sunshine, I need to go. I want to deliver the best closing argument I've ever given. I really want to beat these bastards."

We left. I returned to the cabin and went to work. I dissected every sentence, every paragraph, and practiced every inflection of my voice.

*****

It was Donnie Lee's turn to prove that he was, in fact, in charge of the courtroom. He rose. He looked Anthony Jacobs in the eye. "Mr. Jacobs, you are still under oath. Do you know what that means?" It got worse. "You do plan to tell the truth, do you not, Mr. Jacobs?"

"Mr. Booker, you can't intimidate me. Of course I do. Like I have been doing throughout this trial."

"We shall see, Mr. Jacobs, we shall see."

It was the war of the titans, just like in the movies. I just hoped Donnie Lee didn't carry it too far. Donnie then backed off his attacks on Jacobs' credibility and began to methodically attack his testimony in a rapid-fire manner. His line of attack had been planned for months. Donnie Lee's questions were carefully planned and designed to impeach Anthony Jacobs. Anthony Jacobs' answers had also been well- planned in advance. It was obvious that both sides were well prepared and everyone considered this to be the pivotal point of the case.

Then it happened. Finally Donnie Lee found the crack in his testimony. Donnie Lee touched a raw nerve with Jacobs. "Mr. Jacobs, why did you illegally foreclose on the homes of those poor people and put their wives and children out in the street?"

Jacobs exploded. "Listen, you goddamn little shit. You know better."

"Objection!" Brad King shouted.

"Wait just a minute," Judge Randall shrieked. "Mr. Jacobs, you are the president of the largest bank in the town and you should know better, but as long as you are in this court, you will conduct yourself according to the rules of law. No man or woman is above the law. If I hear an outburst like that again, I will hold you in contempt of court. Do you understand what that means?"

Jacobs turned white. A female judge had finally humbled him.

"Mr. King, do you still insist on your objection or do you want me to rule on it?"

"I withdraw my objection, your honor." Brad King was stunned.

"Then, Mr. Jacobs, please answer Mr. Booker's question."

Jacobs was hoarse. His voice cracked. "Mr. Booker, I don't know."

"No further questions, your honor."

This was the first time in my life that I had ever seen Anthony Jacobs visibly shaken. He moved back to the defense table. His eyes looked towards the floor. His shoulders were bent.

"The defense rests, your honor," said Brad King.

"Very well, gentlemen. I would like to give the jury an hour break for lunch and we shall reconvene at one o'clock."

We adjourned to Judge Randall's chambers and discussed the charges to the jury. They were the same as in the last trial.

We went to lunch. My stomach was in knots. It soon would be my time to perform. We adjourned to the deli down the street. I ordered a chicken salad sandwich and tea. I nibbled at the sandwich. I was not hungry. "Well, Jake, it's in your hands now," said Donnie Lee. "Give 'em hell, chief."

I had rehearsed what I wanted to say over and over, but somehow it wasn't what I wanted to say. We were suddenly back in the courtroom. The jury was in the box. "Mr. Booker, you may proceed."

"Your honor, Mr. McDonald will be giving the closing argument for the plaintiffs. But the plaintiffs will waive opening and reserve closing."

"Very well. Mr. King, please proceed."

Brad King looked tired. For some reason, I felt he didn't have his heart in this case. He was a good trial lawyer, one of the best. I had won some cases against him and I had lost some cases against him, but I had the gut feeling that he was having an off day.

He approached the jury slowly. Methodically he went through the evidence and all the exhibits. For some strange reason he had a fixation on his expert witness's testimony—Zembrowski, the banker. I guess if your client had paid $70,000 for a hired gun, he'd better talk about him in closing argument. His argument lasted exactly one hour. He closed on an emotional appeal. "You should not punish First Fidelity because it is a bank. They have created wealth in this community. They have created hundreds of jobs. They have financed businesses. They have made it possible for people to own their own homes and businesses and cars and send their kids to college. Don't reward those who did not pay what they agreed to pay, by punishing those who gave them a chance in life."

I was fortunate that Judge Randall granted a thirty-minute recess after Brad King's emotional close. I wanted the jurors to go to the snack bar, drink a cup of coffee, smoke a cigarette, and forget what he had said. I felt Judge Randall was setting the stage in our favor with the timing of the breaks and recesses. She had been a trial lawyer herself, and she understood timing. I drank a glass of water. Soon this case would be on my shoulders. Somehow I felt relieved. In a couple of hours my part would be over and this case would be in the hands of the jury, and I could go back to Terri Beth. I wondered what ring she had picked out.

The jury was in the box. "Mr. McDonald, you may proceed," said Judge Randall.

"May it please the court, your honor, and may it please you, the ladies and gentlemen of the jury, Mr. King in his closing remarks asked you not to reward those who didn't pay what they agreed to pay. I ask you not to reward the bank, which took more than it was allowed to take. Michael Douglas, in the movie *Wall Street*, in a stockholders' meeting said, 'Greed is good'. No, ladies and gentlemen of the jury, greed is not good. It is theft. It is taking what does not lawfully belong to you. They balanced their books on the backs of the poor.

They took money illegally from those who could least afford it and fed their fat-cat officers and directors big pay checks, bonuses, free automobiles, expensive trips to resort areas like the Cayman Islands and the Bahamas, and fattened them further with memberships at fancy exclusive country clubs. Then these greed gobblers ask you to believe through the mouth of a paid gunslinger from Philadelphia whom they paid $70,000 to come to our fair city and tell you that what they did was right. I submit to you, ladies and gentlemen of the jury that you don't have to be a Harvard scholar or even a banker from Philadelphia to know what theft is. Even our children at Scenic Heights Elementary School down the street from here can tell you the answer. It's taking what doesn't belong to you. Send a message to Mr. Zembrowski and all those like him. Send a message to this greedy bank and all of them like it. Make it loud and clear. Let the message say: You're not going to steal from the people of Conecuh again. Send Mr. Zembrowski back to Philadelphia together with his $70,000 fee from the bank."

The jury was nodding. All of them were sitting on the edge of their seats. I had their attention. I looked back at Donnie Lee and Dixie. Donnie Lee winked at me. I continued.

"Give them a message they will never forget. Let them feel the sting. They must feel the sting in the only way a bank understands, and it is in the pocketbook. They need to know the struggle that these hundreds of people who are represented here in this class action have gone through. They all lost their homes. They have no place to live. Their wives and children were put out in the streets. They were homeless, and all because this greedy bank violated the Georgia law and illegally foreclosed on them."

Eight of the jurors were crying. The other four hung their heads. I argued for an hour and then I concluded by telling the story of Rudy and Angel Tolbert and their three children. I told how the bank had illegally attempted to foreclose on them and how it was stopped by a court injunction. I told about how strangely their house burned down several days later. The jury was very attentive. They hung on my every word. I glanced towards the back of the courtroom. There was Terri Beth seated three rows from the front. I had not noticed her before. I wondered if she had been there the whole time.

And I concluded. "And do you think this greedy bank stepped forward to help this poor homeless family? They didn't lift one finger. Not one employee at the bank even sent them a basket of food, or a blanket, or a stitch of clothing for three hungry, homeless children. Instead, they took all of the $52,000 in insurance proceeds and put it in their coffers. And they paid a fat cat foreign banker from Philadelphia to come to lie about it. Ladies and gentlemen of the jury, if it looks like a duck, and it walks like a duck, and it swims like a duck, I think we would be naive to call it a rooster. A thief is a thief. There is only one way to treat a thief, and that is to punish him. We ask that you bring back the maximum penalty that you think is appropriate. Rudy and Angela Tolbert and their three children and the other plaintiffs represented here have no homes. Please remember that when you go to yours tonight. I thank you."

All the jurors were crying. I sat down. It was over.

Dixie said, "Jake, that was the best closing I've ever heard."

Donnie pinched me. "Damn good. Damn good."

Brad King and his team of lawyers were stoic and white.

Judge Randall began her charges to the jury. Both sides had argued the charges in the judge's chambers. We knew what she was going to say and we had already entered our objections and exceptions. She charged the jury for one hour and fifteen minutes.

"Now, ladies and gentlemen of the jury, you may retire to the jury room and begin your deliberations. Select one of your members as foreman. Remember that your verdict must be unanimous. You may retire to deliberate at this time."

The jury left. I went over and shook Brad King's hand. "You did a good job, pal," Brad said.

"You did too, Brad. It was hard fought, but no hard feelings," I said.

Brad was packing up his briefcase. "Hey, it's just another case."

Terri Beth came up to me and gave me a big hug. She was still crying. "You were wonderful. I didn't know you could argue like that. That was the first time I ever heard you in court."

"Were you in here the whole time?"

"Sweetheart, I heard all of the closing arguments."

"I don't know about y'all, but I'm going to find me a Coke." I left and went down the hall towards the snack bar. Don Pollard was standing next to the elevator. "Jake, I've been waiting for you. It's urgent that you meet me in my office right now."

"What is it, Don?"

"We can't discuss it out here. Let's go to my office. Can I get you something to drink?"

"Yeah, I could use a Coke. My mouth is real dry."

"Hey, I heard your closing argument. It was terrific. You sounded like a good prosecutor in there."

"Don, that's an oxymoron — good prosecutor."

He laughed. "Have a seat. This is very serious. You must swear that what I am about to tell you must never leave this room. I must have your promise."

"You have it."

"This involves you personally, and I've been debating how to break it to you, Jake. The GBI, the state fire marshal's office, and my office did an exhaustive investigation of your fire. It was definitely arson. Kathy was murdered."

I turned pale. I felt very ill.

"This next one is not easy for me and it won't be for you. We know who did it."

"What?" I exclaimed.

He opened his desk drawer. He pulled out a stack of folded papers. I had seen these forms many times before. They were criminal indictments.

"Jake, the grand jury has been meeting in secret session for the last three weeks. We have a case we can prove."

I was about to jump out of my seat. "Who did it, Don?"

He shoved the indictments across the desk towards me.

"God damn it ! Are you kidding me?"

"Nope. Rube Wiseman and a thug from Chicago did the actual killing. Look at the other indictments."

"Oh, hell." There they were: Anthony Jacobs, conspiracy to commit murder, hiring one for the purpose of committing murder, conspiracy to commit arson, conspiracy to commit burglary; Robert Banks and another bank vice president were charged with identical offenses. I exploded. "God damn it. I'm going to kill that bastard right now." I ran towards the door.

Don tackled me and knocked me to the floor. Don's assistant District attorney, Phil King, came in and helped restrain me. I started to bawl. "They killed my wife. They killed Kathy." I cried. Don put his arms around me. "Phil, get Jake a drink. I mean a real one." Phil brought me a bourbon and Coke.

"Jake, listen to me. Please listen to me. We need your absolute cooperation in this. We can't blow this. I have held up on the arrests because of your case. I know how hard you've worked on it, and I didn't want to cause a mistrial. I did it as a favor to you, my friend. As soon as the verdict is announced, a GBI agent will arrest Jacobs. We have five GBI agents posted near the bank. When I give the signal, they will move in and arrest the other bankers. The sheriff will personally arrest Rube Wiseman. He is under surveillance now. He will not get out of our sight. The Chicago thug is under surveillance by the FBI. When I call them, they will arrest him and extradite him back here. Jake, I know this is very tough on you, but you must not do anything drastic. We cannot act as if you know anything. I just want to tell you that I'm going to do everything that I can to put Kathy's killers in the electric chair. I will be there to personally pull the switch."

"Don, do me a big favor. When they are sitting in the electric chair I want to be there to look them in the eye when they die. I want my face to be the last one they see before you send them to hell." The bourbon and Coke burned as it went down. "I had better get back to the courtroom. They're probably wondering where I am. Have you got any mouthwash? They don't need to smell liquor on my breath in there."

"Sure."

I gargled with Scope and rose to leave.

"Jake, two more things. I don't have any interest in your case one way or the other. I'm a prosecutor, not a civil lawyer. But I'd love to see you beat those bastards. It would be great to tell everybody that I have a friend who's a millionaire. And one more thing, Jake. I can't tell you any more about what I'm about to say. But I'll tell you, your case is only a small part of a much bigger one. You just stirred up the hornet's nest. Unfortunately, Kathy was murdered. There are forces working as we speak to right the wrongs that you, your clients, and the others have suffered. Just keep that in the back of your mind. I'll keep you posted."

I returned to the courtroom. "Where in the hell have you been, hot shot?" Donnie Lee asked.

"I had to get away. I went down to see Don Pollard."

"Yeah, he was here during your closing. What did he think?"

"Unofficially and off the record, he said he hoped we whipped the bastards."

"Look, this jury is going to be here a long time. The judge said she was going to let them go in an hour. Let's leave Dixie over here just in case something happens and let's go back to the office and relax. Terri Beth said she would wait for us."

We returned to the office. Terri Beth met us at the door. "Jake, I was about to come over. Brad King just called and said for you to be sure you called him before you left. He said it was urgent."

"Sweetie? You talk nice to your secretary when the trial is over."

Donnie Lee laughed. Terri Beth blushed.

"Shall I call the enemy?" I asked. "I wonder what he wants."

"He probably wants you to pay Zembrowski's fee for insulting him so much." We all laughed.

I dialed the number of King, Golden and Bonner. I knew it by heart, I had dialed it so many times during our representation of the Jack Owens estate.

"King, Golden and Bonner, may I help you?"

"Brad King, please. This is Jake McDonald."

"One moment, please."

Brad King immediately picked up. "Jake, how are you? I'm sitting here just thinking how badly you beat up on me over there."

"I don't know about that, pal. You did an outstanding job yourself."

"Listen, let's cut out the bullshit and lay it on the line. My clients have expended an enormous amount of money defending this case. Two trials, two appeals, all the expert witnesses."

I laughed. "Okay, okay, you got us on that one."

"You said one thing that was true in the trial. My client makes a lot of money in the banking industry. They see some possible exposure here and they want to minimize any possible losses. You know how paranoid and conservative the banks are. They're willing to make you an offer of settlement. Of course, there would have to be no admission of liability and there would have to be an agreement that the terms of the settlement would never be disclosed."

I was silent.

"Well, Jake, I could nickel and dime you and we could make offers and counteroffers, but I'll just give you my top and final offer—fifty million dollars."

"Fifty million. I don't know about that, Brad." I sounded disgusted. "I'll run it by my clients in the morning and I'll get back with you. Gee, I don't know." I hung up.

Donnie Lee said, "Did he say fifty million? Hell, Jake could buy him a Mercedes for that. . . . Jake, they're scared."

"Donnie Lee, I'm scared. I've never been offered that much money in a case before. What if we lose it?"

"Jake, you are no poker player. Sit on it a while. We have to notify the clients of the offer. Dixie and I will call the principals tonight and have them here at seven in the morning. Court starts back at nine. That will give us two hours to talk about it. Okay?"

"Okay."

I escorted Terri Beth to the door. "Sweetheart, I'm totally exhausted. Do you mind if I go home tonight and just collapse in my bed?"

"Jake McDonald, I am proud of you. You are a real fighter and my hero. I love you so. We're going to win. I can feel it." She giggled. "While you were goofing around in the courtroom, I went to Elfdorf Jewelers. I found a setting I fell in love with, assuming I still have the love, affection and commitment to marry me from a certain young attorney."

"Assuming? You'd better be there when the verdict is read."

"You bet, boss."

"And one more thing. When we're married, you must still call me boss."

She laughed out loud. "You silly goose. Go home and go to bed."

I collapsed into bed, thinking of what forty percent of fifty million dollars was. Twenty million dollars divided between Donnie Lee's firm and ours. I would never have to work again. Terri Beth and I could travel all over the world and do nothing but make love.

*****

I awoke to the real world. We had a very tough decision to make. I arrived at the office early. Terri Beth was already there with coffee on my desk.

"How are you, future wife?" I asked.

She laughed. "Thanks, I needed that. Everybody is in the library waiting for you."

"Thanks," I said. "I didn't sleep a wink last night."

"Neither did I," said Terri Beth.

I gulped down the cup of coffee and entered the library. There was a tremendous round of applause. I couldn't believe it. They were all there—Bill, Betty, Randy, Angela, and eight others. "Gee, has the verdict been announced before I got here?"

They all laughed.

"I don't know about you all, but I didn't sleep well last night. I couldn't help thinking about your case and the thieves on the other side. It's been hard on us. I know it's been hard on you. However, regardless of our feelings, let me put reality on the line. Late yesterday evening I received a call from Brad King. He indicated that the bank was willing to offer a compromise settlement to cut their losses. I hope so. If they're paying their witnesses $70,000 plus, I'm afraid to ask what they are paying their lawyers."

Everyone laughed.

"Bottom line, they have offered us fifty million dollars for all the claimants. That's fifty million less our forty- percent contingency fee, or a net to all of you of thirty million dollars. We have to be in court at nine. You guys can stay here and discuss the settlement offer. Of course, if the jury reaches a verdict anytime soon, then their offer is off the table."

Betty stood up. "Jake, I don't know about the rest of the folks here, but I want to speak on behalf of Gene and me. I deeply appreciate the way you and your firm and Donnie Lee have poured your souls into our case. I believe that the truth will come from the jury. Fifty million dollars excites me, but I will never feel comfortable if I took a compromise settlement from these crooks. I feel that y'all proved that they were crooks and I'm willing to let the chips fall where they may. If we win, then we will be compensated for our losses. If we lose, then we fought the good fight and lost. I believe in those jurors. Let's let them decide. Tell the crooks to go to hell."

One by one our clients stood and reiterated the same sentiment. That made it easy to respond to Brad King's offer. Our clients voted to reject it. It did not make it easy on me. Twenty million dollars in legal fees was hard to gamble with. I felt sick.

I called Brad King. It was 8:45 a.m. "Brad, I have met with my clients this morning. They have decided to turn down your clients' offer."

He was shaken and angry. "God damn it, Jake, they're stupid. Don't you have any control over your own clients?

Twenty million in legal fees. Are you willing to piss that away?"

I became very angry. "Listen, Brad, your clients can buy their way out of their problems. My clients can't. They voted against your offer. They have faith in the jury system. Let the chips fall where they may. I'll see you in court. Goodbye." I hung up.

That could turn out to be the most expensive telephone conversation I've ever had in my life. I had possibly just given away twenty million dollars. I felt sick.

Terri Beth came into my office. "Did you do the unpleasant task, my love?"

"Yep. I turned down a certain lifetime of financial freedom together."

"No you didn't, sweetie. I've got money and this isn't the last case you will try. Jake, you are going to win this case. We just don't know for how much yet. We need to get over to the courthouse."

We arrived in Judge Randall's chambers at nine, before Brad King. "Jake," Judge Randall said, "you know that I have always loved your firm. If I could have practiced law with anyone it would have been with Kelli. She was a pioneer for women lawyers. She was fearless. The word from the other side is that you have been offered fifty million and the offer has been turned down. I must assume that your clients turned it down and not you. Kelli would have beaten them to a pulp for that kind of money. What is the matter? I believe your clients are gambling."

"Judge, I didn't sleep last night. I am sick over this case. But my clients believe in this jury. Judge you know what I'm going through. Fifty million dollars on the table and I'm walking away from it. I should have stayed in Florida."

She laughed. "Jake, you're a trial lawyer. You weren't created to check titles."

Brad King arrived. He had a scowl on his face. "Good morning, judge. Good morning, Jake." He was obviously cold. "Guess we'll sit around here until they decide," he said.

"Who knows, Brad? If they come back before ten, I'll bet you won. If they come back at five this afternoon or tomorrow, then I win."

He didn't answer.

I had left instructions with Juanita and Terri Beth that I would be on the fourth floor of the courthouse in the law library. There was no way that I could concentrate on legal research on any case. I went there to b.s. with Bob Montana, the law librarian. He was a colorful fellow who talked a lot, and had a lot of war stories to tell. Bob and I talked all afternoon. There was no way I could go back to the office and answer phone calls and deal with clients. I left it with Terri Beth to handle the routine business.

It was 4:55 p.m., two days after the jury went out. Deputy Ben Taylor appeared at the door of Bob's office. "Excuse me, Mr. McDonald, but I believe the jury has reached a verdict."

The panic sensation struck me. The adrenaline rushed to my head. I didn't remember the elevator ride from the fourth floor of the courthouse to the eleventh. Somehow I made it.

Everything was numb and blurred. There was Donnie Lee and Dixie seated at our table. There were Brad King and Anthony Jacobs and Robert Banks, and their lawyers at their table. The courtroom was packed. The news media had filled most of the spectator seats. Terri Beth was seated on the front row. Judge Randall was seated on the bench. Deputy Taylor stood in front of the courtroom door.

"Are we ready, Deputy Taylor?" Judge Randall asked.

"Yes, your honor."

"Then bring the jury in."

The jury filed into the courtroom. They assumed their seats in the jury box. Juror Robert Alford was holding the paper that contained the verdict. He was a juror that I felt was favorable to us. That was a good sign.

"Mr. Foreman, I understand the jury has reached a verdict?"

"Yes, we have, your honor."

"Is it unanimous?"

"Yes, it is, your honor. All twelve of us agreed to it." "Please hand it to Mr. Booker so that he may publish it." Donnie Lee's hands trembled.

"Then, Mr.Booker, would you publish the verdict."

"Yes, your honor. He read slowly: "We the jury find for the plaintiffs." He paused. "We award damages against the all defendants jointly and severally in the amount of five hundred million dollars. This, the sixteenth day of November. J. Robert Alford, Foreman."

Eighteen

Anthony Jacobs collapsed to the floor in shock. A deputy rushed to his aid. He was quickly revived. The smell of an ammonia capsule permeated the courtroom. Brad King sat stunned.

I began to cry. I lay my head on the counsel table and sobbed unceasingly. Donnie Lee and Dixie were hugging and kissing without shame.

"Ladies and gentlemen, I can understand the emotions here, but this is still a court of law. Please be seated. Mr. King, are you satisfied that the verdict is in proper form?"

"Yes, your honor. I don't agree with it, but it's in proper form."

"Very well, ladies and gentlemen of the jury, you have done your duty. We appreciate your service on this jury. You are dismissed."

Brad King packed up his briefcase quickly. He came over to me. "Congratulations, pal. You whipped our ass. I won't forget this one." He was angry.

"Brad, what went around just came around."

I wasn't about to leave just yet. I knew what was about to happen. Don Pollard entered the courtroom with two men I didn't recognize. They approached Anthony Jacobs and Robert Banks. "Mr. Jacobs, I am Special Agent Brian Matthews of the Georgia Bureau of Investigation." He showed him his badge. "I have a warrant for your arrest for conspiracy to commit murder, conspiracy to commit burglary and conspiracy to commit arson, and the hiring of another to commit murder. You have the right to remain silent. Anything you say can and will be used against you in a court of law. You have the right to an attorney. If you cannot afford one, one will be appointed for you."

"What is this, some kind of joke? Get out of my face, you asshole."

Agent Matthews spun him around and slapped the handcuffs on him and led him out of the courtroom. The television cameras were rolling on the outside.

"Mr. Banks, I have a warrant for your arrest for conspiracy to commit murder, conspiracy to commit burglary, conspiracy to commit arson, rape, and money laundering." The agent read Robert Banks his rights and led him out of the courtroom. Ronald Sherman, another bank vice president, was similarly arrested.

Don Pollard came up. "Congratulations, Jake. You did one hell of a job. When I need a loan, I'll come to you. Certainly not to First Fidelity Bank and Trust. You didn't leave them a dime".

Terri Beth threw her arms around me. "God, I love you. I knew you would do it. Let's go celebrate. The champagne is on ice at the office. I ordered it in advance. I had faith in you. What was that all about?"

"Terri Beth, I'll tell you very shortly. They just indicted Kathy's killers."

"Oh, Jake, are you serious?"

"Hell, yes. The First Guaranty thugs had her killed."

"God, Jake, do you want to go home?"

"No, I want to celebrate with you and our victory team and the wonderful people known as our clients."

We all went to the office. You could hear the celebration going on from the outside of the building. We entered the front door. The crowd let out a roar. A sign was draped across the front wall that said JAKE THE GIANT KILLER, and another one said JAKE AND THE BEANSTALK. Another said GIVE ME JAKE AND DONNIE LEE. Betty was the first to greet me. She gave me a big hug. Then Bill. Then Rudy. Angela was crying in the corner. She was overcome with joy. Dixie shoved a glass of champagne in my hand. Juanita sneaked up behind me and gave me a kiss on the cheek.

"Ladies and gentlemen," Donnie Lee announced, "ain't it great to be in a room where everybody is a millionaire?" Everyone laughed.

The television was on in the corner. The news came on. "Everybody be quiet," Dixie said. She turned it up.

Ford Ashton led off with our story. "The largest civil verdict in the state of Georgia was rendered today against a local bank. The bank president and several officers of the bank were charged with multiple offenses, including murder."

The crowd sat stunned in silence as Ford Ashton revealed the story of our five hundred million verdict and the indictments and arrests of Jacobs, Banks, Sherman, and the others. Nobody could believe what he or she was hearing. A large crowd had gathered outside the office. All three-television stations and several radio stations and the newspaper reporters were gathered outside. "Jake and Donnie Lee, they want an interview," said Juanita.

"I guess we had better accommodate them, Jake," said Donnie Lee.

The lights of the cameras were blinding. The reporters rushed forward. "Mr. McDonald, what is your reaction to the indictment and arrest of Anthony Jacobs for his involvement in the murder of your wife?"

"Sir, I'm leaving that in the hands of Don Pollard, the district attorney. I'm sure he will do his duty. He always does. I just hope whoever killed my wife gets the electric chair."

"Mr. McDonald, were you surprised with the size of the verdict and do you think it will be overturned on appeal?"

"No, sir, we left the amount up to the jury. We never suggested an amount to them and they just did what was right. And no, sir, I don't think it will be overturned on appeal. Judge Randall tried a good clean case. She was fair to both sides, and the jury rendered a fair and just verdict."

I left the reporters with Donnie Lee. It was his time to be in the spotlight. He was the real hero, not me. Without him this would not be possible. I was sorry that Kelli and Kathy were not here to celebrate with us.

The crowd had cleared out. There were four of us left in Kelli's office—Donnie Lee, Dixie, Terri Beth, and me. Dixie refilled all of the champagne glasses. Donnie Lee lifted his champagne glass. "I propose a toast to the greatest law firm in the world, and to my future wife, my fiancee Dixie."

"All right!" We all cheered. "But Donnie Lee, we really suspected this. After all, I caught you two kissing two years ago in the library." Everyone laughed at the inside joke.

"I would like to make a special toast myself. I would like to propose a toast to a very special lady who has been with me during all my recent trials and tribulations and who is my best friend and soon to be my wife—I toast my fiancee Terri Beth."

Everyone let out a cheer. Dixie and Terri Beth hugged one another.

"When did this happen?" Dixie asked.

"Just before the trial. I must confess that I have loved Jake from the day we first met."

I looked at Donnie Lee. "Sorry, pal, but no double wedding. This lady won't share the spotlight with anyone. Let's flip a coin to see who gets to bite the dust first. The winner gets married first." I flipped a coin.

"Heads," Donnie Lee said.

"Heads it is. Donnie Lee and Dixie get married first. What's the date?"

"April fifteenth. That's the date we will have to pay forty percent of our recovery to the IRS."

"That's my birthday," said Terri Beth.

"Well, let's all get married on Terri Beth's birthday. We'll go at four o'clock and you can bite the dust at five."

"Hell, this is stupid," I said. "Let's go to Las Vegas and get it over with now." I gave Terri Beth a long and passionate kiss.

"Are you sure we can't just go to Judge Randall and let her do it now."

"Jake, I need to talk with you in a serious vein tomorrow morning."

"Okay. Can I have some time with you alone?"

"Absolutely, my love."

I had no trouble falling asleep. I was exhausted. The champagne helped it along. The next morning I awoke at five. I hoped I was not dreaming. I got a copy of the newspaper. Our case was the morning headline. Our verdict and Jacobs' indictment was screaming across the front page. It gave me real pleasure to see a picture of that low life bastard in handcuffs on the front page of the paper. The other thugs' pictures were next to his. There was a story on the Chicago mob hit man who had been arrested by the FBI and who was on his way back to Georgia under a writ of extradition. And then there was my least favorite scumbag, Rube Wiseman. I wanted to be present when the switch was pulled on him. It looked as if we had hit the grand slam.

I got dressed and drove to the office. I entered the back door and sneaked into my office. There was a note on my desk. It was in Terri Beth's handwriting. "Sweetheart, I will not be in today. I hope you will understand. There's a lot that you don't know about me yet. I am all right, but we need to have a long talk before we get married. I think a lot of this will make sense to you if you can bear with me. I love you. Terri Beth."

I wondered what in the world was going on. All day I worried about her. The day was spent with well wishers and news reporters. I was operating on adrenaline. At 5:30 p.m. Juanita buzzed me on the intercom. "Jake, it's Terri Beth."

"Sweetie, where have you been all day? I've been worried about you."

"Jake, meet me at my apartment before six. I don't have time to explain. Just meet me there, and hurry."

I ran out the back door, got in my car, and drove over to Terri Beth's apartment. She met me at the door. "Come in, sit down and don't say a word until it's all over."

"What are you talking about?"

"Just watch."

The six o'clock news came on CBS. "This is Dan Rather. In a massive nationwide sweep the FBI, in conjunction with federal, state and local law enforcement agencies, raided some of the largest banks and financial institutions in this country. Secret federal grand juries have been meeting all over the country and hundreds of banking officials are expected to be arrested for bank fraud, racketeering, money laundering, extortion, and other offenses, including murder and arson. The Justice Department is calling this the biggest bank fraud case in the history of this country. The FBI was able to crack this case primarily due to the efforts of undercover special agent Terri Beth Flynt, head of the FBI's Bank Fraud Division. Allegedly a number of major bank branches were controlled by the mob, and Mafia chieftains were conducting their money laundering operations. The Justice Department is moving against the banks with criminal RICO indictments to freeze and seize the assets of all the banks and bankers involved. Now let us take you to our Washington correspondent John Dowling, who is on the scene with Special Agent Flynt."

I was stunned. I sat in total disbelief as I saw Terri Beth being interviewed by the news reporter.

The interview was over. She shut off the television. "Jake, I wanted to tell you the truth for so long, but I couldn't. So many lives would have been lost. We couldn't have prevented Kathy's death, I promise you. But I will tell you, I was the one who was responsible for nailing that bastard Rube Wiseman. He was the man who killed Kathy. My job at the law firm was a cover for my undercover operation. I fell in love with you while I was doing my job with the Bureau. My love for you is so deep. I hope you still want to marry me after all of this. Today I resigned from the Federal Bureau of Investigation. Jake, please tell me you love me."

"I don't know, Terri Beth. Sleeping with a federal undercover agent might be pretty tough. On the other hand, you're used to these under the covers operations. You won't need to sleep with your gun, will you?" I laughed.

"You silly goose. Kiss me."

I reached into my pocket and pulled out a little box. "I've been sneaking around too," I said. "Try this on for size." I grabbed her left hand and slid the ring on her finger.

"Oh, Jake, it is so perfect."

"I guess I can forgive you for not telling me under the circumstances. Is there anything else you haven't told me?"

"Just three things."

"What are they?"

"I'm rich, my daddy owns a liquor store, and I'm a nymphomaniac."

I laughed. "Let's get married."

EPILOGUE

A Caribbean sunset is almost as beautiful as when the sun sets over the Gulf of Mexico. The first day of our honeymoon was ecstasy. Terri Beth was tanned and beautiful in her sundress. She was now my wife, Mrs. W. Lancaster McDonald. She looked up at me and put her arms around me. "Jake, do I really have to call you boss now?" she queried.

"Yes, boss, you still have to call me boss," I laughed.

"Jake, you know that day when you and Kathy and I were on the firing range. Did you suspect something then?"

"I thought it was odd that someone who wasn't supposed to know anything about shooting handled a pistol as well as you did."

"I did miss a few on purpose, Jake to throw you off."

"The FBI does teach you how to shoot."

"Jake, I did love Kathy. I would never have done anything to interfere with your marriage to her, I promise you. There was nothing the Bureau could have done to stop her murder. It was two days after the fire before we got a solid lead. Both Don Pollard and the U.S. Attorney have solid cases against Rube Wiseman, Jacobs, and the others. I hope Don gets to try them first. I'll have to testify in the federal trials against First Fidelity and the Costellano crime family. We have solid cases which should result in long jail terms for a lot of thugs. One other thing will come out. Anthony Jacobs sent one of his paid hit men to kill one of the mob's hit men here in Conecuh.

Jacobs' hit man killed the mob's hit man first. It happened at the hotel right next to Roosters, Ford Ashton's place."

"Terri Beth, for some unknown reason I believe God made all this happen the way it did. We were brought together, not by accident, but by divine design. I believe Kathy was called away only because God needed another angel, and you were sent to me because I needed another angel."

She kissed me on the cheek. "And, Jake, God sent me to you at the right moment. I was ready to end it all. That time we met in the snack bar in the courthouse was the turning point. You gave me hope after John's death."

"You know, Terri Beth, there's one thing I haven't figured with that case. I guess I never will."

"What's that, boss?" she smiled.

"Remember all those postcards I got from the Caymans saying that my case was there?"

Terri Beth started laughing.

"What are you laughing about?" I asked.

She said, "I must confess, I had them sent to you by an FBI agent of ours in the Caymans. I just wanted to get your blood pressure up." She laughed.

"You little devil, you."

"First Fidelity was laundering money there, but I didn't think you'd ever figure out my trick."

The reggae band started to play. I never knew how relaxing a cruise could be. There were no phones, no televisions, and no clients. Nothing but me and the beautiful woman I had just married. I didn't know what our future would be. Could we ever work together in the law firm? I didn't know. Probably not. I never thought we would ever collect a dime of our judgment against the bank. That somehow was a fairy tale. If we never saw a dime, at least we had shut down a vast criminal conspiracy. At least I had the satisfaction of knowing that Kathy's death was for a purpose. And oh, how I missed my poor old dog Loophole.

Terri Beth and I returned to our room. There was a telegram lying on the bed. "What's this?" I asked. I opened it.

It was from Donnie Lee. It read: "Sorry to bother you on your honeymoon, but I thought you'd like to know that Jacobs and his bankers have agreed to enter pleas for reduced sentences of twenty years each. As part of the plea they have agreed to pay our judgment in full with no appeals. Wiseman is headed to the electric chair. Congratulations, Mr. and Mrs. Multi-millionaires. P.S. Tell Terri Beth that I picked up your wedding present this afternoon and it will be here upon your return. Donnie Lee and wife, Dixie Booker."

I started to cry.

"What is it, sweetheart?" asked Terri Beth. "Oh, Jake, that's wonderful. It's over. What are you going to buy me?" she teased.

"A cook—one that knows how to cook fried chicken, turnip greens, corn, okra, catfish, butter beans, collards, and corn bread."

"You sweet little redneck." She laughed out loud. "And what is this wedding present that you had Donnie Lee pick up for me?"

"I won't tell. You'll see when the time comes."

I threw her on the bed. Terri Beth was the most wonderful soul mate that God could ever bless me with. Somehow Kathy had talked with God about me needing another angel in my life.

We landed at the Conecuh airport ten days after the wedding. I was totally relaxed. For the first time in years I was happy. I was rich and I was in love again. We stepped off the plane. I was surprised to see Donnie Lee and Dixie there to greet us. "Mr. and Mrs. Donnie Lee Booker, I presume?" I laughed.

"Mr. and Mrs. W. Lancaster McDonald, I presume?" He laughed. "Multi-millionaires?"

"The same." I hugged Dixie and Donnie Lee. They hugged Terri Beth and me.

Donnie Lee was holding a purebred black Labrador retriever puppy on a leash. "Who is this?" I asked.

"Well, this is sort of a surprise. Your bride has conspired against you again. You know how these undercover agents for the feds are. She has been sneaking around. She asked me to pick up your wedding present. His name is Cracker. That's the perfect name for a South Georgia boy's dog don't you think?"

The black lab puppy looked at me and I looked at him. He had bright brown eyes. "Cracker," I said, "come here." He came to me, licked me on the hand and sat at my feet. I looked at Terri Beth.

*****

Saint Paul says that all things work for good to them that love the Lord. The reason for the early deaths of Kathy and Kelli can only be answered by Him. For they have crossed the river that runs by the city of Conecuh, and into the promised land to receive their rewards of milk and honey. They have found peace under the shade of the trees on the other side. Everyday in the city of Conecuh somebody is praying for a miracle, and sometimes they happen.

– THE END –

ABOUT THE AUTHOR

E. Wright Davis, Jr., Esquire, is a true product of the Old South. Born and raised in Americus, Georgia, he graduated from Mercer University in Macon, Georgia, and received his Juris Doctorate in law from the Walter F. George School of Law at Mercer. He practiced law for fifteen years as a trial lawyer in Georgia, and is a member of the State Bar of Georgia.

Wright is an entrepreneur, having been involved in broadcasting, marketing, politics, insurance, farming and real estate.

An accomplished speaker and humorist, he won the Georgia state championship of humorous speaking as a member of Toastmasters International. He was selected as one of the Five Most Outstanding Men of Georgia by the Georgia Jaycees.

CPSIA information can be obtained
at www.ICGtesting.com
Printed in the USA
LVHW111258020519
616402LV00001B/66/P